SPRING BREAK
AT THE
VILLA HERMES

XAVIER MAYNE

Published by
DREAMSPINNER PRESS

5032 Capital Circle SW, Suite 2, PMB# 279, Tallahassee, FL 32305-7886 USA
http://www.dreamspinnerpress.com/

Spring Break at the Villa Hermes
© 2015 Xavier Mayne.

Cover Art
© 2015 L.C. Chase.
http://www.lcchase.com
Cover content is for illustrative purposes only and any person depicted on the cover is a model.

ISBN: 978-1-63216-651-7
Digital ISBN: 978-1-63216-652-4
Library of Congress Control Number: 2014921661
First Edition April 2015

Printed in the United States of America
∞
This paper meets the requirements of
ANSI/NISO Z39.48-1992 (Permanence of Paper).

Again and always, for J.

By XAVIER MAYNE

The Accidental Cupid
Husband Material

A BRANDT AND DONNELLY CAPER
Frat House Troopers
Wrestling Demons
A Wedding to Die For
Spring Break at the Villa Hermes

Published by DREAMSPINNER PRESS
http://www.dreamspinnerpress.com

CHAPTER ONE
VOYAGERS

"I CAN'T believe it's only three months away," Donnelly said, his steady voice giving no sign of the pounding pace he was maintaining on the treadmill.

Next to him, Brandt kept stride. "What do you mean? We've been planning this wedding for approximately... eternity. Stars have extinguished while we sat picking out colors for tablecloths."

"It hasn't been so bad," scolded Donnelly, cranking up the speed a little more. "Wendell has taken care of most of it, and Bryce has been handling the rest."

"Yeah, about that. Did I mention I'd heard from one of the caterers Bryce 'handled'? He's not going to file a complaint, but...."

"I'll talk to him. It's not like it's the first time. Remember when we asked him to pick up our car from the garage?"

Brandt chuckled at the memory. "But that one turned out okay. The mechanic was down for it, and we got free oil changes for a year. Bryce must wrestle above his weight class."

Donnelly laughed so hard he nearly stumbled off the treadmill. "Look at you with your wrestling talk. Gearing up for the finals at the university?"

"Figured I should practice. I don't want to embarrass Jonah and Casey by shouting the wrong things during their bouts."

"Oh, did I mention Mal got back to me? He's going to stay with us during the finals meet weekend."

Brandt shot his partner a dagger-y look.

"In the guest room, of course." Donnelly looked quite pleased to have incited a jealous reaction.

"Remind me to set up that trip wire in the hallway I've been thinking about." Brandt smiled and cranked up the speed of his treadmill to meet, then exceed, Donnelly's. "You know, after all the wedding planning, and the wrestling finals, it might be nice to take a little break."

"What did you have in mind?"

"Well, I was kind of thinking we might take a week off and head down to one of those honeymoon spots Bryce has been going on about."

"A whole week? In March?"

Brandt squinted at his partner. "Yes, at the end of March."

Donnelly looked blankly at him. "What's special about the end of March?"

"It's only the one-year anniversary of your proposal, that's all." Brandt's voice was casual, but he beamed; his track record of remembering significant relationship dates was so much worse than his partner's. He was surprised when Donnelly stopped running and disappeared from his vision. Brandt hit the stop button on his treadmill and dropped off the back as the belt slowed suddenly. He stood next to Donnelly, whose face betrayed his astonishment.

"You remembered," he said, his voice mystified.

"As a matter of fact, I did."

"I love you." Donnelly pulled Brandt into a tight embrace, right there in the gym. "You are amazing."

"Does this mean you're going to run away with me for a week?"

"I would go anywhere with you," Donnelly said, smiling broadly. "Anywhere."

"I'll call and confirm the reservation."

"You already made the arrangements?" Donnelly seemed unable to catch his breath.

"I did. I guess this is what they call sweeping you off your feet."

Donnelly leaned close to whisper in Brandt's ear. "My feet will be in the air all night."

"Fuck," breathed Brandt.

"DO YOU have everything, Teddy dear?" his mom called from the living room. "Your swim trunks and sunscreen?"

"Yes, Mom," Ted called back.

"Clean underwear?"

"It's not like I'm going to pack dirty underwear, Mom." Exasperation was creeping into his voice.

"You're going to be there for a whole week. You'll need seven pairs of underwear, plus an extra."

"I can count, Mom," he shouted, losing the battle to keep his voice down.

"Do you have a hat?"

Ted slumped on the bed, exhausted from his mom's hectoring. This was supposed to be a quick shot home to pick up clothes for a spring break that had suddenly turned into a whole week at the beach, thanks to Ted's rich friend Howie. A week in the warm sun would be a welcome change from the layers of ice and snow that blanketed his university campus through the winter. But he was starting to think a day back home to pick up warm-weather clothes was too great a price to pay.

"I have a hat," he called back wearily.

"And sunscreen?"

Ted flopped back on the bed, arms out, wishing for death to just take him already. This couldn't get any worse.

"And condoms?" his dad called. "You got enough condoms?"

It just got worse.

"ALL RIGHT, bitches, let's count up the score," Bryce called, waving a square of cardstock at the others.

"I thought watching an entire day of college wrestling would have been excitement enough for you," Brandt observed.

"Of course I appreciate the efforts of those sweaty, muscular lovelies as much as the next man," Bryce sniffed. "But this adds an extra measure of fun, don't you think?"

Mal leaned close to Donnelly. "Is he always…?"

"Oh, yes," Donnelly replied. "Inexhaustibly."

"All right, then. I got a bingo during the first round. Here's what I marked off: visible jockstrap, semiboner, finger-in-cleft, wedgie tug, and the bonus middle square—teabag. Is that what everyone got?" Bryce looked around the group, smiling brightly.

"You missed singlet malfunction," Donnelly noted, looking at his card.

"Which kind?" Bryce asked, pencil at the ready.

Donnelly checked his card. "Round one was… buttock." He looked up. "Round three was the ball slip."

"I can't do this," Brandt muttered, heading for the tub full of beers on the dining table, shaking his head and chuckling. "Can I get anyone another?"

"That would be great, thanks," Mal called, holding his empty beer bottle aloft. "Oh, and I also got cut versus uncut."

Donnelly turned to him with his mouth open. "How did you see that?"

Mal held up the binoculars still hanging around his neck.

"So, that's round one," Bryce announced, taking careful notes on his master scorecard—the one with pink glitter around the edges.

"It was nice to see Jonah and Casey doing so well," Brandt said, returning with a beer for Mal and one for himself. "They seem to really be fitting in at the university."

"I'll say," Mal replied, taking the bottle from Brandt. "They pretty much delivered the championship today."

"I'm just glad to see their team so supportive of them and their relationship," Donnelly added. "They deserve that, after all they went through in fucking Woodley." He took a drink, then his eyes went wide and he swallowed quickly. "Oh, sorry, Mal, I forget you still kind of have to live there."

"Funny you should mention that," Mal said. "I've been thinking for a while about getting the hell out of there. You know the café we went to yesterday, after the early rounds of wrestling? The one on the south end of Alta Avenue?"

"Nice place," Brandt said. "I think it's the best coffee on the avenue."

"Well, I had a chat with the owner yesterday, and he's getting ready to retire. He's kept the place up really well, but there are some things I would do differently. Like, he's got a full kitchen but doesn't serve lunch, and he brings in all of his baked goods on a truck the night before rather than making them fresh. Seems like I could make a pretty good go of it."

"So you'd sell the place in Woodley?" Donnelly asked. Mal's café was the only thing that had kept him going when they were in Woodley last year helping out with Jonah's case.

"Actually, I already have an offer on the table for it. There's a developer who wants to tear down half the block to put up some horrible chain restaurant. Which I figure is pretty much all Woodley deserves, so I'm inclined to sell out. It's a great offer, and it will give me enough to buy the place on the avenue, plus some to make improvements."

"It would be awesome to have you here," Brandt said, genuinely happy for Mal. Anyone who escaped Woodley should be congratulated.

"Thanks," Mal said. He took another drink of his beer. "So what's this I hear about an exciting spring-break trip for you two?"

"Well, it's not exactly a spring-break trip," Brandt said. "We're just going to get away for a week and have some quiet time together."

"Good for you," Mal replied. "Though from what Jonah and Casey were saying, the entire university is decamping for the beach that week. You'll probably have some company."

"I don't think the college crowd is going to be descending upon the Villa Hermes," Donnelly said. "It's this little boutique B&B up on the bluffs above the beach. It'd be pretty hard not to notice it's a gay-focused business when the photos on their website look like an Andrew Christian commercial."

"Sounds… hot," Mal said, eyebrows up.

"We've never really gone in for the gaycation," Brandt said. "But after all of this political crap we've been dealing with on marriage equality, I would just like to be someplace where I can kiss my fiancé by the pool and not feel like people are staring at us."

"People gonna be staring," Nestor said liltingly.

Brandt blushed.

"As long as they are staring because they want a better view of my stud in a Speedo, I'm okay with that," Donnelly said with a laugh.

Brandt looked at him with an eyebrow raised. "Speedo?"

Donnelly ran a playful finger down Brandt's chest from his collar to his belt buckle. "For me?"

Brandt put his arm around Donnelly and kissed him on the cheek. "Anything for you."

"Oh!" Bryce called. "Nestor, get your phone. You know how I like photos of our troopers being cute."

"The phone say it full," Nestor said, holding it up and shaking his head. "Too much cute already."

"So when do you leave for your week in paradise?" Mal asked, once he had finished goggling at Bryce and Nestor.

"We fly out Friday after work," Donnelly replied. "That gives us a few days to find the right color Speedo for you." He nudged Brandt in the ribs. "Of course, they said on their site the pool is in a courtyard, so it's clothing-optional."

Brandt turned a stunned face to Donnelly. "You aren't seriously considering…?"

"Who knows? An allover tan might just be the thing to lift the winter doldrums, don't you think?"

"Who are you, you manslut?" Brandt cried in a voice full of mock outrage. "And you might want to look into getting that jaw rehinged, Mal." He burst out laughing at Mal's surprise in being called out on his reaction.

"I like this Malcolm person," Bryce said to Nestor. "He has good instincts."

"TAXI'S HERE, motherfuckers," boomed a commanding voice from downstairs. "Finish packing your panties and get the fuck down here."

Ted threw a last few things into his backpack: laptop and cables, the novel he was supposed to have finished for his Irish literature class last week, a baseball cap. He grabbed his suitcase and bolted into the hallway, where he collided with Thor, his roommate across the hall.

"Sorry," Thor said, as was his habit. "When Paul cranks up that bullhorn voice of his, it kind of makes me crazy."

"Let's just get down there before he really turns up the volume," Ted suggested, and they headed down the creaky old stairs together.

"Ted, Thor, nice of you to join us," Paul said in a growl. "Did you happen to see the others up there?"

"Chad was in the bathroom, probably trying to figure out which hair product goes best with humidity," Ted replied.

"Howie came downstairs a while ago," Thor said. "I haven't seen him come back up, so he must be down here somewhere. Did you check the kitchen?"

"No, I've been trying to convince the taxi driver not to leave us here because we can't get our shit together," grumbled Paul. "Can one of you ladies go check the kitchen?"

"I'll go," Ted volunteered.

"And see if you can rustle up Bark while you're back there," Paul called after him. He stepped out into the late-night gloom to be sure the taxi hadn't pulled away.

Ted walked through the sparsely furnished living room and into the kitchen beyond. "Howie, it's time to go. Paul's going to kill one of us if we don't get moving." Ted looked around the corner, where the downstairs toilet and the back door were hidden. "Bark? You in there?"

"He's not back there," Howie replied, rinsing the last of his mac and cheese out of the cracked bowl he'd been using.

"Know where he is?"

"Left about twenty minutes ago. Said he needed a last run before being cooped up on a plane all night."

"He's out running? Shit, Howie, the taxi's here right now."

Howie shrugged and walked past Ted, brushing his shoulder on the way out.

Ted followed him back into the living room. Chad had finally emerged from the bathroom, so now their group numbered five, including the glaring Paul, who had returned from the curb with a new string of expletive-laced invective to motivate his roommates.

"Where the fuck is Bark?" he demanded.

"He went out for a run," Ted said, knowing the abuse he was letting Bark in for.

"It's ten fucking degrees outside, and that cocksucker goes for a little jog? At exactly the time he knew we have to leave? What the fuck was he thinking?"

"I was thinking I didn't want to get all fat and grumpy on the plane," Bark said, having appeared in the doorway behind Paul while he was ranting. He poked the big man in the belly and walked around him. He was wearing a black compression suit for cold-weather running.

"Can we get the hell out of here, please?" Paul shouted at him. "And for the record, this is not what fat looks like." Paul lifted his flannel shirt and showed the six ingots of hard muscle arrayed on his hairy torso. "So fuck you."

Bark smiled at him and started to pull the compression shirt off over his head. Ted watched with alarm, afraid of his reaction to Bark's body but knowing that looking away would be as conspicuous as watching his every move. Shit.

Bark threw the shirt over to the sofa and then kicked off his running shoes. He stuck his thumbs in the waistband of the compression pants, and Ted's heart skipped another beat. Maybe three, based on the sudden pounding in his head. Down and off went the tight black leggings, leaving Bark standing completely naked in the middle of the living room.

"Do you lie awake at night figuring out ways to get naked in front of other people?" Chad asked. "I mean, come on, dude."

"What, it's only appropriate when you're being paid for it?" Bark jeered good-naturedly. "Like you?"

"You wish you got paid for it," Chad retorted, somewhat lamely.

"If I played lacrosse like this, you know attendance would go up at our games," Bark replied. "That would be payment enough for me." He reached casually to a neat stack of clothes on the couch and within thirty seconds was dressed in low-slung cords and a thermal Henley—but, Ted noted, no underwear. He slipped on his boots, cinched them up, and stood upright. "Well, what are we waiting for?"

"Let's move, bitches," Paul said, his voice calm for the first time since the taxi arrived. He held the door open, and the group trundled with their luggage down the snow-covered steps of the old house.

On the way to the airport, Chad turned to Howie. "What kind of place is it?"

Howie shook his head. "All I know is that it's on the bluff above the beach. The whole city was pretty much sold out, but my dad's travel agent got us in as a kind of apology for messing up his last vacation."

"What happened on your dad's vacation?" Ted asked.

Howie grunted. "It was a mess. Dad told him to book the biggest suite at the hotel, and then we get there and find there's a bigger one he didn't even tell us about. Dad tore him a new one about *that*. So he made these arrangements for us as a kind of peace offering."

"I think it's really awesome you're treating us to a spring break someplace warm," Thor opined from the last row of seats. "I just hope it's not one of those places where the tourist area is fancy and nice and the locals live in poverty. That would be a bummer."

"Well, I'm sure you'll be organizing community protests by the end of the week," Howie said with a roll of his eyes.

"Not all of us come from money," Thor replied without rancor in his voice, as if just stating a fact.

"How long are the flights?" Chad asked.

"We gotta take some little propeller thing to O'Hare, and that takes like an hour. Then we have a two-hour layover, and then it's another four hours down there. So basically all fuckin' night."

Ted looked at the snoozing form to his left. Of all the people he knew, Barclay Burnett was the only one who could fall asleep anywhere, anytime, and wake up instantly when he needed to. It was like his body was a precision machine that responded to his every whim. And that body was a machine like no other.

Ted recalled the first time he saw it—the moment he found out he would be rooming with the man who possessed it. It was during freshman orientation, more than three years ago, and he was desperately trying not to get lost while looking like he was not the kind of person who had to worry about getting lost. He arrived at what would be his dorm room and found someone already there, unpacking. It was late August, and a heatwave that was merely uncomfortable elsewhere was simply unbearable in the unventilated freshman dorm. So it shouldn't really have surprised Ted that his new roommate would have taken off his shirt as he went about the work of unpacking and arranging his stuff. But Ted wasn't ready for it, not by a long shot. He opened the door and saw the broad, muscled back of his roomie, and he struggled to draw his next breath. Ted had never played a sport in high school, so his locker-room experience was limited. That was fine with him, because a sight like the one he was now looking at would have resulted in a distinctly awkward reaction.

And then the guy turned around. If his back was breathtaking, his front was exquisite. He was built like some exotic jungle cat, packed with muscle but capable of a fluidity that was mesmerizing. Ted had seen many men with such a physique, but only late at night on the Internet when he trolled Tumblr, hoping his parents wouldn't see the blue glow under his bedroom door and burst in while he surfed one-handed. But he had always assumed the men with builds like this were lit by professionals and smoothed in Photoshop—surely no one could be that perfect. And yet, here he was, a ginger vision. Ted couldn't think of a thing to say to this perfect creature, which was unfortunate given that Bark had asked him his name.

Though things got less awkward between the two of them during that year, they never approached normal, at least not for Ted; he never found out what it was like to have a normal pulse when in Bark's presence. But they were happy enough in the blending of their personalities that they roomed together again sophomore year, and then in their junior year, they had found the old house for rent. The other guys had jumped at the chance to get off campus and keep the dorm group together. It was a good move for Ted, as he gained his own room and no longer had to suppress his reaction when Bark was naked. And naked he tended to be, whenever a chance—or even half of one—presented itself.

The six of them had, in a lot of ways, grown up together, but this would be their last spring break as students. A few months from now, they would graduate and go their separate ways, a prospect that made Ted far too sad to contemplate.

Ted closed his eyes and tried to think tropical thoughts.

"IT'S BEAUTIFUL here," Donnelly said as the taxi took them through the still-warm evening toward their vacation destination.

"Anything's got to be better than what we left at home," Brandt replied. "Can you believe we got snow this week—the last week in March?"

"Ah, just look at that ocean," Donnelly said, pointing out the window. "Enough to make you forget there's anything like snow in the world."

Brandt sat back and contemplated his partner for a moment. "I don't think I've ever seen you this excited. If I'd known this is how you'd react to a vacation on the beach, I would have done it sooner."

"It's kind of like a pre-honeymoon," Donnelly said, beaming. "Try it out. See if we might want to come back after the wedding."

"Anywhere in the world will be fine with me once I'm your husband," Brandt replied, taking Donnelly's hand.

The taxi ride from the airport was a good half hour, but the time flew by for the troopers, so happy to be on vacation.

"Villa Hermes," announced the driver as he pulled into the semicircular driveway at the front of the inn.

Perched on a bluff overlooking the finest of the area's white-sand beaches, the Villa Hermes was a classic Greek cliff house, brilliant white among its pink stucco neighbors. Lit by a hundred beams emanating from the shrubbery, its bright blue doors and window shutters were a Santorini postcard rendered in the tropics. Brandt and Donnelly stepped out of the taxi while the driver pitched their bags onto the stone drive. Donnelly paid him while Brandt stacked and counted their luggage.

"Enjoy your stay… gentlemen," the driver muttered as he got back into the car.

"I don't think I like the way he said that," Donnelly remarked. "Did that seem—"

"It seemed like something a taxi driver would say," Brandt said soothingly.

Donnelly shook it off. "You're right. Sorry. I'm just really sensitive to what people are saying when they pause like that. It's like I'm hearing things, and all those things are homophobic."

"Good thing we're getting away from the job for a week, then, isn't it?"

Donnelly nodded and picked up his suitcase. "Let's get this R&R on the road, shall we?"

"Oh, you're here, you're here," called a lilting voice from the front door of the hotel. "Please, come in, come in!"

They carried their bags through an open iron gate into a small courtyard where a fountain splashed with an elegant trickling sound, to be greeted by a tall, slightly built man in his early sixties who smiled broadly as he approached them with extended hands.

"You must be the Misters Brandt and Donnelly," he exclaimed, shaking their hands in turn. "Welcome to the Villa Hermes. I am the proprietor, Winston Eubanks, but please, call me Winnie."

"It's a beautiful place you have here," Brandt remarked, looking about the small courtyard.

"Why, thank you, sir," Winnie said as he led the men into the small office off the courtyard. "It's a labor of love; it really is. We've only been open a year, but Vic and I began working on it nearly five years ago. It's like my little Greek paradise in this wasteland."

"I've only been here for an hour," Donnelly remarked, "but the area seems very pretty."

"Oh, it is, it *is*," Winnie replied. "I spoke only in terms of culture, or the lack thereof. But there is so much natural beauty, which is only enhanced during spring-break season when even more natural beauties fly in to take a week off from studying and fill the entire town with skimpy bathing suits and hormones. It can be quite intoxicating." He looked up at the men, who seemed perhaps not as enchanted with this vision of hordes of horny college students. "But we don't get that kind of clientele here, of course. Our little villa is a respite from all of that, though if you wish to see what all of that looks like, I can direct you to a vista point on our balcony from which you can observe the mating rituals on the beach below." He looked from Brandt to Donnelly and back again. "If you're into that sort of thing."

"What I'm into," Brandt said, looking at Donnelly, "is spending some quiet time with my fiancé and relaxing by the pool."

"Then you have come to the right place. Let's get you registered, and I'll show you to your room. You have the finest accommodation we offer, the honeymoon suite. Privacy, luxury, and a view of the ocean. Come, let's get you settled in."

A short time later, they stood on the terrace off their bedroom, looking at the stars twinkling over the ocean. A hundred feet below them, the surf lapped gently at a beach that glowed white even in the pale moonlight. They could also see the pool, illuminated by torches where the infinity edge dropped off toward the sea.

"This is perfect," Donnelly said as he wrapped his arms around Brandt and nuzzled his neck from behind.

"It is," Brandt agreed. "Seems like we're the only people here, doesn't it?"

"Winnie mentioned they were fully booked, so more people will probably be getting here tomorrow."

"So what you're saying," Brandt said, pulling Donnelly close so he could growl in his ear, "is that if I want to do something outrageously inappropriate to you on this balcony, I should do it right now, when there's no one to hear you?"

"No one to hear me… what?" Donnelly murmured.

"Beg me for more," Brandt whispered into his ear.

"Oh, fuck." Donnelly took a couple of quick breaths. "Go ahead and assume that's what I want, even if I don't say it."

"Then hold on tight," Brandt said, slipping out from Donnelly's embrace and circling around behind him.

Donnelly grasped the top of the solid, whitewashed half wall of the balcony with both hands while Brandt dropped to his knees behind him. He unbuckled Donnelly's belt, unbuttoned and unzipped his pants, and slid them down to his feet. Then he ran his hands up the strong, smooth legs until his hands slipped into the leg openings of Donnelly's boxer shorts. Donnelly took in a surprised breath as Brandt's hands converged where his legs met.

"Hello, boys," Brandt growled. He let go of Donnelly's dangly bits to take hold of the cuffs of his boxers and yank them down to join the khakis pooled at Donnelly's feet. He lifted each foot in turn and then tossed the pants and drawers behind him.

Donnelly now stood in the moonlight naked from the waist down. Brandt sidled up close, still on his knees, and pushed Donnelly's knees apart.

"My, that sea breeze reaches places that don't normally blow in the wind," Donnelly said as he leaned forward and thrust his smooth and muscled ass back.

Brandt ran his fingers down the small of Donnelly's back, fanning them out across the tight, powerful globes of his buttocks. He was delighted to see goose bumps flash into being in response to his tickling touch. Placing his hands around Donnelly's hips, he closed his eyes and insinuated himself into the cleft, seeking that hot center he knew so well. Donnelly leaned forward a little more, opened himself to Brandt's seeking lips. As soon as he made contact with that tight ring of muscle, Brandt darted out his tongue, teasing it with his hot, wet touch. Donnelly groaned, and the knot untied itself slightly, then puckered up tightly once more. Brandt pushed forward, his tongue slipping inside the hot center of the man whose legs were beginning to quiver with the exertion of remaining upright under Brandt's assault.

Brandt laid the most delicate of kisses on Donnelly's twitchy anus and then stood behind him. He reached into his pocket and pulled out a small tube of slippery stuff he had stashed there on the off chance a suitably inappropriate opportunity might present itself. With an adept flip of the cap and a precisely aimed squeeze, he slicked up the erection caused by his tonguing of Donnelly's ass and aimed it at the opening he had moments before been teasing.

"Wha…?" Donnelly wondered aloud at the intrusion. But surprise quickly gave way, and he moaned his assent.

Both men were startled by voices coming from the pool area below them. "Well, I don't know," a voice Brandt recognized as Winnie's said. "The travel agent called and asked if we had room for six, and I said we only have four rooms and one of them is taken, so if they don't mind doubling up, it should be fine."

"Is it some kind of group thing?" a much deeper voice asked. "We wouldn't want a bunch of spring breakers showing up thinking this is party central."

"I don't know who they are. But the agent knows what kind of place we're running, so…."

Brandt, having frozen at the sound of voices, pushed forward once the voices died away. He wasn't going to lose the chance at his partner's ass just because they'd overheard some voices. Donnelly, however, seemed to think otherwise, as he tried to step back from the railing. Brandt held firm, though, and Donnelly's backward motion served only to impale him on the first few inches of Brandt's eight-inch erection.

"Ethan," Donnelly whispered in a panic, "we should go in."

"I'm planning on going in," Brandt answered, and thrust his hips forward, forcing the next several inches of his cock into Donnelly.

"No, I mean we should go in the room," Donnelly replied more loudly.

"I know what you really mean," Brandt huffed. "You're begging me for more." He lunged forward, burying himself to the balls in Donnelly's ass.

"No... oh God," Donnelly babbled but ultimately surrendered to the force of Brandt's onslaught. "Fuck... fuck that feels good."

Brandt could feel the tension leave Donnelly's legs, and he began to slide back and forth with a gentle rhythm that soon had the two of them swaying on the balcony, lost in their union.

"Oh, there they are!" called Winnie's voice from below. "Settling in all right?"

The men looked down at the pool deck and saw Winnie in a floral dressing gown waving up at them. Donnelly relinquished his hold on the balcony ledge long enough to wave back.

"Lovely view, isn't it?" Winnie asked.

"It's... beautiful," Donnelly replied, clearly trying to keep his breath under control.

"The rhythm of the waves is contagious," Brandt offered, and he started thrusting imperceptibly into Donnelly again while both men smiled down at the proprietor of the inn.

Donnelly brought his free hand down and slapped Brandt on the hip, clearly trying to get him to back off. But Brandt was undeterred, intent on making a complete break not only from their daily life back home but the inhibitions that came with it. Suddenly he wanted to be the kind of person who has sex on a balcony on vacation. He kept the motion confined to his hips so it was not visible to the pool deck below, but it was certainly apparent to Donnelly, who squirmed a little as if trying to shake him off.

"Please let me know if there's anything you need," Winnie said. "And I'd like you to meet Vic, my partner in the villa and in life."

A towering slab of man stepped into view and waved cordially up at the balcony. "Evening, gentlemen."

"Nice to meet you, Vic," Brandt answered, a small thrust of his hips accompanying each word.

Donnelly had to grasp the ledge with both hands in order to keep from pitching forward completely. Brandt took advantage of this by reaching around and taking hold of his penis, which protruded upward and, from the feel of it, had begun to drip precum in response to the pressure of Brandt's cock on his prostate. Brandt's hand was still slick with lube, and he slid it rapidly along Donnelly's girthy prick.

"Well, we'll leave you two to your romantic evening," Winnie said, taking Vic's hand. "We'll see you for breakfast in the morning— just come down anytime."

"Sleep in if you like," Vic said, in the manner of someone used to toning down the enthusiasms of a voluble partner.

"Thanks, guys," Brandt said, thrusting more vigorously now. "We'll see you tomorrow."

The proprietors walked out of sight.

"I can't believe you," Donnelly scolded, but his voice was husky and his breath short.

"Want me to stop?" Brandt teased.

"Fuck no." Donnelly began to push back against Brandt, matching his thrusts and meeting him halfway.

Brandt surged more forcefully, building a fuck rhythm that had Donnelly gasping.

"Not going to last long if you keep that up," Donnelly managed to say.

"Sometimes it's not about the journey," Brandt grunted. "It's about the destination." He felt the orgasm building deep inside, and it wouldn't be long until it overwhelmed him.

Donnelly bucked and writhed and clamped down all along the length of Brandt's invading cock. This was the clear sign he was about to come.

"Oh, and one more thing," called Winnie's voice from below.

"Fuck," blurted Donnelly.

Winnie appeared on the pool deck once again. "We have a group arriving tomorrow, first thing in the morning, so if we're a little busy please bear with us. Looks like we'll have a full house for the coming week!"

"That's… great," Donnelly managed to get out before the orgasm swept away his ability to speak. The splatter of his semen on the balcony wall was, apparently, below the range of Winnie's hearing.

But the sound of it put Brandt right over the edge, and he froze in midthrust as his cock jetted deep into Donnelly—who moaned quietly as Brandt flooded him.

"Well, good night, then," called Winnie as he walked back out of sight below them.

"Good night," Brandt managed as the tightness in his chest caused by their public performance began to recede.

Once they were alone Donnelly slumped forward onto the balcony wall. "Holy fucking shit," he panted out.

Brandt leaned forward, covering him, wrapping his arms around him. "That was amazing," he whispered, kissing Donnelly's ear.

"Do you think he noticed?"

"I think he's noticed just about everything about you," Brandt said. "But I tried to be super subtle with my thrusting."

"Subtle like a grizzly bear." Donnelly laughed, then abruptly stopped. "Don't make me laugh while you're still inside me. I want to keep you there as long as I can."

"That might lead to a repeat performance," Brandt replied.

"I'm up for it if you are," Donnelly said. "But I'm kind wondering about one thing: you're carrying lube in your pocket now?"

"I figured we're on vacation, I might as well be ready for a good time." By the feeling in his groin, his body was getting ready for another good time already.

"I like the way you think," Donnelly said, then wiggled his hips a bit. "I like the way you do a lot of things."

"I'm glad. I'm planning on doing a lot of things a lot over the next week. A lot."

"Best vacation ever," Donnelly said, leaning back to kiss Brandt.

CHAPTER TWO
THE VILLA HERMES

"HOW CAN all of our suitcases be missing?" Howie demanded of the stone-faced woman at the service desk. "One, maybe two I can see— but all six? And just ours? Everyone else got their luggage but us."

It was five in the morning, and the guys were gathered listlessly around Howie, who was positively inflamed about the airline losing his luggage. All of their luggage.

"As I explained, sir, the baggage door on your aircraft into O'Hare apparently froze shut during the flight, and it wasn't defrosted until after your flight here had departed."

"Froze shut? How does that even happen?"

"It's winter, sir. Things freeze. Your luggage will be on the next flight from O'Hare. Or the one after that at the latest."

"When will that be?"

"There's no afternoon flight on Saturday, so it will be tomorrow morning, or late afternoon if they can't fit your luggage on the morning flight. Or possibly Monday morning, seeing as the flights this weekend are overbooked. It's a very busy time, sir. We will deliver your bags to the hotel within four to six hours of their arrival here."

"So you actually have no fucking idea when our luggage will get here? What the hell kind of operation are you running here?"

"Now, Howie, let's calm down and see if we can find a solution here," Thor counseled.

Ted had seen this drama performed many times over the years: Howie blowing up at some poor service worker, Thor attempting to exercise his middle-school conflict-resolution skills. His interest in predawn airport drama exhausted, Ted stepped away from the desk to wait for the Howie and Thor Show to reach its inevitable conclusion: Howie would offend every single person within earshot, and Thor would nauseate everyone with his "can't we all get along" bit. Ted didn't need to see it again, in an airport, before dawn. He walked over to the row of seats where Bark was once again snoozing, a look of perfect peace on his face. He sank silently into the seat next to him.

"They doing the bad cop/crazy cop thing?" Bark asked, blinking awake the moment Ted sat.

Ted nodded. "They're still in the first act. Gonna be a few minutes before Howie pisses her off enough to get her supervisor."

"Any chance pitching a fit is going to make our suitcases show up?"

"Nope. They're still in Chicago."

"Then why don't we just go to the hotel and start our vacation?" Bark asked.

"You know Howie once he smells blood. It's already not about the luggage. We've been traveling all night, and he's waging moral warfare."

"Wake me when he finally gives up or someone tases Thor," Bark said. "Those are my favorite." He closed his eyes again.

Chad and Paul returned empty-handed from their mission to find an open snack bar just as Howie and Thor retired from the field of moral warfare.

"Gentlemen, here's the situation," Howie said. He was always formal when he was coming down from a conflict with someone he considered far his inferior. "Our luggage won't be here until tomorrow morning at the earliest, and it may be later than that depending on when this airline gets their heads out of their saggy asses."

"As I mentioned during our conversation with Denise," Thor interjected gently, "'saggy' is not a helpful value word when trying to reach resolution."

"So let's get a taxi and get the hell out of here," Paul ordered, ignoring the nuances of the conflict. Without waiting for anyone else to submit to his command, he strode off toward the sign that said Taxi and disappeared outside into the pink light of sunrise.

The rest of the group picked up their packs and carry-ons and followed Paul out to the curb. A line of taxis idled there, even this early in the day, and Paul had already chosen the largest one; it would have been a tight fit with luggage, but they didn't have to worry about that now. Soon they were on their way.

The taxi pulled up outside the Villa Hermes half an hour later.

"It's kind of small, isn't it?" Chad asked, stepping out of the little van. "Not gonna be a lot of action here."

"The travel guy said it was 'quaint,'" Howie replied, "which I thought meant the place was kind of a dump, but with spring break we were lucky to get anything. This actually doesn't look so bad." He paid the taxi driver and led the way through the wrought iron gate and on to the front desk. Seeing no one, he briskly pounded on the silver bell that adorned the counter.

Almost immediately, footsteps clattered along the corridor that ran behind the front desk.

"Oh, you're here," sang out a voice, and a slight man in an exotic silk dressing gown burst around the corner and then stopped short. He looked the group of six college students up and down. "Oh my."

"Checking in?" Howie blurted impatiently.

"Yes, of course," the man said. He seemed to be having trouble tearing his eyes away from them. "I'm Winston, your humble proprietor—please call me Winnie—and you must be the Hayes-Morton party?"

"That's us," Howie replied. He handed over his credit card, the one that bore the name Howard Hayes-Morton III but was paid for by his father, Howard Hayes-Morton II.

"The reservation is for three rooms, seven nights, correct?"

"That's right," Howie replied.

"Excellent. I'm so glad you'll be staying with us." Winnie's fingers danced on the keys of the front desk computer. "I'll need ID from everyone, and then I'll get you your keys and you can settle in."

The guys handed over their driver's licenses, and Winnie entered the vital information from each. "Now for keys," he said, pulling six cards out of the bin and running them briskly through the encoder. "Who's together?"

Howie turned to the group. "Usual?"

Everyone nodded, except for Ted, who simply shrugged. Rooming with Bark, which was his "usual," meant he would spend the week with an increasingly painful erection from watching Bark walk around the room naked. But to object would mean having to explain, and as a result, possibly hurt his feelings, so Ted said nothing. As usual.

"Here are your keys, then," Winnie said, handing pairs of key cards to Bark, Chad, and Howie. "Now let me show you around." He stepped around the desk and looked, puzzled, at the group. "No luggage?"

"The damn airline left it all in Chicago," Howie groused. "They'll bring it here tomorrow. Or they'll fuck it up again somehow."

"Oh, that's too bad," Winnie replied with a furrowed brow and empathetic frown. "But you'll find we're very casual here, so no worries about feeling underdressed. Come this way." He led them back into the courtyard, past the fountain, and out onto the pool deck that formed the center of the hotel. The infinity pool glittered in the morning light, and the ocean beyond was deep blue.

"Wow," Thor said, looking out over the view. "This is really beautiful."

"Thank you, dear," replied Winnie with just enough modesty to convey his deep pride in the hotel.

The pool deck formed a horseshoe around the pool, and the rooms opened onto it with large french doors, mostly made of glass. There were several umbrella tables tucked under the balcony of the second-floor suite, and a number of brilliant white sun loungers around the pool.

"Room one is over there," Winnie said, pointing to the room on the far left side of the pool. "That's you, dear." He pointed to Bark. "Room two is here, and that's yours." He nodded to Chad and gestured to the glass door to the left of the entrance. "Over here is room three." He pointed to the room on the right side of the courtyard. "Breakfast is served on the pool deck here pretty much anytime you'd like it. Are you starving?"

"Hell yeah," answered Paul. The others nodded their agreement.

"Well, I don't want to keep a... *man* waiting for his breakfast," Winnie replied with an appreciative glance at Paul, who winked at the effusive innkeeper, a courtesy that had him blushing as he scurried off toward the kitchen. "I'll have it out in a few minutes."

The guys drifted off to their respective rooms. Bark opened the door of his and Ted's, and that's when Ted saw it: the bed. *A* bed. King-size, but just one. Shit.

"There's just one bed," Ted muttered, knowing Bark would not find this an impediment of any kind because Bark didn't have personal space. Ever.

"Then you can keep me warm," Bark said sweetly, and brushed his fingers along Ted's cheek before walking off, laughing, to check out the bathroom.

Standing perfectly still, trying to convince his rising boner to go back to sleep, Ted willed himself to think of other things. That's when he realized he should have taken his mom's advice about packing an extra change of clothes in his backpack. All he had was his laptop, a book, and an overpriced car magazine he'd bought during their layover in Chicago.

"Sucks not to have our suitcases," he remarked to Bark. "I don't have any clothes other than what I'm wearing."

"Eh, whatever," Bark said, as he often did. He came back from the bathroom. "We can just wash some stuff tonight after we get back. It'll be fine."

"Back from what?"

"From whatever we get up to tonight," Bark replied with a sinister laugh. "It's spring break, man! There are honeys out there who need to get with this." He pointed, of course, to himself. To his crotch, specifically.

Ted smiled and nodded, as if he too were interested in nothing so much as finding a "honey."

They stood for a moment, looking down at the beach and the ocean beyond.

"Breakfast," called Winnie from the pool deck.

"Fuckin' starvin'," grunted Bark, and he lunged for the door.

Ted followed, trying not to think about the hell of sleeping right next to Bark for the next week.

Winnie, and the strapping salt-and-pepper man he introduced as Vic, had very quickly arranged a substantial breakfast buffet on a large table near the pool. They were placing the last few items as the guys approached the spread, taking plates from a stack at the end of the table and surveying the food.

"Everything looks amazing," Thor said. "You did all of this yourself?"

Winnie, looking deeply flattered, put an arm on Vic's shoulder as he placed a large tray of fruit at the center of the table. "My man here just loves to cook up a storm," he gushed, "and with so many strong bodies to feed we're going to be getting a workout this week."

Howie looked around the pool. "Kind of a sausage fest, isn't it?" He turned to Winnie and Vic. "Any chance the suite up there is filled with women?"

"Oh, you must be the funny one," Winnie replied, laughing, as he hustled off to refill the orange juice, already running low. Vic followed, carrying metal covers from the trays of eggs and bacon.

"Anyone else think the smaller one might be a little...," Howie said, "oh, I don't know... gay?" His voice dripped with sarcasm.

"He was kind of staring at me," Chad offered.

"I thought you lived to have people stare at you," Paul said, before shoveling another huge bite of scrambled egg into his mouth. "You're not going to have a very long career as an underwear model if you don't like people staring at you."

"I'm serious. I think he was checking me out."

Ted quietly piled breakfast on his plate and took a seat away from the others. Bark joined him shortly.

"Pretty good spread, huh?" Bark asked, then tucked into his breakfast.

"Yeah, it seems like a nice place."

"If only the owners would stop looking at Chad," Bark said with a laugh. "That guy, I tell ya." He shook his head and attacked some french toast.

"These seats taken?"

Ted looked up and saw two newcomers—men, of course—standing at the table, hands on the two empty chairs.

"No, please, sit," Bark said.

"Thanks," said one and sat, while the other went to the buffet table. "You must be the group Winnie seemed so excited about. I'm Gabriel Donnelly." He smiled at them.

"I'm Barclay, but everyone calls me Bark. And this is Ted. Everyone calls him Ted."

"Pleased to meet you, Bark, Ted," Donnelly said, extending a hand to each in turn. "You guys just get in this morning?"

"Yep," Bark said with a weary nod. "Would have been here sooner except the airline decided we should travel light, so they left our luggage in Chicago. Took a while to sort that all out at the airport. But we're here now, and with any luck we'll have clothes and stuff tomorrow."

"Well, with a day as beautiful as this, it's hard to complain about anything," Donnelly said, taking the coffee the other man had brought back from the buffet table. "Bark, Ted, this is my partner, Ethan Brandt."

The word made Ted's heart skip a beat, then two. He smiled weakly and extended a hand. "Pleased to meet you, Ethan," he managed to say, far more quietly than he would have liked to. He shook his head to clear it of whatever short circuit had been caused by meeting the two handsome... partners.

Ted turned his head and nodded across the pool. "That's the rest of our group. The angry-looking one is Howie. He's fine—that's his normal face. Next to him is Chad, and the guy piling six pounds of scrambled egg on his plate is Paul." Ted lowered the hand he'd been using to point out the guys and scanned the pool deck. "Ah, there he is. Thor's the one over there trying to rescue that beetle that fell into the pool."

"Here for spring break?" Brandt asked.

"Oh hell yeah," Bark answered. "It's gonna be awesome." He looked around the pool deck. "Assuming, of course, there are actual women somewhere around here. No offense."

Brandt smiled. "None taken. We may seem elderly, but I remember spring break."

"You don't seem old," Ted mumbled, barely audible.

"Why, thank you, Ted," Donnelly said. "Ethan here likes to remind me I'm closing in on thirty, but I still have a couple of good years in me yet." He turned to Brandt. "All right, first shot of caffeine is on board. Breakfast?"

"Sounds good."

They rose and headed for the buffet.

"They seem nice," Ted said to Bark.

"Sure, I guess. Though I was kind of hoping what Howie said— that the penthouse up there was full of women having pillow fights and wondering if what they say about lacrosse players is true."

"That they're all conceited windbags who think they're God's gift?" Ted replied, smiling.

"Green is not your color, buddy," Bark shot back, but with a genuine smile. "I'm heading back in—need anything?"

"Grab me one of those scones?"

"You got it." Bark went back to the buffet, passing Brandt and Donnelly on their way back.

"So, Ted, where you guys from?" Donnelly asked once he and Brandt had sat back down.

"Polytechnic State, way up north," Ted replied.

"Must be frigid there this time of year," Brandt said.

"It is. It's kind of a shock, being here. It was ten degrees when we left home last night."

"Oh, man," Donnelly said with a shiver. "I thought our winter was bad."

Winnie made the rounds of the guests, making sure everyone had enough to eat. Then he stood by the pool and called for their attention. "Welcome, everyone, to Villa Hermes. If there's anything we can do to make your stay more comfortable, please don't hesitate to let us know. We're delighted we'll have all of you here for the coming week. Now, here are a few things to remember. First, access to the beach is by way of the bluff stairs, just outside the property and to the right. Three flights of steps and you're on the sand. Second, most of the spring break fun will be happening at the bars and clubs along the north end of the beach. Just follow the hooting and pheromones! And finally, since your luggage has not yet arrived, you'll be happy to know the pool area is swimsuit optional. Cover up or go bare, as you wish. We're all men here!" Winnie finished his speech with a joyful giggle.

"Hell yeah," said Bark, who had returned to the table during Winnie's talk. "Here's your scone." He handed Ted the small plate he'd brought back to the table, then stood up and yanked his shirt off over his head. He unbuckled and unbuttoned his pants, and, sliding them to the ground, he was suddenly and exuberantly naked.

"Cannonball!" he cried, launching himself through the air. A titanic splash and wave erupted across the previously calm pool.

"That's the spirit," Winnie cheered, once he had caught his breath. The sight of the naked and airborne Bark had apparently winded him.

Bark flipped over onto his back and floated, paddling lazily out to the edge of the pool where it seemed to disappear over the bluff and fall down to the ocean. Once there, he hiked himself up onto the ledge and looked over, his bright white ass displayed to the assembled company in all its glory. Ted looked down at his plate.

"Your buddy Bark is an enthusiastic guy," Donnelly remarked.

Ted whipped his head back to the table; Donnelly was looking at him carefully. "He's all enthusiasm when it involves getting naked," Ted replied. Bark always tortured him this way, a torture made worse by the fact that Bark had no idea the pain he was causing.

"If I were in that kind of shape, I'd probably be the same way," Brandt said.

Ted noticed the look Donnelly shot Brandt in response to his remark. He had never spent much time in the company of anyone in a gay relationship, and the first thing he noticed was how... normal it was. This interaction—one partner appreciating the beauty of a younger person, the other casting a warning glance—was exactly the kind of interaction any other couple might have.

"I think you are in that kind of shape," Donnelly said. "Feel like you might want to jump in?"

"Wouldn't that seem a little creepy, jumping naked in the pool with him?" Brandt countered, giving no indication he was even considering this.

"Don't worry about that on Bark's account," Ted said to Donnelly. "He's happy to have anyone looking at his body, male or female. It's kind of his thing."

"I think I'll hold off for the time being, thanks," Brandt said.

"This is a...," Ted began awkwardly. He leaned over the table and whispered, "a gay hotel, isn't it?"

Donnelly seemed surprised by the question. "Um, yes, it is." He sat back and looked at the group of college guys finishing their breakfast. "Did you guys not know that?"

Ted shook his head. "Not only that, but none of us are gay. Howie's dad's travel agent set it up for us at the last minute."

Donnelly was about to reply when Paul stood up and stepped to the edge of the pool. He stripped off his shirt and shucked off his jeans and plaid boxers and stepped off the edge into the deep water of the pool.

"All right!" called Bark, who appeared quite happy to have company in the water.

He splashed at Paul, who strode powerfully over to him and simply smash-dunked him under the water. Bark popped up just out of his reach, and splashed away giddily. Paul lunged at him, grabbed him around the waist, and hefted him out of the water. Bark yelled and laughed and slapped at Paul's bulging muscles but Paul simply turned about with Bark over his head as if he were a lumberjack trophy, rotating in a case. Bark shook water everywhere as he struggled, his legs kicking, his cock flopping madly about.

"I should go, um… do something," Ted mumbled. "Nice to meet you."

"Likewise, Ted," Brandt said.

Ted made a point of not looking at Bark as he walked quickly into their room. Once there, he flopped down on the bed and covered his head with the pillow so he wouldn't be able to hear Bark's naked hooting. He didn't know how much more he could take.

AFTER THE splashy hubbub of breakfast had subsided, Brandt and Donnelly sat finishing their coffee. Bark and Paul lay on loungers at the edge of the pool deck, absorbing the sun's rays across their entire bodies, while the other guys huddled over a table discussing their plans for the first day of spring break.

Winnie walked over and took a chair at Brandt and Donnelly's table.

"Well, gentlemen, what do you think of our new arrivals?"

"They seem like a friendly bunch," Donnelly said.

"I wouldn't mind getting friendly with either of those," Winnie said with a head-tip toward the loungers. "The muscly ginger is simply breathtaking, but his strapping lumberjacky friend the otter… well, I don't know that my heart could take it."

"Um, Winnie," Brandt began, "do you know much about these guys?"

"Only that they filled my little hotel during a week when we would have been empty save for the two of you, and that means the books may balance this month after all." He looked at Brandt's face. "Is there something I should know?"

"We talked to one of them—Ted," Donnelly said. "He told us the group didn't know this was a gay resort."

Winnie's mouth dropped open.

"And that none of them are actually… gay."

Winnie's mouth snapped shut. He furrowed his brow and took a rather flustered breath. "Not even the lanky ginger who nuded up so quickly?"

"Apparently not," Donnelly answered with a shrug.

"Well, this is bad. This is very bad indeed," Winnie lamented.

"They seem to be okay with the place," Brandt offered. "Maybe they don't even care."

"The problem is… well, the problem is much larger than that."

"What's the problem?" Donnelly asked.

"You may not know, but this area is pretty conservative, politically. Sure, they love the money horny college kids bring, but there are a lot of people here who don't like the idea that we cater to a gay clientele. Imagine, if you will, a group of business owners who turn a blind eye to a whole line of football players slurping Sex on the Beach body shots off of mostly-naked sorority girls down there at Señor Horny's Hideaway but think because we provide a discreet yet refined resort experience for men that we're the immoral ones. All the little bigots on the chamber of commerce have been dying for a reason to shut us down."

"But how will hosting a group of straight college guys get you shut down?" Brandt asked.

The intricate relationships among sexuality, commerce, and morality still mystified him, despite his experience over the last year working to implement his own state's equality statutes.

"Last fall, when we'd been open only a few months, we had a group we thought looked perfect: a dozen young men here for a pre-Thanksgiving holiday. We only had two rooms open, but we put out some cots and they piled in. But it turns out they were missionaries staying here for a few days before shipping out to Eastern Europe, and they only stayed here because everyone else in town was closed for the holidays. Well, we couldn't exactly afford to do that, since we had just opened, so we were happy to have them. The problem was that we already had a few guests that week, and they were taking full advantage of our clothing-optional policy around the pool. We were able to sort it all out pretty quickly, once we fished that one poor missionary out of the hot tub, where he had fallen into the arms of another guest. And just between us girls, he was definitely not objecting to the attentions he received. But when their mission leader found out what kind of place they were staying in, he rousted them from their beds and marched them out of here in the middle of the night. I think he spent every waking moment for the next month writing angry letters to newspapers and church groups and the chamber of fucking commerce, pardon my French."

"It was a misunderstanding, that was all," Brandt said, indignant. "Why did they make such a big deal about it?"

"Because it gave them a shot at getting us shut down. I tell you, it got weird after that. At one point there was a helicopter hovering over the beach so someone could take telephoto pictures of our pool deck. I think they wanted shots of guests *in flagrante*. But we got lucky because that week we were hosting a group of retired librarians from Iowa, and all they saw were knobby knees and the covers of old books."

"Exciting stuff," Donnelly said with a smile.

"Right? I'd much rather watch Ginger and Otter over there cavort in the pool, but business is business. The problem is that if any of these straight college boys feels oppressed by the gay agenda while he's here, the flames could be fanned. This is why we reworked the website to be clearer about the kind of clientele we market toward."

"That explains the photos of boys by the pool," Donnelly mused.

"Oh, that was a fun weekend," Winnie said with a distracted smile. "I asked all of my gentlemen friends of a certain age to contribute to the cause."

Donnelly frowned. "Not one of those guys looked to be over twenty-five."

"Exactly. I asked everyone to bring their pretty young thing of the week, and we let them loose on the pool." He smiled dreamily. "It was quite a weekend. But it didn't really help us," Winnie continued. "If anything, it made it worse. The website showed potential guests what they could expect, but the locals got wind of it and claimed it proved we were running a brothel or something." He looked out over the group, the snoozing Bark and Paul, the conferring Chad and Howie and Thor. "A full house of straight boys. I don't know what to do."

"I'll tell you what we *don't* do," Vic said, coming up behind Winnie and taking the fourth chair at Brandt and Donnelly's table. "We don't freak out, and we don't make a big deal where there isn't one. We just trust that this generation really is over the whole gay panic thing, and that it won't be a big deal. We can't live like we're under siege, Winnie."

Winnie put his hand on Vic's, and beamed at him. "That's my man. My rock."

"So how did you two end up here, running the inn?" Brandt asked, trying to get the conversation on something more pleasant than whether a helicopter would shortly appear above to gather incriminating evidence.

Vic nodded to Winnie, a tacit acknowledgment of his partner's role as the storyteller.

"We met nearly thirty years ago," Winnie said, looking with loving eyes at Vic. "This guy was in the front row of a show I was in, and I saw him standing there, glassy-eyed and star struck, and I just had to meet him. I asked the house manager to invite him to my dressing room after the show, and he came."

Vic cleared his throat. "I was there on a dare. I was in college, the same age as our guests over there. Some buddies of mine bet I wouldn't go to a gay club and sit in the front row during the drag show they did on Saturday nights. Now, I'm not one to walk away from a dare, so I went. It was the most awkward thing I'd ever done. Awkward, that is, until Winnie LaPugh here showed up on stage."

"I made a bit of an impression on this poor boy," Winnie said with a laugh.

"Then after the show, when I got the note inviting me backstage... well, I didn't really know what to do about that. My buddies were waiting for me outside the club, but then it seemed rude not to go." He looked at Winnie and smiled. "That decision changed my life."

"We've been together ever since that night," Winnie said, resuming the thread of the story. "We met in Austin, but I was working at my family's business in a raggedy little town out in the middle of nowhere. Once Vic finished school, I finally came out to my parents, and... well, that began our life on the road. We landed in a string of poky little towns, because that's the only life we really knew. Vic's a wonder with the welder, and I was a CPA, so we always found work. We managed to save up a little nest egg, and when my parents finally kicked it and went to whatever hell awaits virulent homophobes, I inherited enough to allow us to purchase the wreck that was on this plot five years ago. Four years of blood, sweat, and tears—"

"The blood and sweat were mostly mine," interjected Vic.

"The tears were almost always mine," Winnie said with a faux moue. "But we persevered and became the area's prime gay resort."

"In a not very crowded field," Vic added. "We're also the area's only gay resort."

"Which is one too many for some of the redneck locals," Winnie concluded.

"I don't think you have much to worry about," Donnelly said, nodding to the college crowd. "They don't seem to be obsessing about it."

Chad was walking back out of the room he appeared to be sharing with Thor. "This is all I brought," he said to the others, holding up four book-size boxes.

Howie burst out in derisive laughter. "You're the only one who thought to put extra clothes in your carry-on, and that's what you brought? Four boxes of underwear with your picture on the front?"

"Fuck off, Howie," was Chad's reasoned reply. "These have gotten me more tail than you'll get your entire life."

"You have sex with a woman and then give her a box of underwear?" Thor asked. "Men's underwear? With your picture on the box?" He shook his head in wonder.

"Hell yeah. Chicks go crazy for that shit." Chad smiled a crooked grin that was doubtless part of his seduction routine. "I'll even sign it for them, if they deserve an extra thrill."

Watching this scene from the table across the pool deck, Winnie leaned over to Donnelly and whispered, "You know, I'm starting to think they actually are straight."

Donnelly stifled a laugh by clamping a hand over his mouth.

"So if we go out tonight, four of us will have clean underwear," Howie summed up. "And the other two will either have to stay here or go commando."

In unison, Bark and Paul raised their hands. "Commando," they said, then went back to lounging in the sun.

"Well, I guess that's settled," Howie said. "Now, let's see what we've got." He yanked a box out of Chad's hands and started to open it.

"Hey," protested Chad, "those are the ones I'm going to wear."

Howie tossed the box back to Chad, and grabbed the other three when Chad dropped them on the table. "Here," he said, tossing a box to Thor. "I'll take these, and Ted can have these." He looked up as if realizing Ted wasn't there. "Hey Ted! Get out here."

Ted appeared in the doorway of his room, and then walked over to where the other guys were gathered. He smiled at the table of older men as he passed.

"What is it?" he asked Howie.

"Chadwick has provided us with clean drawers for this evening," Howie answered, handing Ted a box.

"Um, thanks?" Ted said as he looked at the box. He opened it and pulled out a sheer black brief; he held it up to the sun. "I can see through this," he said, plaintively.

"You can't once you have it on," Chad said. "Unless you look really close. But if she's looking that close, then they've pretty much done their job, haven't they?" Chad nudged Ted in the ribs with his elbow.

"Heh, great," Ted replied, running the slip of black fabric through his fingers. "Thanks, Chad." He walked back to his room and disappeared inside.

"Well, I'm beat. I'm gonna go take a nap," Howie said to the guys, and then he walked into the room he shared with Paul.

"I'm gonna try out the hot tub," Chad said, taking off his shirt. "You comin'?"

"Sure," Thor said. "I'll bet the view is beautiful."

Chad shucked off his pants. "I just want some hot bubbly water to wash off the airplane stank." Clad in just his plain tighty-whities, Chad walked over to the hot tub.

Thor followed, wearing a pair of somewhat dingy green boxer briefs. "Those what you underwear models wear on your days off?"

"I tell ya, you get kind of sick of smashing your junk into tiny weird thongs. It's nice just to have some soft cotton around the boys sometimes." Chad slipped into the hot tub. "Ah, that's the stuff."

Thor stepped in after Chad and settled in on the side that cantilevered out over the edge of the terrace. "The beach is gorgeous. Looks like everyone's sleeping off their Friday night, though. There's no one down there."

Chad, however, was lying back with his eyes closed and failed to keep up his side of the conversation.

"What do you think about a walk on the beach?" Brandt asked Donnelly.

"Sounds wonderful." He turned to Winnie. "Thanks so much for a great breakfast. And it really seems like you don't have anything to worry about from these guys. They seem perfectly content here."

"I hope you're right," Winnie replied. "I'd hate to have anything get in the way of my blueberry pancakes for Sunday morning."

"Best. Vacation. Ever." Donnelly, beaming, took Brandt's hand and they walked out through the courtyard to the beach steps.

Chapter Three
Spring Broken

IT WAS late afternoon when the guys gathered again on the pool deck to discuss their plans for the evening. Ted's internal clock was a mess, with the overnight travel, jet lag, and then a huge breakfast; he had slept right through Bark coming in and lying down on his side of the bed after the sun grew too warm for him.

Winnie scurried out of the kitchen area with a large box in his arms. "Now, I know your luggage hasn't arrived yet, so I pulled out my lost-and-found box. Most of it is clothing that for some reason got flung over the edge of the pool deck or wedged between a bed and the wall." He looked up at the startled guys. "You know how people can be on vacation. Anyway, I washed them up, and you are welcome to anything you like."

"Thanks, Winnie. That's very thoughtful," Thor said, ever the group's diplomat.

Ted and the other guys rooted through the clothes bin. The look in general was 80 percent tropical and 20 percent slutty, with an emphasis on bright colors and stretchy fabrics. Ted pulled out a pair of cargo shorts that at least came down past midthigh, but all of the shirts seemed to be clingy V-necks in children's sizes. He chose the largest one he could find, in a deep blue, and retreated from the box to try it on in the corner of the pool deck nearest his room.

Bark, starting from naked, simply slipped on the first pair of shorts he found right where he was. He grabbed out a shirt in a complementary color and stretched it over the muscles of his torso. It was a tight fit, and he looked somewhat more naked with it on than he had before.

"Wow," Winnie said appreciatively. "That looks like it was made for you."

"Let's hope the ladies I meet tonight agree with you," Bark said with a courtly bow to Winnie.

Chad, Thor, and Howie also found clothes they could wear, and soon the pool deck looked like a circuit party in Palm Springs. The exception was Paul, who seemed content to get back into his jeans and flannel shirt regardless of the weather.

"Now, I would be a terrible host if I sent you out to the clubs with nothing in your tummies," Winnie exclaimed, "so hold on and I'll bring out a little something for you to nibble on." He hustled away excitedly.

"Is it just me, or does he seem to be getting off on having us here?" Howie asked. "It's like we're entertainment for him or something. Kind of creeps me out."

"Me too," Chad added. "When I got out of the hot tub he was totally staring at me."

"Oh shut up," growled Paul. "He's a nice guy, and he's gone out of his way to help us. It's not like he's been pawing you or anything. Grow the fuck up already."

Brandt and Donnelly returned to the villa as the guys were packing away the discarded clothes, Thor attempting to fold everything as carefully as it had been when Winnie opened the box for them. Vic walked out to light the torches that were placed every few feet around the deck and out along the edge of the terrace. Then Winnie arrived with a huge tray of cold cuts and veggies. Placing them on the table, he scurried back and returned immediately with several bottles of wine. Vic brought out some glasses, and they opened the bottles and began pouring and handing around glasses.

"Now don't you worry your pretty little heads about drinking," Winnie hooted merrily. "You won't have to drive for an entire week, and if you can't find your way home, just give us a call and we'll come get you."

Ted took his glass of wine and walked over to the table he had shared with Brandt and Donnelly earlier. They were already there, sipping wine and talking about the day's adventures.

"May I?" Ted asked.

"Please, sit," Brandt answered. "How was your day, Ted?"

"I didn't see much of it, honestly. After breakfast everyone kind of crashed for the middle part of the day. We all just got up, and

Winnie found these clothes for us to wear." He looked over at Bark and then quickly back to the two men. "What did you guys do?"

"We walked all the way down the beach to the south until we got to this stretch that was kind of industrial and not all that pretty," Donnelly replied. "Then we turned around and walked all the way up into town. It's not a bad little shopping district, and we found a sidewalk café for lunch. Most of the places, though, seemed to be of the 'drink until your clothes fall off' variety. They weren't even open yet, so it was actually a pretty nice stroll."

"You guys going to go out tonight?" Ted asked.

"We'd like to," Brandt answered. "But I think we'll be looking for a rather different experience than you guys seem to be going for. Winnie mentioned a great seafood place over on the wharf we might try."

Ted nodded. "Are you guys—no, that would be rude to ask."

"You can ask us anything, Ted," Donnelly said warmly.

"Are you guys married?"

"We're engaged," Donnelly answered. "It just became legal for us to get married in our state about a year and a half ago, and we're planning on getting married in June."

"Congratulations," Ted said, blushing for no reason he could fathom. "I think that's great."

"Thanks," Brandt said. "You know, Winnie was very worried you and your friends might not be okay with this being a gay resort."

Ted smiled. "I think the reactions vary. Bark, as you may have noticed, will probably only go to gay resorts in the future because he can be naked all the time. Nothing bothers Paul, ever, so he's good. Thor tries to get along with everyone, so even if it did bother him, you wouldn't know it. Chad's a weird one. He's been modeling for a couple of years now, and because he's got that allover tan from his mom being Latina, he gets a lot of underwear shoots. You would think that would make him like Bark, but it doesn't. He'll walk into a room full of women in a jockstrap, but if there's one guy out there, he freaks out. Now, Howie, he's the strangest one of all. He's pretty chill about most things, but when it comes to sex, his conservative parents have really done a number on him. I wouldn't say he's full-on phobic, but he can get a little twitchy about it."

"Sounds like you know the guys pretty well," Donnelly said.

"We've stuck together since we were on the same floor freshman year," Ted replied. "I roomed with Bark, and the other guys were in the other two rooms in our pod. I think we got thrown together by random chance, but it seems to work. Howie and Thor only *seem* like they're going to kill each other—it hasn't come to that yet, anyway."

"Bottoms up, Theodore," called Bark. "The fair maidens of this hamlet await their first taste of our manhood."

Ted rolled his eyes. "He gets Shakespearean when he's horny," he said apologetically to the older men. "Have a nice evening."

"You too," Brandt said as Ted walked over to where the other guys were gathered.

"ALL RIGHT, men, here's the plan," Howie said to the assembled group. "We walk to town, find females, get drunk, and get lucky. Any questions?"

The plan seemed simple enough, and they struck out for the beach steps. It was a quick walk down to the beach, and within ten minutes they were at the edge of the town, where several neon-lit bars stood watch over the sand. Groups of already drunk spring breakers made mostly futile attempts to keep a volleyball in play on sand courts adjacent to the bars. The group passed by these first establishments on the strength of Howie's belief that the outskirts were for the unsophisticated.

A little farther up the street, they were assaulted by booming music coming from a club on the ocean side of the main drag. Strobes and black lights dominated the atmosphere inside the large bar and its dance floor, visible through large windows giving out onto the street. Howie pointed to the front door and cocked an inquisitive eyebrow at the gang; the response was strong enough that he turned and opened the door for all to follow him. Ted brought up the rear. As usual.

Howie handed the bouncer at the door several bills, and the group entered the club. The scene inside was a sweaty jumble of bodies, bobbing in time to the relentless beat thudding through the speakers. Winding through the crowd were young women in go-go boots distributing free shots into the mouths of dancers by way of hoses connected to tanks on their backs. Ted hadn't intended to partake, but he happened to open his mouth to say something to Bark when a passing shot girl squirted a jet of fruity rum right in. He nearly choked, and by the time he had stopped coughing he was pretty buzzed. He didn't drink much, and it occurred to him that his habitual abstinence from alcohol had lowered his tolerance dramatically. He sought out a place to sit along one side wall of the club. He was joined shortly by Thor, who handed him a tall, fuchsia drink with a parasol stuck in it, keeping one for himself.

"Well, that didn't take long," he observed, practically shouting into Ted's ear. He pointed to where Bark was dancing with a dangerously top-heavy woman; next to him Chad was the meat in a sandwich between two women who might or might not be twins.

Ted scanned the crowd for the others. He spied Howie at the bar using the tools at his disposal, buying expensive, exotic cocktails for a woman whose interest in him probably extended no further than his credit line. Paul was nowhere to be seen, but Paul could take care of himself. Ted sipped the drink Thor had brought him and found it to be both overwhelmingly sweet and powerfully alcoholic. The business plan of the club seemed to be to get people shitfaced on cheap, strong drinks and then get them to spend more money on the expensive stuff later in the evening. It was largely working, from what Ted could see.

"Aren't you going to dance?" Ted asked Thor.

Thor shrugged. "I'm always kind of uncomfortable in this setting," he replied. "It's really hard to get to know someone when all you can hear is the music and you're getting knocked around by a dozen other people trying to share the same square foot of floor."

"I don't think getting to know people is what Bark and Chad have in mind," Ted said. The dancing was quickly turning into a full-on contact sport. Bark and his dance partner writhed and jiggled until they were, by popular acclaim, launched up onto the bar to continue their dance with a spotlight on them.

"Next round's on me," Ted said, taking his empty glass up to the other end of the bar and asking for two more of the same. As the drink was a specialty of the house, it was dispensed at high velocity from a gun kept under the counter, and Ted was soon on his way back to Thor with two more bright pink glasses. "Cheers to the lonely ones."

Thor drank, but as soon as he had swallowed, he made his objections known. "Here's what I don't get, Teddy," he slurred a bit, leaning toward Ted so violently Ted thought he might end up on the floor. "You could be doing exactly what Bark does, but you don't."

At that moment Bark was stripping off his shirt so he could come into even more direct contact with his dance partner, to the hoots and catcalls of an adoring mob.

"Yeah, I kind of doubt that," Ted answered Thor, shaking his head and chuckling. "I guess we'll just have to content ourselves with taking the high road and drinking alone."

Thor raised his glass, returning the salute, and took another long swig of the potent punch. "To the high road," he said, his voice somewhat unsteady.

Ted drank to this toast as well, and from that moment the evening got a bit blurry.

THE BED is shaking.

Do they have earthquakes around here?

Someone's moaning. Why is someone moaning in my bed?

Oh, shit.

Ted felt something against his leg. Something warm. A leg? At first he thought it was Bark's leg, but it was smooth and slender, unlike the lacrosse calves Bark had worked so hard to develop.

Whoever's leg it was, it was moving. It seemed increasingly likely that it belonged to whoever was moaning. Next to him. In his bed.

Ted opened his eyes to find the room mostly dark. The light from the bathroom illuminated a streak across the foot of the bed, and he could see the duvet moving rhythmically. He wasn't sure he wanted to know what was going on next to him, though by this point he knew full well what was happening. He looked at the pillow next to him and saw a tangle of long blonde hair. She, whoever she was, was facing away from him. Her arms were wrapped around Bark and his around her. They were writhing together on their sides—how were they even doing that? Ted tried to imagine what mechanics were in operation under the covers, but then realized he was trying to picture his best friend having sex. He closed his eyes again.

He wanted to get up, to slip out of the room before the congress next to him reached its inevitable conclusion, but that seemed awkward. Perhaps less awkward than lying there pretending not to exist, but overall Ted was more comfortable with his complete erasure than he would have been with the visibility of stalking across the floor while they went at it.

Plus, from what he could tell, he was naked.

Where the see-through black briefs had gone was just one of the mysteries of the evening. A mystery, Ted knew already, he would prefer to let recede into the mists of time. He probably had barfed all over himself and had to be hosed down and put to bed. And of course Bark would figure that if he was too far gone to keep from soiling himself, he would surely sleep through Bark and his new friend working through the *Kama Sutra*. This was the kind of insane reasoning that added up only on spring break.

Ted decided to play dead and wait for it to be over.

A few minutes later, however, as the pace quickened and the moaning rose an octave, he felt compelled to open his eyes. What he saw was worse than he could have imagined.

It was Bark. Looking back at him.

He held his lady friend close, strong arms holding her as his rhythmic thrusts grew more urgent. He was flushed and a bit sweaty, but his green eyes were locked on Ted as he moved up and down with the effort of sliding his—Ted knew this as much as he tried not to know it—nine inches of stiff cock in and out of her.

Ted tried to look away, made every effort to close his eyes, but he could not. Seeing Bark this way, transported by physical pleasure, so transfixed him that he was powerless to break their connected stare. His eyebrows rose in panic as the sheer obscenity of the situation overwhelmed him.

Bark's eyebrows rose along with his.

Ted's chest grew tight. He closed his eyes for a long blink and opened them.

Bark did the same.

Oh, fuck.

Bark's pace was growing ever faster; the moans of his companion were rising to a staccato frenzy of yelping. And still his eyes remained locked on Ted's.

Ted took a deep breath. He couldn't live with himself if he didn't try to determine whether Bark's mirroring of his motions was coincidence or intentional.

He opened his mouth, and bit the right side of his lower lip. It was a move every movie heroine does when she wants to convey simultaneous innocence and sexual availability. He did it because he had to know.

Bark's eyes crinkled for an instant, just as they did when he was about to burst out laughing, but he didn't laugh. No, instead he opened his mouth and bit down on the left side of his lower lip, exactly mirroring Ted's motion.

We're really doing this.

Ted didn't remember feeling the erection grow, but he was now certainly aware of its presence on his belly. It throbbed in time with Bark's thrusting, and now he felt it slipping crazily side to side in a slick pool it had produced near his navel. Ted hadn't touched it, but he felt its eager presence, the warmth it created radiating out from his groin.

Bark's eyebrows began to peak, and his breath was short. Ted knew he was close, and he watched with fascination the changes that swept over his friend's face as the moment neared. His cheeks flushed, and he licked his lips as if they were dry from the exertion—Ted did the same, without even thinking—and sweat beaded on his forehead, dampening his hair to a dark copper. Then, the spasm started. He froze at the peak of a thrust, and made a dozen tiny little jabbing movements while his eyes rolled upward. His mouth formed into an O, and his cheeks pulled in and puffed out with frenetic bursts of breath. He writhed, arms and legs in motion, and then...

And then.

Ted's world stopped spinning when Bark's hand touched his shoulder. Hot and sweaty and strong, at first it seemed accidental, a byproduct of his grasping for leverage, a better angle from which to pound away at his lady fair. But then it flopped over, palm pressed against Ted's clavicle, and the fingers gripped his flesh. Ted looked down at it in a panic, and then back up to Bark's face, which was contorted and red. No breath, no sound. But his eyes never looked anywhere but at Ted's.

Bark was frozen this way for several long seconds, and then a growl unlike anything Ted had ever heard rumbled through his chest and out his throat. His hand, though—his hand never released its grip on Ted's chest. The fingers grasped and released but then grasped again even harder. Bark wouldn't let go of him.

Then, suddenly, his expression changed from one of angry exertion to one of surprised bliss. Eyebrows peaked, mouth open as if chasing its next breath. It was a look of pleasure and innocence, as if Bark were experiencing this for the very first time, as if this orgasm were a roller coaster he had saved all of his summer chore money to ride, one time, before school started. It was the entire story of his life in one look, and it was what did Ted in.

As Bark cried out in ecstasy, Ted's lonely member responded in kind. As he watched Bark's primal thrusting, their gazes still locked on each other, his cock suddenly erupted. The orgasm took him completely by surprise, and he thrashed in its grip while Bark shivered out the last spasms of his.

And still he held Ted tightly, never taking his hand back, never looking anywhere else.

As the spontaneous orgasm waned, Ted's chest tightened. What the fuck had they just done? His heart pounded. But then the hand that had come to rest on his heart relaxed its grip. Ted was relieved that this bizarre physical connection would be broken. But Bark didn't lift his hand off Ted's chest, despite its panicked heaving, driven by the breath he couldn't seem to catch. Instead, the fingers began to move in little circles, small tickling movements that sent goose bumps springing all across Ted's chest. The sheer insane intimacy of this motion made the blood drain from Ted's face, but Bark simply smiled as his breathing slowed to normal.

And then, with a wink, he pulled his hand back and wrapped his arm around the woman who was between them. He closed his eyes and his head sunk back to the pillow and out of sight.

Ted tried to work out his next step, but nothing came to him. He was in a bed with his best friend and the woman he had obviously brought back from a bar; those two had just had sex with each other, and Ted had accidentally done so as well, but with himself. Now they seemed to be snoozing, and he was wet and mortified. There was nothing in Ted's experience to prepare him for this situation, which, he was certain, had never happened to anyone ever.

He decided he just needed to get the hell out of there. As he slid out of the bed, he did his best to wipe off his torso on the sheet. It would be an awful mess—Ted didn't think he had ever come so much in his life—but it was better than walking out of the room dripping with spooge. He stood up, searching the floor for something, anything, he could put on. Luckily, though his underwear were still missing in action, his cargo shorts were conveniently wadded up in the middle of the floor. He stooped down to put them on.

"Oh, is your friend leaving?" a woman's voice asked from the bed.

Bark only grunted uncertainly.

"He's welcome to stay and join us… I mean, if you're into that. It would be fine with me."

"Thanks, but I was just leaving," Ted said inanely. "You two have fun." He opened the door and stepped onto the pool deck.

CHAPTER FOUR
WALK OF SHAME

THE PINK light of dawn was just beginning to bathe the pool deck in its warm glow as Ted stumbled out across it. He plopped down in the first chair he came to, which happened to be the one he had sat in the day before when talking with Gabriel and Ethan.

He didn't know what to do, what to think.

He stared out at the horizon, the pinky-gray promise of a new day, and felt hot tears invade his eyes. What the fuck had just happened? What had he done? What had Bark done?

Ted simply had no place in his brain to hold the reality of what had transpired in that bed. He could still feel the weight of Bark's hand on his chest, the tender spirals he had drawn in the afterglow. But why had he put his hand there? It had to have been accidental. That was it—the entire thing was an accident.

The horizon reserved judgment.

If it had been an accident, wouldn't he have pulled it away immediately, once he realized it had come to rest on Ted and not whoever that woman was in bed with him? Ted's chest wasn't exactly hairy, but surely it felt different enough. But Bark had looked at him, right at him. And he had smiled. And winked. And there was no way that was an accident.

The very top of the sun broke over the flat, distant horizon of the sea. It was a fierce red jewel for a moment, and then it widened and glowed more golden. The daylight was here.

Bark had done it on purpose. He had reached out and touched Ted, had meant to touch him, and kept touching him while he had sex. While he thrust his way to coming. While he came. Ted closed his eyes under the weight of it. Bark had touched him and looked right into his eyes, even after he came.

This was the part that made Ted's head hurt, his chest pound. He had, in his brief and largely uneventful sexual history, had orgasms under the influence of things that seemed like a good idea at the time, but once the surge and splatter had passed, all he felt was shame. A sort of minor version of this happened every time he viewed porn while jerking off; most times he tried to close his browser window just as the last throb of ejaculation faded so as not to be reminded of what had pushed him over the edge once the thrill had gone. The most violent reaction he had ever suffered was the first time he had accidentally clicked on a gay porn video and ended up watching it with a shocked curiosity. His orgasm had been unplanned but driven to completion by the sheer novelty of watching male bodies fit together in ways he'd never even let himself imagine. The desolation he felt once he had soaked the carpet under his desk, however, was unprecedented in his entire life. He didn't touch his penis for weeks after that, except to try to scrub it clean in the shower. It was months before he even looked at porn again, and more than a year before he allowed himself to open another gay video, this time in less accidental circumstances.

This he knew: if Bark had not wanted to do what he did, had not done so consciously and on purpose, he would not have been able to keep his hand on Ted's chest after the orgasm had finished with him. He would have pulled back and looked away and maybe even shoved him out of bed.

But he had smiled. And winked. And touched him so delicately and lovingly Ted could still feel the traces of his fingertips from his clavicle down to his nipple. That touch was real. What feelings lay behind it—well, that he needed to figure out.

The sun was stronger now, emerging from the haze of the ocean horizon, and Ted blinked away from it. He noticed there was something on the lounger out by the edge of the terrace. It looked like a pile of towels.

But it moved.

Ted leaned forward and squinted a bit to bring focus to the movement. He saw a foot sticking out from underneath the pile. He got up and walked around the corner of the pool to the loungers, and there he saw it wasn't a pile of towels. It was a blanket. Two, actually—one on each lounger. Under one was Thor, and under the other was Howie.

"Morning," Thor said sleepily, looking up at Ted.

Howie grumbled and turned over, pulling the blanket over his head.

"Decided to sleep outside?" Ted asked, unsure why anyone would want to do this, despite the warm weather.

"Chad brought home some company, and the bed wasn't big enough for all four of us."

"Four?" Ted said, surprised.

"Yep. You know Chad once he gets going. At one point he had three of them, but we lost one along the way. I think she'd had a little too much to drink. Plus some nachos, based on what the gutter looked like when she was finished. We dropped her off at her hotel on the way back here."

"So he spent the night with two women?"

Thor nodded. "For once he lived up to his own hype."

"What's Howie's story?"

Thor shook his head and gave a shrug.

"Howie's story, if you must know," Howie said groggily from under his blanket, "is that Paul disappeared from the club, and we thought he had gone to some girl's hotel room." He pulled the blanket off his face and looked up at Ted. "But when we got back here, I went to open the door to the room and heard an ungodly sound of demonic possession. It was like he was in there having sex with a wolverine. An angry, sex-crazed wolverine. I don't know where he found her, and I have absolutely no desire to actually see her, so I came out here and joined my good friend Thor, previously dispossessed of a bed by the animal appetites of his own roommate." He gave a world-weary sigh. "And that, my dear sir, is our sad tale of disappointment. I'm assuming by your presence here that perhaps Bark was also one of the lucky ones?"

"I guess you could say that."

"Well, then, gentlemen, perhaps we can rustle up some coffee and make this a respectable little support group of the vaginally excluded?"

"As long as you agree never to call it that," Thor said, disgust on his face. He sat up and threw off the blanket. He was still wearing the clothes from last night, and he tried gamely to smooth out the wrinkles in the tight turquoise fabric of his shirt. "I'll go see if there's coffee on."

"How much does this suck?" Howie asked as he got to his feet. "We come all this way, surround ourselves with horny women, and end up like this—alone, balls as blue as the sea." He spat over the edge of the terrace. "Shit."

"Come on, you reject," Ted said, putting an arm around Howie. "Let's get some coffee in you and the old spirit will come back. I'm sure you'll find your own wolverine tonight."

"Thanks, Ted. That means a lot coming from someone as sexually stunted as you."

"Fuck off, Howie."

"Love you, man." Howie dropped into a chair just as Thor came back around the corner, with Winnie following right behind.

"I found coffee," Thor said happily.

"And more than that," Winnie cried. He was carrying a coffee urn and a basket of pastries, which he set on the table. "We will have a hot breakfast for you in a bit—we tend to have leisurely Sunday mornings here."

"This is really great, thanks," Ted said as he took a mug from a stack Winnie pulled out of a cabinet nearby.

"It's my pleasure, gentlemen. We often have some guests who feel a bit peckish when the sun comes up, so I keep a few things at the ready." He watched, beaming, as the guys helped themselves to coffee and muffins. "How was the night on the town?"

"You're looking at the rejects," Howie groused. "The others are still enjoying the company of their new acquaintances."

"Oh, I see," said Winnie in a mock-scandalized tone. "Well, there are more fish in the sea. Enough for all of you to fetch on board this week. Now I must help that man of mine get the breakfast fires burning. Let me know if you need anything more, all right?"

"Thanks, Winnie," Thor said between bites of danish. "You're the best."

"Oh stop it, you," Winnie said modestly. "Well, don't stop altogether. You're such a charmer." He waved and walked briskly back to the kitchen.

"The old faggot makes decent coffee," Howie observed.

In a blur of motion, Thor's hand clamped down on his wrist.

"Ow!" Howie cried.

Thor just shook his head slowly, a look on his face Ted could only describe as venomous.

"Sorry, sorry," Howie said, pulling his wrist back and rubbing it with his other hand.

"You don't have to approve, but you *will* be civil," Thor growled.

Ted had never known Thor to react so aggressively, but he had to admit he was glad he did. Howie had grown too free with his moral disapproval lately.

The tension around the table was dispersed by the opening of the door to Chad and Thor's room. From the room stepped a tall brunette with a deep tan and high-heel shoes that would clearly be useless on the sand. She was followed by an almost identical model with a slightly darker tan and somewhat lighter shade of hair. Both wore tiny boy shorts, and halter tops that barely contained their impossibly spherical breasts. They tottered out onto the pool deck, giggling at something— or perhaps nothing. Next to step out of the room was Chad himself, bearing two boxes of underwear. These he presented to the women with a bow and a thousand-watt smile. This would have seemed strange to anyone who didn't know him, but Ted was fully expecting it. What he wasn't expecting was what Chad was wearing: a pair of bright blue briefs with no back. Like a stylized jockstrap, the briefs left his tanned and round ass completely exposed.

It wasn't a bad look, Ted reflected before he shook his head to clear it of such a perverse thought.

"Ladies, thank you for a lovely evening," Chad said to them as he took their arms to lead them out through the courtyard.

Ted was momentarily distracted by the undulations of Chad's buttocks, framed by bright blue spandex, as he walked away from the pool deck. He again shook it off, annoyed at his inability to keep the reins tight on whatever perversity had been unleashed by Bark's touch.

A taxi pulled up into the circular drive just as the trio reached it, and into this Chad deposited his guests. He turned and padded back down through the courtyard to the pool deck, and joined the three rejects for a cup of coffee.

"Morning, gentlemen," he said as he poured himself a cup and stuffed a pastry in his mouth. He stood rocking back and forth and grinning while he chewed.

"That's a… good look for you," Thor said, glancing at Chad's ass.

"Thanks. I got a ton of these after a shoot a couple of months ago. I was worried that it seemed kind of… you know, gay… what with being assless and all. But the chicks really seem to dig it. And the brunette was really into it. The stuff she did to my ass, man… I've never had anyone get into it like she did."

"Way, way, way oversharing, dude," Howie said with a wrinkled nose.

"Sorry. Kind of punch drunk right now. Girls did a number on the Chadster."

"Is that what we're calling your dick now?" Howie asked.

"Funny. I'll laugh at your lameass jokes when you can land two hotties in one night. Until then, I can't really be bothered." He sat down and put his feet up on another chair to drink his coffee and bask in the golden dawn light.

"Seems to me we need to set some ground rules on the sharing of beds," Howie continued, undaunted. "The three of us vacated the premises so you three could get your rocks off, and we're going to need equal time."

"Seems to me," countered Chad, "this is pretty much an academic question until you can locate a female who wants to get busy with you. I don't like your chances."

"Eat shit, asshole," grumbled Howie angrily.

Tempers might have flared were it not for the opening of another door. Bark chivalrously held the door for the leggy blonde who had just recently been rubbing up against Ted in their bed. She was attired similarly to her counterparts from Chad's room, and Bark was wearing… Ted's sheer black briefs.

Ted stared, his mouth hanging open.

"Guys, this is Darlene. Darlene, this is Chad, Howie, and Thor, and of course Ted, whom you've already met."

"Nice to meet you all," she said, smiling prettily. "And Ted, I wish you had come back to bed. It would have been fun."

The other three guys turned wide eyes to Ted as Bark escorted Darlene through the courtyard and to another waiting taxi. Ted simply shrugged, as if he had no idea what she had been talking about.

"So how are we this morning?" Bark called as he returned to the group. He poured himself a cup of coffee and came to stand next to Ted's chair. He put his hand on Ted's shoulder, at exactly the same place he had put his hand before, when they were in bed. Together.

Ted felt an electric charge surge through his body from where Bark's hand rested. It was harder and harder to breathe, but he willed himself to be calm and pretend not to notice.

"Sounds like you and Ted got up to some fun last night," Thor teased. "Ted hadn't even mentioned it."

"That's because Ted is a gentleman, and gentlemen don't tell." Bark leaned down to look Ted in the face, though upside down. "Do they, Ted?"

Ted shook his head with a sly grin, which he hoped achieved the two effects he intended: first, he wanted to let Bark know he wouldn't talk about what had happened in bed earlier, and second, he wanted to hint to the other guys that maybe something had in fact happened with Darlene in bed earlier. This latter effect would not only put them off the scent of anything happening between Bark and himself, but also—just maybe—make Ted seem like something other than a complete washout when it came to sex.

Bark smiled broadly and clapped his hand on Ted's shoulder again. "Good man," he said heartily and then took a chair and reached for a muffin. "Good man."

"So who else got some last night?" Bark asked the group.

Chad raised a lazy hand, as if bedding two beautiful women was a nightly occurrence for him. "Twice," he said suavely.

"Just twice?" Bark scoffed. "Really? I lost count at six."

"No, I mean I slept with two women at once last night."

Bark gave Chad a congratulatory nod. "Kudos," he offered. "They just do you, or did they get with each other a little?"

Chad's grin erupted enthusiastically in response to Bark's question. "A little," he replied with an enigmatic shrug. He seemed content to let the group do the math on that one.

"Excellent," Bark pronounced with a sage nod. "How about the rest of you?"

Howie and Thor shook their heads, but all Ted could do was look—look at the man with whom he now shared a far deeper connection than they ever had, or he had ever dreamed of. He couldn't say he hadn't gotten lucky, because he had. He just didn't know whether it was the best luck in the world or the worst luck imaginable.

The sound of Paul's door opening distracted Ted from his musing; in fact, all heads swiveled toward the sound. Paul stepped out of his room, in just his jeans, and turned back to smile at whomever was about to emerge onto the pool deck in this bizarre "morning after" pageant they were experiencing. All of them, but Howie in particular, watched expectantly for her to make her appearance.

But it wasn't a her at all. It was a… him.

He was as tall as Paul and built as solidly. He even wore jeans and a plaid shirt like Paul favored. They stood there, bearded and handsome, for a second or two. Might have been an hour, actually, as time seemed to have stopped for Ted and probably everyone else watching. Five gaping faces were turned toward them, but they didn't seem to notice.

Paul held out a fist, and his guest bumped it. "Good shit," he said, in his deep, rumbling voice.

The other man nodded. "Fuck yeah," he replied, then turned to walk out through the courtyard.

"Remember to ice that," Paul called after him.

"Nah," the other man called out, not even turning around. "Bruises are trophies." As he reached the front drive of the hotel, he slung his leather backpack over his shoulder and just kept walking.

Paul grabbed a cup of coffee and sat among the astonished, the utterly breathlessly astonished, men. He took a long sip and looked at the horizon for a moment. Then he seemed to realize no one had recovered their power of speech.

"What?" he asked, to no one in particular.

"Dude," Howie managed. "Dude, that was a… dude."

"Very good, Howie. You nailed it."

"But…" was all Howie could muster as a follow-up.

Bark leaned over and presented his own fist for bumping. "He was hot, man," he said with a wink.

Paul fist-bumped and nodded his appreciation for the compliment to his taste in men.

"But," Howie finally was able to say, "you're not gay."

Paul looked at him as if he'd sprouted another head. "The hell you talking about?"

"I'm talking about how you are the fucking manliest man I know. You're not gay."

"Wait. I thought you all knew." Paul looked from face to face, met each time with an uncomprehending stare. "I haven't exactly hidden this from you."

"Uh, yes you have," Howie replied more assertively.

"I think what's got us confused," Thor offered, shifting into conflict resolution mode, "is that you've never brought a guy home."

"I didn't want to make anyone uncomfortable," Paul said simply. "But you know I go out on the weekends, and I tell you about the guys I meet."

"I don't remember you ever doing that," Chad said, his face a replica of Howie's—confused and growing upset.

"Last weekend I came home in the morning and told you about this guy I fucked. How much clearer could I be?" Paul's voice was growing a little angry now.

"I thought you meant you'd fucked a guy *up*," Howie retorted. "You know, got into another bar fight."

"Another bar fight? I've never been in a bar fight in my life!"

"But you always talk about these guys who come at you, and then you whale on their asses…. Oh," Thor said, a light dawning on him. "Oh, I get it now."

"All this time I've been telling you about guys I hooked up with, and you thought I was raging through every bar in the city beating people to a pulp? What the fuck?"

"You don't act gay," Howie snapped, suddenly flushed with anger. "You don't seem like one of them."

Paul leaned toward Howie, and his voice was quiet, deadly. "I understand this is a shock, though I still don't completely get how that happened. But I strongly caution you that saying anything stupid about sexual orientation will get you seriously fucked up, my friend. And I mean actually fucked up, not just fucked. So just take a moment to let this all sink in and don't say anything for a while. Okay?"

Howie, clearly terrified, nodded and fell silent.

"Who wants sausage?" rang out Winnie's voice from behind them. He walked out onto the pool deck with the first of many platters of breakfast food, and the group seemed to appreciate the distraction.

Ted grabbed a plate and sat at his usual place, where he was shortly joined by the guys from upstairs.

"Looks like some of the guys had an interesting night," Donnelly remarked, looking from Chad's jockstrap to Bark's sheer black briefs to Howie's perturbed scowl. "How was yours?"

"It was—" Ted stopped short when Bark walked past his usual chair, taking his breakfast over to a lounger near the hot tub to eat looking out over the ocean. "—complicated," he said with a sigh.

Donnelly looked confused and a little concerned but let Ted off the hook from explaining.

"And how was yours?" Ted asked, recalling his social obligation to keep the conversation going, regardless of the turmoil in his chest.

"It was nice," Brandt answered. "We went to that restaurant out on the wharf, and then my buddy here dragged me to a club. I think there was dancing involved, but it's all kind of fuzzy."

"Dancing on the bar, at one point," Donnelly said with a grin. "Or don't you remember that?" He chuckled at Brandt's mystified reaction, then turned to Ted. "Tequila will do that to you."

"You let me drink tequila?" Brandt moaned. "Well, that explains the touring company of *Stomp* currently performing in my head." He rubbed his brow miserably.

"That's okay," Donnelly said. "It will all come back to you when we go back there later. They said they'd have your picture on the Wall of Shamelessness by tonight."

"There are pictures?"

"Oh yes. Especially once you flung your shirt off. That caused quite a stir." He looked at Ted with a scandalized expression. "There were injuries in the scrum."

"Oh fuck." Brandt lowered his head to the table.

Ted felt the angst lift for the first time since he awakened. "I think that's awesome," he said to Donnelly. "You guys should cut loose on vacation. Good for you."

"Thank you," Donnelly replied triumphantly, as if Ted had won some long-standing argument on his behalf. "My partner here is somewhat less inclined to letting his hair down. At least last night he loosened up a bit." He reached over and stroked the back of Brandt's neck. "Don't worry, love. You didn't embarrass yourself. Much."

Ted and Donnelly shared a laugh while they ate their breakfast, and after a few minutes, Brandt recovered enough to join them.

Bark walked by again, bussing his plate to the tray Winnie had provided for the purpose, and then once more as he returned to the hot tub. Once there, he slipped off the briefs and stepped, naked, into the water.

Ted watched this performance as if it were in slow motion. When he turned back to his breakfast companions, he noticed them sharing a glance.

"Ted, would you like to take a walk?" Donnelly asked. "I think my usual walking partner needs some additional time to clear his head of the agave fog."

Ted was surprised by the offer, but the prospect of getting away from Bark was something he couldn't turn down. "That would be nice," he said. "Just along the beach? Or should I grab a shirt?"

"Come as you are," Donnelly replied, smiling. He stood and kissed Brandt on the top of the head.

Ted and Donnelly walked out through the courtyard and around to the beach steps. Donnelly kicked off his sandals once they reached the sand, and set them on a rock along with his shirt. Then the two men set off down the beach, which at around eight on a Sunday morning was completely deserted except for the occasional portly old man in long shorts waving a metal detector across the sand.

Ted hadn't realized Donnelly was in such good shape. His pectorals bulged with power, like Bark's. His abs stood out in sharp relief, just as Bark's did. His shoulders were pronounced and rounded with muscle, just like Bark's.

Shit. It's like wherever I look, all I see is him.

"So, Ted," Donnelly said as they walked along. "How are you?"

It seemed like idle, polite conversation, but it also seemed to Ted to be quite a personal question.

"Fine," he answered lightly.

Donnelly nodded and kept walking along, looking at the scenery. "How are you, really?"

If the first question was mere politeness, this one cut right to his heart.

"How did you know?" he asked, nonsensically. He suspected Donnelly would make sense of his response immediately.

"Well, first, I'm a police officer, and we get pretty good at sensing when something's not right. And second, when you're a gay police officer, you get even better at it, especially when you think you might help someone who looks a little lost."

"Is it that obvious?"

Donnelly nodded sagely, his eyes kind. "Want to talk about it?"

Ted was quiet for a long moment as they walked along the sand. "I don't know how," he said finally. Then he shrugged. "That sounds stupid."

"No, it's not stupid at all. That's actually a really common response people have when they start to consider that maybe what they've always thought about themselves isn't true."

Ted turned to Donnelly, amazed. "Seriously, how do you do that?"

Donnelly grinned. "It's not a superpower or anything. It's just a sense I have. I'm usually pretty good at reading people."

"Wow."

They walked along for another few minutes. Ted took a breath and opened his mouth to say something three separate times but still could come up with nothing he could put into words. Finally he sighed and just looked down at the sand passing under their feet.

"How about you start with Bark," Donnelly suggested gently.

Ted stumbled and nearly fell at the mention of his name. Donnelly put out a hand to steady him.

"Seriously, you have to tell me how you do that," Ted said once he had recovered his footing.

"I will. Promise. But first let's talk about what's going on with you and Bark."

Ted nodded. For some reason he felt he could trust Donnelly, and more than that, he seemed to want to tell him the things he couldn't even tell himself. But he still didn't have the words.

"Take as much time as you need," Donnelly said. "It's a slow Sunday morning, and the beach goes on forever."

"It feels really weird to talk about this," Ted said eventually. "I mean, there's stuff I haven't even figured out inside my head. Stuff I've actually worked really hard not to think about."

"Uh-huh," Donnelly said encouragingly.

"Is that normal? To feel like there's stuff inside of you that you don't really want to feel, but you can't make yourself not feel?" Ted sighed. "Shit, I'm not making sense."

"Actually, what you're saying makes a lot of sense. I've come to the conclusion that the most normal thing about human beings is that we're all completely convinced we're not normal—as if no one has ever felt what we're feeling. I guess one of the things that comes with getting older is seeing that nothing we feel is new, no matter how weird or scary it seems to us. If we feel it, then over the history of the species many, many, *many* other people have felt it too."

"Wow."

They walked along in silence for another few minutes.

"So," Ted began, "it's about Bark."

Donnelly nodded and waited.

"He's my best friend, and he's the greatest guy."

"He seems like it," Donnelly added.

"It's just that... sometimes, I feel like... I don't know...."

"Take your time."

"Sometimes I feel like I don't know what I'm supposed to feel about him... you know, as my friend." Ted moved his hands as if trying to sculpt meaning out of the air around him. "Being around him makes me feel like... like I'm real. When he's not around, I miss him more than I think a friend should. And when he comes home, the first thing I want to do is see him and talk to him. And just be near him."

"And is that different from how you feel about your other friends?"

Ted considered this for a moment. "I like the other guys in the house, and I have friends I don't live with, and seeing them every once in a while is fine. But I don't get that feeling with them. The feeling that maybe this time we'll finally do or say something that will explain why I'm that way around him. Why my stomach kind of flips when he puts his arm around me, or when…."

Donnelly looked at him as they walked. "When… what?"

"When he takes his shirt off," Ted mumbled, then covered his face with his hands. He could feel hot tears rolling down his cheeks, now he'd said it out loud. The thing he'd only been able to say to himself, and only when he was too tired to fight it off any longer.

Donnelly didn't say anything. He simply reached out his arm and put it around Ted's shoulder. Ted leaned into him, the casual embrace providing him the strength to face down this demon inside him. He sobbed a couple of times, forcing the tears out. They walked along this way for a little while, and then Ted sniffed mightily and righted himself.

"I've never told anyone that," Ted said simply.

"I am honored to have heard it," Donnelly said with a smile. "And speaking as someone who has also seen Bark take his shirt off, I agree."

Ted chuckled before he could catch himself. "He does tend to get naked a lot. It's kind of the worst thing in the world for me."

"And that's the feeling that makes you think Bark means more to you than just a really good friend?" Donnelly asked.

Ted shrugged helplessly.

"Have you ever talked with Bark about this?"

"Oh fuck no," blurted Ted. "Oh, sorry. I didn't mean to swear. It's just I could never…." He shivered as the horror of articulating his feelings to Bark washed over him.

"I can see that would be a really hard conversation to have. But have you ever given him any indication you feel this way? Or has he ever caught you looking at him in a way he thought was funny?"

"No. I haven't even really been able to think it to myself, much less let him see it." Ted tried to imagine what it would be like not to feel ashamed of his attraction to his best friend. "You are so lucky," Ted said with a sigh.

"Me? Why?" Donnelly asked.

"Because you can say things like you notice Bark's body, and you're okay with it. It's just part of who you are."

"You mean, because I'm gay?"

Ted nodded.

"You want to know a secret?" Donnelly whispered conspiratorially.

"Sure," Ted answered. He figured he was about to get some kind of gay code that would unlock his conflicted feelings about Bark and himself and everything.

"I wasn't always gay."

Ted stopped dead. Just stopped walking and stood gaping at Donnelly. A stride and a half later Donnelly must have realized he was alone, and he turned around. He tipped his head and raised his eyebrows as if expecting an explanation for Ted's sudden disappearance.

"What?" Ted asked, his voice tight and a little panicked.

"I said I wasn't always gay."

Ted shook his head, still sure he had misunderstood. "That can happen?"

"Yes, it can. Until I met Ethan, I was completely straight. Or, I guess I should say, I was interested only in women, sexually."

Ted, still trying to take this bizarre information in, started walking haltingly forward again. "Then what happened?"

"Well, Ethan and I were partners on the force for about two years. We became good friends, but that was it. Like you and Bark, we saw a lot of each other. We were practically living together as well as working together every day. Then we got an assignment that… well, it showed me a different side of him. Or, probably a better way of saying it is that it showed me a different side of my feelings for him. All of a sudden, when he took his shirt off, my stomach starting doing a little flip," he said with a smile.

"And you told him? About how you felt?"

Donnelly took in a breath through gritted teeth. "Well, it wasn't as simple as that."

"Why not?"

"Because he was straight too. At the time. At least I thought he was, and he thought he was, so… yeah."

"Wow. Complicated."

"Yes, yes it was. I tried to bottle it up, because it honestly scared the shit out of me. I was sure if he ever found out he would kill me. Not a figure of speech—like he would actually kill me. But eventually I couldn't keep it locked up inside anymore."

"How did you tell him?"

Donnelly cast a thoughtful eye to the clouds overhead. "Looking back on it, I probably could have chosen a better way to let him know. I just kind of dropped it on him in a moment of complete emotional exhaustion."

"What did he do?"

A smile broke over Donnelly's face. "He kissed me."

"Dude, no way."

"Way," Donnelly replied with a laugh.

"So, that happens?" Ted couldn't wrap his head around two straight guys just sort of… doing that.

"It did for us. We went about it in a way most people would probably never believe, but as I said before, there's nothing new in the human heart. It could very well be that until recently there wasn't a way for two guys to fall in love like we did. It would have been too dangerous. But luckily, things are changing, and I think it will get easier and easier over time."

Ted just shook his head at the bizarre tale Donnelly had told him.

"Can I ask you something?" Donnelly said.

"Sure," Ted answered, kind of relieved to have the other man drive the conversation.

"What forced this crisis? Why is the situation with Bark suddenly more than you can keep tamped down?"

Ted studied the ocean for a bit, not at all sure how to go about answering this simple question. "It was something that happened last night," he began. "Or, I guess, this morning. Bark brought a woman back from the club, and somehow—I was kind of drunk, so I don't know exactly how—we all ended up in bed together."

Donnelly's eyebrows shot up. "Well, a threesome is one way to break through the tension."

Ted laughed. "It wasn't a threesome. Not really, I guess." He pondered how to describe it. "It was more like he was having sex with her, but sharing the emotional part of it with me."

"Neat trick. How'd he do that?"

"While he was… involved… with her, he reached out and put his hand on my chest. Right here." Ted thumped his chest, right where Bark's hand had rested.

"You're sure it wasn't an accident?" Donnelly asked, squinting at Ted.

"I thought it was, at first," Ted replied. "But then he just left it there. And then he started, like, pawing me with it, dragging his fingers along my skin as he was putting it to her. And then… and then it got weird."

"He was petting you while having sex with a woman right next to you, and *then* it got weird?"

Ted chuckled and nodded. "He looked at me. Looked right into me. I looked back at him, and we just… connected. His eyes never left mine, even when he was… reaching completion. We just stared at each other the whole time, like it was us, like she wasn't even there."

"Oh, wow," Donnelly said. "That changes things."

"I know, right?" Ted replied. "And then, when he was finished, he kept his hand on my chest a while longer, just kind of making little tickly circles with his fingertips. It's like we were cuddling afterward."

Donnelly nodded thoughtfully. "I can see why this would have you confused about the nature of your relationship." They walked a little farther. "Seems to me you two have taken a kind of baby step toward something that's more than friendship. But there are a lot of possibilities in that direction, so you kind of need to figure out what you want from it, and what he wants from it."

"I think I know what I want from it. From him."

"You do?"

"I do. While I was watching him I kind of… experienced something… amazing."

"Oh," Donnelly said, an expression of comprehension appearing on his face. "So while he was involved with her, you took matters into your own hands?"

Ted smiled at the decorous language but shook his head. "Actually, my matters kind of took care of themselves."

Donnelly cocked an eyebrow at Ted as they walked. "Really? Just like that?"

Ted nodded. "Just like that. It was messy and kind of gross, actually. I mean, in the moment it was awesome because it felt like for the first time in my life my body was getting what it has always wanted. It did what it wanted to do, even though I've fought against it for years. But once it was all over, I had no idea what to say to Bark, or even if should say anything at all. I just kind of slunk out of there, and figured I would figure it all out later." He turned to Donnelly and looked up into his kind face. "I'm really lucky you came along to help me work all this out."

"One of the things I think you'll appreciate about the universe is that once you are honest with yourself and the people around you, you'll find support all over the place. People can sense when they are getting glimpses of the real you, and they will help you when you need it."

"I get the sense you are a super optimistic person, Gabriel. I kind of want to live in your universe, where everything you feel has been felt before, and there are people waiting to support you if you give them a glimpse of your true self."

Donnelly laughed. "I've been accused of having a relentlessly upbeat attitude. In fact, Ethan accuses me of that on a regular basis. But I still believe it's true we are never as alone as we think we are, and others can only support us when we let them see who we really are. Be true to yourself, and the rest of it will fall into place."

"I like that," Ted said, a ray of hope shining into his life for the first time today. "Now I just have to figure out who I really am."

"I think you're getting a pretty good start on that," Donnelly replied.

"Maybe. But I don't think I'm ready to do what Paul did this morning."

"Oh, what did I miss? Do tell."

And as they walked back to the villa, Ted brought Donnelly up to speed on what he'd slept through that morning. As they mounted the beach steps, Donnelly was obviously still trying to grasp how it had all happened.

"So, he honestly thought everyone knew?" Donnelly asked.

"That's what he says. And once he explained it all, it was pretty easy to see how we'd misinterpreted everything, mainly because we were all assuming that there's no way a guy who's so macho could possibly be gay. I guess we were all stuck on the stereotype."

"That's just one more thing for you to break through," Donnelly said as they walked through the courtyard and onto the pool deck. "I guess spring break is an appropriate time to break with the past, right?"

"Right," Ted declaimed with what he hoped was actual resolve. That would remain to be seen. "Thank you, Gabriel, for taking the time to talk with me. I really appreciate it." He held out his hand.

Donnelly took his hand firmly and gave it a bracing shake. "You're going to be fine. Start with being honest with yourself, and with him."

Ted nodded. He knew what he had to do. The trick was whether he could actually do it.

Chapter Five
Storm Warning

While Donnelly and Ted walked the beach, Brandt had slowly been recovering from his tequila-fueled misadventure the night before. The college crew lounged about lazily, napping, sunning themselves, and snacking on the breakfast buffet, which turned into a brunch and then into a lunch.

Brandt was sitting under an umbrella reading when Winnie plopped himself into a chair across from him.

"Good God, straight boys can eat," he said, wilting with dramatic exhaustion. "I keep bringing out more food, and they keep putting it away. They may look like pool boys, but they eat like football players." He wiped his brow and winked at Brandt. "Or so one would imagine.... I haven't fed a football player in some years now."

Brandt set down his tablet. "I was the youngest of three boys," he said. "My mother said that if she'd had another, she'd have had to start robbing grocery stores. My little sister was quite a relief to her."

"So there *are* more like you at home," Winnie said slyly. He glanced along Brandt's biceps for a long moment.

"And every one of them straight... so far as I know, anyway."

"Much like our little group here, I'm afraid." Winnie looked across the pool deck at the lounging boys. "Such a waste," he said, shaking his head.

"I'm sure next week you'll once again have a full house of gorgeous gay ones, and all will be right with the world," Brandt replied.

"It can be a bit of a mixed bag during the spring-break weeks," Winnie said. "I'm afraid I'm going to end up with a houseful of old creepers who just want to sit on the edge of the terrace with their binoculars and watch the young lovelies they can no longer attract—or afford."

"I've never really understood the fascination with 'young lovelies,' myself," Brandt replied. "Much nicer to have someone fully grown to build a life with, isn't it?" Brandt said. "I didn't think I'd find that at my age, and I never in a million years expected it to be a man."

Winnie's eyebrows shot skyward. "Do you mean... he *turned* you?"

Brandt considered Winnie's insinuation for a moment. "I wouldn't say that. More like we turned each other."

"My, my, what a world I've lived to see," Winnie said, fanning himself delicately. "Back in my day there were only the normals and the queers. And if you were one, you could never be the other. I guess today there are more options available. How much better it is to be young and gay today."

Brandt nodded. "I think it will be better still once we get past labels altogether. Honestly, just between us, I don't really consider myself gay, actually. I fell in love with a man, and he was kind enough to return the favor, but I'm not at all sure the label fits me, or us, or what we are to each other. I get that it's politically important to have the labels, because that's what allows us to push for equality. But once we have achieved that—and I have to believe it'll be soon—I hope we can ease up on the labels and let people just love the people in their lives."

"I hope you're right, Ethan. You describe a world I hope I will see. But until then, I'm glad to be able to provide a place where the labeled ones can sun themselves and dream of a world that accepts them as equals."

"That's very philosophical of you," Brandt said with a smile. "And here I thought it was all just about college guys parading around in jockstraps."

"Oh, the politics are secondary to that, make no mistake," Winnie replied, laughing. "The views this week are the finest we've had."

At that moment Chad walked by their table on his way from the hot tub to the breakfast/brunch/lunch table. He still wore the bright blue jockstrap, though now it was dripping wet and clung to every curve and ripple of what it concealed. Winnie watched him intently as he passed, head swiveling like an owl.

"It *is* you!" he cried as Chad completed his transit.

Chad stopped and turned around. "Excuse me?"

"Oh, I'm sorry," Winnie said, clapping his hands to his mouth. "That was very rude of me. It's just that... well, I'm such a fan."

Chad squinted at him, obviously lost. He shook his head and waited for clarification.

"I mean I'm a huge fan of"—Winnie leaned toward Chad and whispered loudly—"Chaz Mannington."

The blood drained from Chad's face, which wore an expression of pure stupefaction. "I don't understand."

"Who's Chaz Mannington?" Thor asked from a lounger nearby.

Chad, appearing mortified by the entire conversation, clearly felt he needed to explain. "It's the name I use when I'm modeling."

Thor's brow contracted in confusion. "Why would you do that? What's wrong with Chad Menendez?"

Chad sighed resignedly. "My agent thought my last name might keep me from getting some jobs."

"Well, that's just wrong," Thor replied, his tone indicating that his social justice gene had been activated.

"I know, and I wouldn't have ditched it just because of some dumb prejudice. But there was another reason. I wanted something that sounded... I don't know, masculine. There are so many gay people who work in the fashion industry. I didn't want them thinking I was... available, I guess? Sorry, Winnie, no offense."

"None taken, Chaz dear."

Howie stuck his head up from the next lounger. "And Chaz Mannington is what you came up with?" he asked before bursting into laughter. "Nothing gay sounding about that."

"Fuck off, Howie." Chad turned back to Winnie, his face still pained. "Here's what I don't get. I only use that name when I'm working, and it never appears in the ads or anywhere else. How did you find out about it?"

"Oh, honey, you don't know?" Winnie's expression was instantly one of concern.

"Don't know about what?" Chad asked, his voice smaller and more anxious now.

"Oh, dear. Well, I wasn't going to say anything, of course, because I wasn't sure it was you—celebrities look so different in real life. But when you walked past just now, I saw it."

Chad's eyes narrowed. "Saw what?"

"Your birthmark," Winnie said, wincing a little bit as if aware he might cause offense.

Chad took a step back and brought his hands down to cover his ass. "You are seriously freaking me out right now. My birthmark has never shown up anywhere. It's always either covered, or they put pancake on it to smooth it out. One time they had to take it out in editing, but that was just because the swimsuit I was wearing tore. There's no way you could know about it."

Winnie seemed truly horrified about the upset he had caused and looked to all sides in a panic, as if searching for an escape route. "I don't know if I should…."

"You have to tell me," Chad implored. "I need to know."

"All right, all right," Winnie said, flustered. "Ethan, can I borrow your tablet?"

Brandt was surprised to be asked to participate in this drama, but he handed over his tablet without a word.

"Thank you. Now, Chad, I assume you're familiar with Tumblr?"

Chad nodded. "Of course I am. Isn't everyone?"

"Are you acquainted with a certain Tumblr in particular, called… now, don't get upset, dear, I'm only the messenger here. I have nothing to do with it. It's called 'fuckyeahchazmannington.'"

Chad dropped into the empty chair next to Winnie as if he'd been sucker-punched in the chest. "You are shitting me right now."

"I'm afraid, dear boy, I shit you not." Winnie swiped and typed on Brandt's tablet until the Tumblr interface appeared and then filled in with picture after picture of Chad. He set the tablet on the table and slid it over to Chad as if it were a bomb he was being called upon to disarm.

"Oh," Chad said as he looked at the pictures. "I guess that's not so bad."

"Scroll down a bit, dear."

"Oh fuck," Chad whispered when he had followed Winnie's instructions. "Oh fucking fuck."

Thor and Howie stepped up behind him to get a look at the screen.

"Whoa, there!" Howie jumped back in apparent surprise. "Chaddy boy, you never told us you did soft-core." He leaned closer to the screen. "Good man," he murmured, patting Chad's shoulder.

"Fuck off, Howie. I didn't—these aren't…." He looked plaintively at Winnie. "Where did these come from?"

"The person who runs this particular Tumblr says he gets them from photographers and makeup people and others who happen to find themselves at the shoot. They're kind of like outtakes."

"Chad, you're, like, completely naked in this one," Thor said, pointing to the screen.

"I know, I know," Chad replied miserably. "That looks like an underwear shoot I did last year where they couldn't decide what color they wanted me to wear, so I had to change like every ten minutes. It wasn't worth running back behind a screen every time."

"So you just change with everyone there, looking at you?" Howie asked.

"Believe me, after your first job shooting intimates you don't care who's looking at you. All they want to do is get the shots they need, and they could care less about what you look like. You just kind of forget that you have a body at all."

"If it's any consolation, dear, you have thousands of fans," Winnie said, laying a hand on Chad's arm.

His moan indicated he was not consoled. "This is just so weird. I mean, these pictures are up for anyone to see. Do you think people—I mean, like, guys—look at these and… do stuff?"

"Oh heavens no," Winnie blustered, rather unconvincingly. "I can't imagine anyone sitting down to look at these pictures, perhaps with a glass of wine, and doing *that*."

"Oh fuck." Chad's forehead met the surface of the table with a gentle thunk.

Thor clapped him bracingly on the shoulder. "Cheer up, Chad. It's not like you didn't know people love looking at the underwear boxes. You've turned those into your business card."

"Yeah, but I give those to women. There's a difference."

"What are we looking at?" Paul asked, emerging from his room, rubbing his short, spiky hair and blinking into the light. He walked over to the table. "Oh." He reached over Chad and flicked through more pictures. "Huh. Not really my type, but—hold on." He leaned closer to the screen and tipped his head to one side with a discerning frown. "Yeah, I'd hit that." He looked down at Chad. "You should wear more leather." He walked over to the pool, shucked off his jeans, and jumped in.

"Fuck. Fuck. Fuck." Chad swore in time with the thumping of his head on the table.

"Chad?" Brandt said, entering the fray for the first time. "You okay?"

Chad stopped banging his head on the table and looked up at Brandt. "It's just kind of… I feel like I've been… violated? I know that sounds stupid, but that's kind of what it feels like."

"I understand completely. The same kind of thing happened to me once."

Chad's mouth dropped open. "You cannot be serious right now."

"I am. I did an undercover job once where I had to… well, getting naked was just the beginning. Then I found out a lot of people saw me doing things that make these pictures of you seem wholesome. But you know what? I was doing a job, and I did it well. If other people want to look at me and get all worked up, then that's their deal. It doesn't mean I'm suddenly dirty or I've done anything immoral. And no, Winnie, a Google search of my name won't show you the pictures," he said as he slid the tablet out from under Winnie's typing fingers and back to Chad. "You've just had a shock, so you need to take a few deep breaths and let yourself get used to the idea of it. Then, when you've had some time to adjust, you should reflect on how this could only happen to someone who works as hard on his career—and his body—as you do. When you get to be old, like my age, you're going to look back on this time and smile because you were able to bring joy to a lot of people just by being you."

"Shit," Howie said approvingly. "You're really good at this. Do you do hostage negotiation too?"

"Fuck off, Howie," Brandt said with a grin. Everyone, including Howie, broke up with laughter.

"What did we miss?" Donnelly asked as he and Ted returned from their walk on the beach.

"Just Chaddy here discovering that he's spank-bank material on the Interwebz," Howie explained. "He's taking it kind of hard, but I think he'll bounce back. You know, Chadwick, you should just add the URL to your signature on the underwear boxes. Call it a bold integrated marketing initiative."

"The whole world's gone fucking crazy," Ted muttered as he walked off toward his room.

AFTER A light lunch, Donnelly disappeared upstairs for a few moments and returned to stand over Brandt with a tote bag. "Come on, mister. Adventure awaits."

"My adventure was going to be finally finishing this book I started nine months ago but don't have time to read at home."

"I have a better idea. Come on, I'll explain while we walk."

"Do I need to bring anything?" Brandt asked.

"I have everything we need right here," Donnelly said, patting the tote bag.

"Please tell me there's beer," Brandt said, rising from his seat.

"Of course there is," Donnelly said with a roll of his eyes. "You think I don't know how to seduce a cop?"

They walked out of the courtyard holding hands and around to the beach steps. Soon they were strolling down the beach, away from the town with its clubs and bars that would not open for several more hours. The beach was nearly full, with seemingly every partier having dragged themselves out to a towel where the alcohol in their systems could evaporate in the sun's rays. A few footballs and Frisbees were in motion, and Brandt could catch snippets of animated conversation about the exploits of the previous night and ambitious plans for the next.

"So where are we going?" Brandt asked after they had walked for a few minutes.

"I was talking to Winnie this morning, and he mentioned that he house-sits for a couple who leaves town every year during spring break season. He says they can't stand to see their town taken over by college kids."

"Just the opposite of Winnie, apparently."

"True. So they take off for another house they own in the south of France and come back once the locals have reclaimed the town. Winnie checks in on their place every couple of days."

"So we're going to Winnie's friends' house?" Brandt asked. "To what, take in their mail?"

"No, we're going to take a dip in their hot tub, which Winnie says has an amazing view."

"But there's a hot tub at the villa."

"Yes, which is occupied pretty much constantly by one or more mostly or completely naked college guys. Not exactly the romantic setting I was hoping for on this trip. But this place," Donnelly gestured at a pile of postmodern shrapnel that rose like an exploded battleship above the dune, "brings the romance."

They walked up to the gate in the security fence that surrounded the base of the house, and Donnelly typed in a code. The lock clicked, and he pushed the gate open. They stepped into a courtyard of sorts, where exotic tropical plants grew among the black granite and twisted steel cable that provided the design aesthetic for the building. The gate clicked softly shut behind them, and suddenly the sounds of the wind and ocean dropped to a whisper.

"Nice place," Brandt remarked.

Donnelly nodded. "Winnie said the hot tub was on the second floor." He looked about for a moment. "Stairs are over there."

He led the way to a DNA-like helix of stacked stone and steel, and they soon emerged onto a terrace overlooking the ocean.

"Wow," Brandt murmured. "When you said hot tub, I wasn't expecting this." He strode across the pebbled granite surface to the neat rectangle cut into the terrace. "It's already running."

"Winnie turned it on this morning from his phone."

"No shit? Who knew there was that kind of money in the world, huh?" Brandt replied. He dipped a toe in the bubbling water. "Perfect."

The pool was surrounded by a semicircle of sheer black granite panels which not only provided privacy but served to focus sound. The only thing Brandt could hear was the crash of the waves and the screech of an occasional gull floating by. It was like they were the only people on the coast.

"Don't see how the spring-break crowds would bother someone living here," Brandt said, looking around the opulent digs. "You don't even notice other people once you step through the gate."

"Which means it's the perfect place for a little skinny dip," Donnelly replied, setting down the tote bag and whipping off his shirt.

"What is it with you trying to get me naked outdoors?" Brandt demanded with an ironic smile.

"You had no problem taking off your shirt—and more—last night at the bar, so...."

"And more?" Brandt's smile evaporated.

Donnelly smiled at him as he dropped his shorts to his feet. "You may have flashed a little skin at the crowd. Nothing tasteless, of course."

Brandt closed his eyes, trying to remember what had happened the night before. All he could get was a sense of being up high and dancing and... oh shit. "I didn't actually wave my dick at them, did I?"

"Of course not," Donnelly replied as he slipped into the water. "I could only see the top of your pubes, but I wasn't as close as some people."

Brandt kicked off his shorts and lowered himself into the churning pool. "How close were some people?"

"Well, there was one young lady who seemed to want very much to find out what you keep in your boxers. She kept grabbing at you, but you managed to retain your shorts, and most of your dignity."

Brandt's eyes widened. "This was at a regular bar?"

Donnelly frowned at him. "Yeah. Where did you think it was?"

"I was just assuming it was at a gay bar."

"Does that make a difference to you?"

Brandt considered this for a moment. "Yeah, I think it does."

"Hm." Donnelly tipped his head thoughtfully. "Why?"

"Because, I guess, we're gay... right?" This sounded like more of a question than Brandt intended it to be, but having said it, he thought maybe it really was a question. It seemed to him this was something he should be sure about. "Aren't we?"

"Depends on how you look at it, I guess," Donnelly replied.

"How can this be something we don't know about ourselves?" Brandt asked.

"Well, if you define sexual orientation by what people do in bed, then I'd have to say we're pretty darn gay. I think you're super hot, but I doubt many straight guys would enjoy taking my place on the receiving end of that huge dick of yours."

"But you used to be a straight guy. I used to be a straight guy. And yet we ended up with two dicks in bed despite that. So were we not straight back then? Or did we change?"

"I don't think—"

"I mean, look at Jonah and Casey." Brandt continued. "Jonah says he knew he was gay from the moment he knew anything. Casey was straight until he found out Jonah was in love with him, and they ended up together. Does that mean Casey was mistaken, or so far in denial he didn't even know he could feel that way about another guy?"

"I don't—"

"But then again, neither of us was gay, or at least we didn't think we were. So it's not like either of us—to use Winnie's cloak-and-dagger phrase—'turned' the other."

"Stop." The command in Donnelly's voice set Brandt back. "You're kind of spinning out of control, and you need to just take a breath and relax. Here." Donnelly reached over into the tote bag and pulled out a silvery cooler pack. From it he produced two beer bottles, twisted the caps off, and handed one to Brandt. "To chilling the fuck out," he said, holding his bottle toward Brandt.

They touched their bottles together and drank.

"Now," Donnelly began before Brandt could open his mouth to speak, "I don't think it matters at all what anyone calls us. Before I met you, I dated and slept with women. A few women. Not that many women, to be perfectly honest. I enjoyed it, but when I look back on it, I have to say I can see now there was something missing."

Brandt grinned. "Another dick?"

Donnelly splashed a jet of water at Brandt's face. "No. I mean, I wouldn't trade yours for anything in the world, but it's not like when I had sex with a woman I was imagining it would be better if she suddenly whipped out a cock."

"Yeah, that would have been a little disconcerting," Brandt agreed. "But then what was it?"

Donnelly was silent for a moment, as if he was trying to find the right words. "It wasn't a thing that was missing. It was something else. It was... what we know." He squinted at Brandt as if he realized he wasn't making sense. "I mean, it wasn't until you and I were together that I realized it. That we both know what it feels like for a man."

"What *what* feels like?" Brandt asked.

"Sex. But not just sex. Love, I guess? Connection? I'm probably not explaining this right, but when you and I first broke through and connected, I felt like for the first time in my life I was with someone I understood and who understood me. I knew what you felt when I touched you, and I knew when you touched me it would be amazing because you already knew what I needed." He looked down at the water. "I'm not making any sense, am I?"

"I totally get it," Brandt said. "I'd never really put it into words, but when I think back on it, I felt the same way." He sipped his beer. "But it's not like all guys are identical. Like that twisty thing you do with your hand when you're jerking yourself? I have no idea why you think that feels good."

Donnelly smiled. "You're proving my point, actually. I did that to you one of the first times we were together. And I could tell instantly you didn't like it, because I can read your body. I saw your back arch a little, just a twitch. I know that's what I do when I'm overstimulated and I need to pull back, so it was pretty clear to me you weren't into it. Though you seriously don't know what you're missing, buddy. That little twist is magical."

Brandt just shook his head. "I will never understand that. But I am endlessly entertained by watching you do it to yourself."

"Again," Donnelly said, "not something a straight guy would probably be into."

"I'm not into it because you're a guy. I don't think I'd really be into watching any other man in the world do that. But I'm into it because of you—because I love you."

Donnelly smiled at him, but then looked off to the horizon.

"What is it?" Brandt asked.

"I was just thinking I would have said the exact same thing a few months ago. That the boner I get when you walk into the room is just because I love you. But I don't think that's really the case. I'm pretty sure I get a boner for you because I'm wired that way. And probably always have been."

"What happened to change your mind about it?"

"Promise not to get mad?" Donnelly asked.

"Seriously? You don't have to ask me that, Gabriel. There is nothing you could say that would change the way I feel about you."

"Well—"

"Unless it's something really stupid," Brandt interrupted to tease. "Then all bets are off." He recoiled from Donnelly's glare. "Sorry. Please, continue with your confession."

"It's not a confession... really."

Brandt looked hard at him, but then laughed again. "Out with it."

"It was meeting Mal that did it."

"Really?" Brandt recalled viscerally how jealous he had been of Malcolm when they'd first met him at his café in Woodley. But then he had convinced himself that it was silly to be, and from then on he was able to enjoy his and Donnelly's cheeky flirtation. Now, though....

"Yeah. He was the first guy aside from you that I've ever really... noticed in that way."

"Is this your way of breaking it to me that you are ending our engagement and running off to start a café in Australia or something?"

"No, of course not." Donnelly slid closer to Brandt and put a hand on his thigh. "It's just that it was a really new experience for me, and it took a while to sort it all out. Almost a year after coming out to everyone in my life, it was the first time I'd really felt... well, gay."

"I knew it! I knew there was something going on there."

"There's nothing 'going on' with Mal," Donnelly said reassuringly. "It's something that happened in me. Or that I became aware of in me, because of him. He was a catalyst."

"So he awakened the gay man inside of you?"

Donnelly chuckled. "I guess you could say that. But I don't want you to think it makes me love you any less. You're still the only man I'd want inside of me." He kissed Brandt, then sat back and looked into his eyes. "What's that look for?"

Brandt studied the surface of the water for a long moment. "That's not the way it is for me." He looked at Donnelly, studying his reaction. "I guess I'm more comfortable than I used to be when it comes to other guys. I can look at Bark and get what's attractive about him, even if I don't go full Winnie on him," he said with a chuckle. "But it's not like I want to drag him into bed or anything."

Donnelly nodded, but didn't say anything.

Brandt took a deep breath. "In the spirit of complete honesty, I also have a confession."

Donnelly simply nodded again, as if he'd been expecting this.

"The reason I was concerned about being in a regular bar last night is that... the idea of women finding me attractive... it still kinda turns me on." He swallowed hard and tried to find the words. "I guess what I'm trying to say is that I think there's a straight guy inside of me."

Donnelly's brow furrowed, and the look in his eyes actually frightened Brandt. He slowly set his beer on the edge of the pool and leaned in close, eyes burning with a furious intensity, right next to Brandt's face. Then he burst out laughing. "Sorry, sorry. I tried to keep it together, but you're just too fucking adorable." He kissed Brandt on the nose. "I know you, Ethan Brandt. I know you. You're not going to shock me by telling me the straight guy I see in you every single day is lurking there." He put his hand on Brandt's chest. "I know he's there, Ethan. I know him and I love him because I love you." He smiled slyly. "You've never really been able to hide him from me. I see him when Bryce says something completely outrageous and you smile on the outside and freak out on the inside. I see him when we hold hands on the sidewalk and you're constantly doing threat assessment on everyone we walk past. But you know when I love to see him the most?"

Brandt was so shocked by Donnelly's reaction he couldn't say anything at all. He just shook his head.

Donnelly slid right next to Brandt, and slid his hand up Brandt's thigh to gently flutter around his bobbing cock and hot, loose balls. "I see him when I'm on top of you, and I push your legs up, and you know what's coming next. You know you want it, but the straight guy inside of you is fighting to keep me from violating him. When I put the head of my hard cock against you, he's in your eyes. They widen because you want it, and he doesn't. And then I slide into you, and he knows he's lost, but he still fights, trying to keep me from owning you, desperate not to feel the full length of my hard dick spread you open, fill you up. He's with us when I pull back and come at you again, and when I start to pound into you, feeling the most male parts of us crashing together. But you know the best part?"

Brandt hadn't drawn breath while Donnelly had been speaking, and his head was light from all the blood rushing to his cock. He shook his head. He had no idea what would come next.

"The best part," Donnelly continued, "is when you're getting close, and I can feel your prostate start to twitch. The straight guy in you hates that you get so much pleasure from that magic spot in your ass. Every time I jab at it, I can see him in your eyes, furious with me for violating you. But you want it, you want to feel that grinding, overwhelming, brutal spasm that only comes from that place, and you bear down, and your cock starts to leak, and I know I've won. You grip me so tight with your ass—it's my ass now, I own it—and then you cry out when the orgasm takes you. It's that sound I love, because it means I've won. My victory dance is coming in you, filling you up, fucking the straight guy right out of you." He glared at Brandt, his expression savage, intense. "But he'll be back—he always comes back. And I'm going to win every time. I'm going to…. Fuck. Him. Up."

Brandt's head was filled with a searing red light that blocked out everything else in the world. "Now," was all he could manage to say.

"Like you have a choice," Donnelly growled. He sprang up and spread out his towel at the side of the pool. "Get up here, straight boy." His cock stabbed the air in front of him, powerful and hungry.

Brandt bolted upright, light sparkling around his field of vision, his head dizzy with blood loss and fuck lust. He sat on the edge of the pool, then scooted over to the towel and lay back. Donnelly was on him in a flash. Donnelly did away with his usual nuzzling kisses and soft attentions; fixing Brandt with a deadly stare, he reached back and grabbed Brandt's legs under his knees. He lifted Brandt's legs to his chest, then reared back, kneeling behind him. Brandt felt so vulnerable.

"There he is," Donnelly murmured. "Straight guy doesn't like that, does he? His legs spread open, his ass exposed and twitching. No straight guy wants that, does he?" He reached into the tote bag and pulled out a small bottle of lube, popped it open, and squeezed a healthy dollop out onto his finger. "He's really not going to like this."

Brandt gasped as Donnelly thrust his finger in one forceful motion through the tight knot of muscle. He pulled it out just as quickly and then came back with two fingers.

"Oh fuck," whispered Brandt.

Donnelly yanked his fingers out of Brandt and slicked up his erection. He leaned forward and touched the head of his cock to Brandt's anus, throbbing from the stretching it had undergone. Brandt closed his eyes and tipped his head back. He needed this, needed it in a way that made him shiver to realize.

"Look at me."

Brandt opened his eyes and saw Donnelly's intense glare focused on him.

"I want to see him," Donnelly commanded. "Show him to me."

Brandt didn't know how to show Donnelly the complex of lust and violation he felt, always felt, at this moment.

Donnelly nudged forward, the head of his cock slipping into Brandt.

Brandt took in a breath, preparing for the onslaught.

"There you are," Donnelly whispered, his eyes fiery. He pushed, driving his hardness into the tight, unyielding muscle Brandt struggled to open to him. "I'm coming for you." He grunted with the effort of forcing himself into Brandt in one great surge. He didn't stop until their pelvises ground against each other.

This moment, Donnelly's full possession of him, was the moment Brandt loved and feared most in the world, and now he knew why. And Donnelly knew it too, and accepted it, and loved him not in spite of it, but even more because of it.

Donnelly pulled back, but only for a split second before lunging forward again. He growled and slammed into Brandt, again and again, only gaining in power and pace. The force of his thrusting took Brandt's breath away. He felt a surge in his own cock, immediately followed by that twanging sparking spasm that only comes from a direct hit on the prostate. This pleasure was one Brandt had never known as a straight man—Donnelly alone could provide it. A slick of precum flowed from his achingly hard cock.

"Gotcha," Donnelly snarled with a wicked grin. He lunged upward with his next thrust, sending his erection crashing into Brandt's prostate. Then he quickened the cadence of his crazed bucking, delivering repeated, focused blows in rapid succession.

Brandt gasped at the change. This was something Donnelly had never done. He looked up in surprise, but Donnelly's expression was just as aggressive as before—he fucked like a man on a mission.

"You're mine," Donnelly growled. "I'm going to fuck the straight man right out of you."

Was it the growl, or the words, or the devastating rhythm of his thrusts that put Brandt over a cliff he'd never before scaled? He didn't know. All he knew was he couldn't fill his lungs, couldn't make a noise, could only hold on and surrender to the orgasm that crept up from his toes and down from the top of his head, prickling and tingling and surging, converging on his groin rather than originating from it. It was like nothing he'd ever experienced. And suddenly his cock throbbed into motion, untouched. It shot thick ropes of white in time with Donnelly's thrusts, every glancing blow to his prostate forcing out another jet of semen. He came without coming, orgasmed over his entire body. He was transported.

"Aargh!" Donnelly screamed, and his entire body tensed, sinews standing out in sharp relief as he spasmed into Brandt. He jolted as if electrified, his breath coming in short, gasping bursts, eyes rolled back in his head. Then, without warning, he flopped forward onto Brandt, their sweat-slicked chests pressed together, heaving. They lay that way for a long moment, recovering from their ecstatic exertion. Donnelly kissed Brandt as their breathing calmed. He looked into Brandt's eyes, a wide smile spreading across his face. "I won." He kissed Brandt again. "Take that, straight boy."

"That was amazing," Brandt sighed once he was capable of drawing normal breath. "I never… I didn't think it was possible…."

"I remember the first time you did that to me," Donnelly said. "Feeling an orgasm just appear out of nowhere—I thought I'd been possessed. By the ghost of a particularly adept whore." He laughed.

"That's not something straight guys get to experience, is it?"

Donnelly shook his head slowly. "Not without a very indulgent woman and some optional equipment."

"But you can make it happen just by being you." He craned his head up and kissed Donnelly again. "I don't think I'm straight anymore."

Donnelly chuckled. "You can't fool me. Straight guys don't give up that easy. Even when you fuck them into oblivion, they always come back. And I, for one, will be happy to see him. Because I will never get tired of fucking him up."

"I am the luckiest straight guy in the world," Brandt said. "But do you think you might withdraw your weapon so I can slip back into the tub? My straight ass needs a little time to recover."

"We have all day, my love."

CHAPTER SIX
STORM SURGE

THROUGHOUT THE afternoon Ted had tried to find the right moment to talk with Bark about… well, about everything. First he joined Bark in the hot tub after lunch, summoning his courage to strip off his cargo shorts and step naked into the water.

"Hey," Bark greeted him sleepily.

"Hey," Ted said.

For the next twenty minutes, he tried to work out just the right words to convey to Bark the complex of emotions roiling inside him. But when he finally thought he had it worked out, Paul and Chad charged naked into the tub, turning the quiet respite into a four-way splash fight.

Later, when Bark was lying on a lounger by the pool, Ted worked up the nerve to walk over to him, resolved to finally start this terrifying conversation. But he found Bark asleep. This would not necessarily have presented an insurmountable obstacle except that Bark was fully erect: all nine inches of his rigid member was pressed against his belly, throbbing red in the sunshine. This was indeed insurmountable; Ted retreated miserably.

Finally, when Winnie had brought out the afternoon wine and cheese, Bark and Ted found themselves alone at the table they normally shared with Brandt and Donnelly. Bark was forcing down the last of the wine Winnie had poured him—beer was his afternoon drink of choice—and Ted seized the moment.

"Hey, Bark?" he said.

"Yeah?" Bark replied, setting down his wine glass and looking right into Ted's eyes.

This was one of the things that always made Ted feel so good in Bark's presence: he had a way of making Ted feel like he was the only person in the world. Bathed in the glow of his attention, Ted swallowed hard and began.

"About last night—" he started.

"Oh, shit, Ted," Bark interrupted. "I am so sorry about that. I didn't mean to make you uncomfortable."

"What?" Of all of the possible response scenarios Ted had run in his head over the course of the afternoon, this was one for which he was completely unprepared.

"I didn't mean to put you in that position. It was really unfair to you."

"No, it was fine." This was not at all what he had intended to say, but there it was.

Bark looked astonished. "Really?"

"Really. In fact, I wanted to talk with you about—"

"So you were okay with me bringing Darlene back to the room? The more I thought about it today, the more I thought that was kind of a dick move. I should have at least asked you if it was okay."

"No, I wasn't talking about her," Ted managed to say out of his confusion.

Bark's brow knitted in confusion. "Then what were you talking about?"

Ted swallowed hard. "About when you—"

"All right, listen up bitches," Paul cried. "It is now sixteen thirty. We will get this party on the road at precisely seventeen hundred. You have thirty minutes to scrub your dainties before we lay siege to the virtue of the fair lasses—and a few brawny lads—of yonder town. May the gods protect the virgins, as they shall not be safe with us!" With a Spartan yell, he sent the guys to their rooms to prepare for the evening.

Winnie had laundered the few pairs of underwear the guys had in their possession and had again proffered the lost-and-found box for them to find clothing for the evening. By five, all six guys were gathered on the pool deck, arrayed in their pool-boy-reject finery—all except Paul, of course, who stayed the course with his freshly laundered jeans and plaid shirt. As they made their way down the beach steps, Bark sidled up next to Ted.

"Tonight we're going to find you someone," he said quietly. "I'll make sure of it."

I've already found you.

"Thanks, buddy," Ted replied. "But don't make promises that my dorkiness won't allow you to keep."

Bark looked surprised. "You aren't a dork, ya dork," he said, cuffing Ted on the shoulder. "Any girl would be lucky to land you."

"You are so full of shit," Ted said, returning Bark's shoulder punch.

"No, I'm completely serious," Bark said. His voice and expression bore out his words. "You are the smartest person I know, but you always have a smile on your face when I see you. I can tell you anything, and you always know what to say. Sometimes, when something shitty happens to me in class or at work, I just think to myself, 'Ted would know what to do.' Then I try to figure out what you would do." Bark laughed. "Which honestly, I suck at, so I have to wait to come home and tell you about it, and then you make it all okay. Sometimes I think I need to marry you because once we graduate, I'll only survive about a week in the wild."

Ted's head was spinning at the turn this conversation was taking, but he tried to hold it together. "And this is going to help me get a girl… how?" Ted asked, mustering up a grin he hoped looked casual.

"If I've fallen for you, then how hard will it be to find a woman who will do the same?" Bark smiled and winked at Ted.

Fuck. That wink.

Ted laughed, going along with what he thought Bark was trying to say—the kind of thing guys say to each other to boost morale—not what Ted would like him to say. Ted was coming to realize there was a frustratingly fine line between "I love you" and "I love you, man." Hearing everything twice was hard work.

The guys—Howie, actually, since he paid cover charges—decided to try new fishing grounds this evening. They passed the thudding and strobing club that had been successful for them last night, and a hundred yards down the boulevard, they found their spot: an indoor-outdoor club where everyone danced with everyone (Howie was clearly trying to keep in mind Paul's newly disclosed taste in dance partners) under a web of colored lights. They entered and joined the bass-driven, bouncing fray.

Howie bought the first round of strong tropical drinks, and Bark nudged Ted over to where two absolutely stunning twins—each a blonde, leggy, mirror image of the other—stood swaying and sipping.

"I'm going in," Bark said. "You ready?"

Ted had no idea how to seduce a woman, and after the events of the day, he had no interest in trying. But this wasn't the time to explain that to Bark, so he simply nodded and followed along.

That was how they made the acquaintance of Mindy and Mandy, from Mobile, who were in town for spring break with just each other because their boyfriends, who went to a military academy, had a different spring break than theirs. It took half an hour for Bark to extract this information from them, upon which he immediately weighed anchor and sailed off with Ted in search of better prospects. Through the course of the evening, they met women who were drinking to forget boyfriends they were clearly not over, women who were underage and had snuck in with a fake ID, and women who had had too much to drink and would clearly be spending the evening with only the toilet for companionship.

Three hours of this, and Bark and Ted ended up back at the bar.

"Well, fuck this place," Bark pronounced as he raised another drink.

"Maybe we should just call it a night," Ted offered.

"I just don't get it," Bark said, slamming his hand on the bar. "I have never had a run like that."

"It can't help to have me as a wingman. I'm just bringing you down."

"The fuck you are. That last girl, the one with the eating disorder? You practically did an intervention when her third order of onion rings showed up. When she cried and told you that you finally made her see her toxic relationship with her father was driving her binge and purge cycles? That's what I'm talking about right there, man. You help people." He punctuated this last statement with a finger poking into Ted's chest.

"But apparently I don't fuck people."

"Don't let one night get you down, man."

Ted laughed morosely. "It's just another in a long line of nights. All of them, in fact."

Bark looked like he'd been slapped. "No," he said, his voice low and serious. "No fuckin' way." He shook his head slowly.

"'Fraid so," he said.

"Never?" It was like Bark was asking him if he'd really never breathed oxygen.

"Never."

"There is no way that someone who looks like you and is as good as you and as sweet as you," Bark rambled, still shaking his head. "No way that happens."

"And this is who you chose to be your wingman," Ted said with a shrug. "Again, sorry."

"No. This is bigger than just this one night. This shall not stand, my friend. This shall not stand."

Ted was about to ask what exactly Bark planned to do about this sexual travesty but was prevented from doing so by a tremendous clap of thunder.

"Looks like we're in for a bumpy night," Thor said, coming up behind them with a weather map on his phone. "The storm that was supposed to miss us has turned in the last hour and is heading right for us." Another clap of thunder, long and rolling, echoed over them, louder even than the music that still pulsed. "You can blame global climate change, gentlemen. We're about to get very wet."

"Unlike the ladies in this place," Bark groused. He knocked back his drink and stood. "I say we drive a wooden stake through the heart of this evening, and head back to batten down. I hear the storms down here can really blow." He grinned. "Unlike the ladies in this place!"

"Hey, where'd you go?" Chad asked, suddenly appearing at Thor's side. He looked at the other guys. "We were ready to close the deal. Then the thunder freaked out the couple of hotties we were working. I was going to pull out the trump card"—he tugged down the waistband of his shorts, showing a black leather thong underneath—"but this guy disappeared, and that freaked them out worse. Thanks, buddy."

"Have you seen Paul and Howie?" Thor replied, ignoring Chad's complaint. He craned around the club, scanning for their compatriots. "There's Howie…. Ooh, that's not good."

The other guys turned to look.

Chad sighed. "Is he seriously going to—"

"Yep, he's got his wallet out," Bark confirmed.

"Has that ever worked?" Ted asked.

"I'm sure there's a woman somewhere in the world whose panties will drop the moment she sees a titanium-plated McFancyPants National Bank credit card," Bark replied, "but Howie's never found her yet."

"Aaand that's not her either," Thor said as the woman turned away from Howie with an exasperated roll of her eyes.

"Bitches don't know quality," Howie crabbed as he joined the guys at the bar.

"We're gonna call it a night," Thor announced. "Soon as we rustle up Paul."

"You aren't the first to try that tonight," Howie said bitterly. "He was getting rustled pretty hard over by the bathroom a few minutes ago. Bastard."

"I know it's not fair, but guys are just easier, Howie," Bark said. "Paul will always draw better than you will."

"I should just fuckin' go gay, I guess," Howie grumbled.

Bark wrinkled up his nose. "I still wouldn't do you," he said, shaking his head sympathetically. "Sorry, you're just not my type."

"Fuck you."

"He just doesn't listen, does he?" Bark said to the others. "No wonder the chicks won't touch him."

Howie turned away from Bark's harassment. "Can I get a shot of whatever?" he asked the bartender.

"Sorry, bud, we're closing up. Storm's going to beat the shit out of this place, and we gotta get the tables and chairs and stuff put up."

"Fuck." He turned to the guys again. "Let's get the fuck out of here. Someone go pry Paul off that dude and let's get moving."

"I'm on it," Bark said, grabbing up a table knife from the counter. "I'll go start prying. If I'm not back in five minutes… it means I've decided to join in, so leave us the fuck alone." He grinned and hauled off for the bathroom.

He returned nearly five minutes later with Paul in tow, brandishing his knife. "They fought me, but I was able to break the suction and pull them apart," he said with a leering snicker.

"Yeah, like I wouldn't drop any guy in here to go home with you," Paul said, stroking Bark's cheek.

"Finally," Bark pouted. "I was starting to think you would never notice me."

"Are you fucking kidding me? I would bend you over this bar right now and make that hot lacrosse body my bitch."

"So romantic," Bark replied with a flutter of his eyelashes. "You'd have to kiss me first."

Paul leaned in until his face was just millimeters from Bark's. "You couldn't handle a kiss from me," he whispered.

"Fuck you," Bark murmured. He bolted forward, closing the gap in an instant, smashing his lips into Paul's.

Paul's eyes grew wide in shock, but he didn't falter in the face of Bark's impetuous lunge. Instead, he wrapped his hands around Bark's head and kissed him like it was a sport. And he was going for gold.

"Fuck," Howie spat and stalked away toward the exit.

Ted stared at Bark and Paul, joined at the lips in some bizarre contest to make the other yield. The walls were closing in on him suddenly, making his chest tight. His pants too.

"If you guys are playing gay chicken, you're doing it wrong," Thor pointed out blandly. "You're supposed to pull away at the last minute, not kiss until someone's tongue is exhausted."

Paul and Bark ignored him for a long moment.

Finally, Paul released his grip. He stepped back from Bark, wiping his mouth. "Fuck, dude," he said.

"Yeah, me too," Bark replied. "Well, gentlemen, I think we're done here."

"What, you're not going to get bent over the bar now?" Chad cried. "No fair."

"We have all week," Bark told him. "If I strike out again like I did tonight, you'll find me here, taking it from this guy."

"It's a date," Paul said with a comic leer.

Bark and Paul cracked up laughing and punching at each other. Ted tried to remember how to breathe normally and hoped the color would drain back out of his cheeks before anyone noticed.

"Let's move, bitches," Paul said, back in charge.

The group headed out for the walk through town and back to the villa. The wind was picking up, and they could see flashes of lightning over the ocean. The waves beat against the shore with a vengeance, glowing white and angry under the gloom of a clouded sky. The breeze off the water, normally humid and warm, grew cold and cutting. Dressed in pool-boy togs, the group was ill prepared for a drop in temperature. Bark, however, was not to be rushed.

"Ooh, swings!" he called.

They were walking past an ancient, spindly swing set whose tired rubber swings creaked back and forth in the wind.

"Ted, swing with me," Bark wheedled, pulling his arm.

"We gotta get back," Ted answered, deeply thrilled to have been asked.

"Guys, there's something important we need to do," Bark called to the others. "We'll catch up with you."

"Whatever," Howie called dismissively over his shoulder.

"We really should stick together," Thor scolded.

"We'll be along in a minute," Bark insisted. "Ted probably won't last more than a couple of swings anyway." He jabbed a finger at Ted. "Lightweight."

"Oh, it is on," Ted replied, grabbing a swing and launching himself into motion.

Bark took the next swing over and jumped wildly into the air to catch up. The other guys continued on.

Ted pumped energetically to gain altitude, pursued by Bark, until his stomach was flopping in the nauseating free-fall zone at the peak of each swing. They laughed and argued about who was higher. Exhausted, Ted stopped pumping and rode the diminishing momentum of his pendulum, drifting lower and lower while Bark did the same. Finally, they found themselves nearly still, rocking gently back and forth, looking at the sea.

The cheap booze, sweet and strong, was still thrumming through Ted's brain, but the cold wind off the ocean brought some clarity. He looked over at Bark, who stared out at the dark, roiling water, lost in thought.

"That was pretty funny, back there… with Paul," Ted said.

Bark grunted out a chuckle.

"The guys'll be talking about that for a long time," Ted continued.

"Do you ever, sometimes, feel like doing something just because it'll make people talk?" Bark said, still looking seaward. "Just to push their buttons?"

"Is that why you did it?"

Bark stared for a moment, pondering. "No, I don't think so."

"Then why?"

He shook his head, then stared some more. "I just wanted to feel something… different."

"I imagine it was, what with the beard and all," Ted replied with a laugh.

Bark turned to face him, suddenly serious. "No, it wasn't that. It was different, like, it was… serious. Paul doesn't fool around when he's kissing someone. He means business."

"Is that what you really want? In a kiss, I mean?"

"Maybe I do," Bark said quietly.

A clap of thunder seemed to come at the same instant as a flash of lightning, and thick raindrops began to pelt down, lashing them with cold jolts.

"Ouch," Ted said as a raindrop smacked him in the head. "We should probably…."

"Yeah," Bark said, his voice still quiet. "We probably should."

They walked along the beach, dawdling despite the growing storm, until the rain grew heavy enough to soak them completely through their clothes. They started to jog, then broke into a run when the wind began to drive the rain horizontally off the ocean at them.

They dashed up the beach steps and through the courtyard, emerging onto a wet and desolate pool deck. All of the doors were closed and curtains drawn, and they sprinted to their room, slipping and sliding on the slick tile. Ted got there first, and Bark crashed into him as he fumbled his card into the slot.

"Hey, I can't get it when you're smushing me," Ted protested.

"Hurry up! I'm freezing," Bark replied, laughing and pressing his entire body against Ted's.

"Back up, dickhead," Ted called, shoving back against the immovable muscular bulk behind him. He laughed, but the feel of his body in full contact with Bark's made his chest pound. He finally managed to insert and extricate the card; the lock clicked, and they crashed through the door as it swung open.

"Ugh, so cold," Bark griped through gritted teeth. "Shower?"

"Uh, duh," Ted replied. It sounded like the best thing in the world.

"I'll go get it started."

Ted stood shivering in the middle of the room, not sure whether to dry off or wait for Bark to finish in the shower. He heard the water begin to run, and the wet slop of Bark's clothes hitting the floor.

"Oh, fuck, that's the stuff." Bark's voice echoed through from the bathroom.

Ted approached the door, listening to the happy splashing of his more-than-friend.

"Ted, where the hell are you?" Bark called.

"I'm right here," he answered through the door.

"Get in here, ya dork."

Ted's mouth went suddenly dry. He put his finger on the door handle, afraid to push it open.

"Ted. Now."

As little as Ted was expecting an invitation, he was even less expecting a command. He opened the door, pulse pounding in his ears. The room was dark except for a night-light next to the light switch, which cast a gentle amber light across the room. Steam billowed from behind the shower curtain, where Bark was splashing and humming to himself. Suddenly, he pulled the curtain open at one end and stuck his head out.

"What is wrong with you? You're shivering. Get in here." Bark whipped the curtain closed again.

Ted was shivering, but not with cold. A strange heat broke over him as he pulled the shirt over his head and tried to steady his fingers enough to unbutton his shorts. Finally they slid to the floor, and he stepped out of them, moving closer to the shower despite his every instinct to back away and… what? Hide? He reached out and pulled the curtain open just enough to slip in between it and the wall.

Then the world stopped.

It's not that Ted had never seen Bark's body. Roommates for two years, housemates for nearly two more, they had been in naked proximity hundreds of times. For the last two days, Bark had been nude far more than he had been clothed, allowing Ted ample opportunity to study any detail he had not long ago committed to memory. But this? This was different. In the dim amber glow, in the billowing steam, in the welcome heat of the splashing water after the frigid rain, Bark stood godlike. He was facing away from Ted, into the water, and Ted took in the sight of his strong shoulders, his muscular back, the fullness of buttocks built over years on the lacrosse field. Massive strength radiated from his legs, his calves rose and fell as he rocked side to side to a rhythm only he heard.

"Finally." Bark turned around and raked Ted up and down with a professional, appraising glance. "Teddy," he said. "You've been working out."

"Um, thanks?" He had no idea how to respond.

"Get in here," Bark said, stepping to the side.

Ted tried to slip past him into the water, but there were inevitable points of contact. These Ted instantly committed to memory, so as to relive the moment later. Then he felt the warm, soothing water rain down on him, and all felt right with the world. Except the part about how he had no idea how one was supposed to behave in a romantically lit shower with one's straight best friend. But the water relaxed him so much he forgot for a moment he wasn't alone. He turned to let the water flow down his back, basking in the warmth. It was only when he opened his eyes that he saw Bark looking at him with a sly grin and a bit of a smirk.

"You might want to turn down the temperature," Bark said, his voice full of mischief. He glanced significantly down to Ted's middle.

The horror of this moment was unprecedented in Ted's life. He dared not look down, but he could feel the weight of his penis as it cantilevered out in front of him. Whether it was a semi or a full-on boner, he couldn't tell, but he knew for a certainty that it wasn't hanging soft like Bark's…

Wasn't.

Ted couldn't take his eyes from it. When he saw it earlier in the day, when he approached the lounger and found Bark dreaming, he had recoiled from the rude javelin of cock. But here, in the glow and the steam, it pointed to him beckoningly. Ted had never had the luxury of looking at it straight on, contenting himself with sideward glances and accidental glimpses. It was beautiful, he could see now, and if he harbored any doubt that his orientation lay along this line rather than what they had been trying to seduce at the club earlier, it dissipated instantly in the face of Bark's fresh-scrubbed body with its prominent, bouncing member.

"Bitches got us boned, didn't they?" Bark said with a grin. "Like I said, you might want to turn the temperature down unless you want this poking at you all night."

Ted swallowed hard. Decision time.

"What, you'll give it up for Paul but not for me?" His heart was pounding. This was not him talking, and yet that was his voice. He was shocked to hear the words, but he knew in that moment he wouldn't take them back even if he could. They were a hail of bullets he had fired at his old reserve, his virginal hesitation. He panted from the effort of willing such a drastic departure from his life's previous course.

"Jealous?" Bark teased.

"No." Ted's voice was strong, filled with the confidence he wished he felt. "Because I know why you kissed him."

Bark's smile evaporated.

"I know why you did it." A promise, not a taunt.

Bark's voice was barely a whisper. "You do?"

Ted nodded. "It's okay," Ted whispered. "It's just us." He held out his arms, reaching out to save Bark from drowning in his turmoil.

Bark raised his hand, but he didn't take Ted's; he placed it, with achingly slow deliberation, on Ted's chest in precisely the same place he had touched earlier when they had been in bed, separated but together. Ted looked down at the point of their contact, feeling his life change in that touch.

"You touched me there," he whispered.

Bark nodded slowly, as if reluctantly realizing the truth of what Ted had said. "I don't know why I did that. Back then, with her in the bed."

"I do."

Bark licked his lips. "Of course you do. Because you know everything."

"I don't know everything," Ted replied.

"Everything that's important to me."

Ted lifted his hand and placed it on Bark's, pressing it even more firmly to his chest.

"That was the most amazing thing anyone's ever done to me," Ted said, his voice low and serious. "It changed me. You changed me."

Bark took in a sharp breath, and let it out slowly, raggedly. "I...." He blinked hard, and his eyes filled with tears. "I'm so scared."

Ted was shocked. Scared was something he had never known Bark to be—about anything. He had no idea what to say.

"Teddy, I am so scared," Bark repeated. He was starting to shiver.

"What are you scared of?" Ted asked.

Bark pressed his hand into Ted's chest. "This."

Ted smiled. "You have nothing to be scared of."

"But I can't keep it… under control anymore. It's too much for me. I can't." Bark stifled a sob.

"Bark, it's me. Teddy. You don't have to." Everything that Ted knew about Bark—his confidence, his essential masculinity, his sheer exuberant physicality—suddenly folded in on itself and reemerged in a new configuration. Now he understood Bark's in-your-face personality was meant to cover over the part of him he didn't dare to show to the world. The part of him that looked at Ted and felt the same way Ted felt when he looked at Bark.

"Shit, Teddy," Bark muttered, his voice anguished. "I don't know what to…."

"Shh." Ted reached out with his left arm and, keeping their right hands joined on his chest, pulled him close.

Bark was strong enough to resist but did not. He stepped forward into the embrace. Under the warm rain of the shower, they stood together, Bark's heaving, irregular breaths against Ted's calm, even cadence.

For the first time in his life, Ted felt like the strong one. As Bark cried into his shoulder, he stood strong, sure of his grip and sure of his love for the man who had finally found his way into his arms.

SAME ROOM, different leg pressed up against his.

Ted woke in the gloom of a stormy Monday morning, hearing the wind and rain lash the thick white walls of the Villa Hermes. But the only sound that mattered to him was the deep, even breathing of his best friend lying next to him. He turned his head and looked at the peaceful face, blissful in slumber, and shook his head in wonder at how they had gotten here.

I was the strong one.

Ted had held Bark tight under the spray of the shower until the spasm of grief and doubt and exhaustion passed. Finally he had calmed, though he never took his hand from Ted's chest. He had taken a deep breath, then two, and then spoke the only word to pass his lips to that point, and the last one since.

"Thanks."

Ted had nodded, hearing in that word his every hope kept alive.

Bark had stepped from the shower, dried off, and then handed Ted his own towel. By the time Ted was dry, Bark was sprawled on the bed, completely asleep. He had passed out under the weight of the entire evening: drinking too much, crapping out with every woman he talked to, kissing Paul, getting rained on, coming undone in the shower. Ted stood watching him for a long while, trying to guess whether after all of that anything had really changed between them. He knew what he wanted to hear in Bark's plea that there was something he could no longer hide, that scared him badly. But what Bark really meant by all of that, those tears and grasping, Ted had no idea. He had fallen asleep the same way he had awakened a moment ago—listening to Bark breathe.

"I love you," he whispered to his sleeping friend.

Bark's eyes opened. Ted nearly jumped out of his skin.

"I must have been a mess last night," Bark said, sleepily but with a wry grin. "I've never been pathetic enough for someone to wake me up by saying they loved me."

Oh. So that's what we're doing.

"You had a bad time. No big deal."

"Did I do anything I'll regret once I remember it?"

"Nope," Ted replied, in the most upbeat voice he could muster. "You drank too much, seduced the ladies too little, got rained on, done."

"You're leaving out a pretty major part," Bark scolded, his eyebrow cocked.

Ted could feel the blood rushing to his cheeks. He had no idea how to describe what had happened between them in the shower.

"Or did I dream it?" Bark asked, narrowing his eyes at Ted.

Ted shook his head. There were still no words.

"Paul's never going to let that one go. Seemed funny at the time, but…."

Ted was both relieved and agonized that Bark was talking about kissing Paul, not about their teary embrace in the shower. The relief passed away immediately; the loss took root.

They were jolted by the ringing of the phone.

Up until that second, Ted hadn't even been aware there was a phone in the room. He stumbled to it, while Bark rolled over, away from the dim light coming through the curtains.

"Hello?"

"Ted? It's Winnie. I'm afraid the storm is getting much worse, dear."

"What?" Ted tried to shake off both sleep and the boner Bark's proximity had occasioned.

"We're going to get everyone into the shelter until it passes. Come to the office as soon as you can, okay? It's important."

"Ah… all right," Ted said into the phone and hung it up.

"What's up?" Bark asked in the tone of someone who doesn't need to get out of bed for some time.

"Winnie says the storm is getting worse, and we should get to the office right now. They have a shelter of some kind we're supposed to go into until the storm passes."

Bark sat up. "Shit. Some spring break. First last night's utter fail, and now I'm going to be locked up in some storm shelter with all of you losers." He flopped back onto the bed, and cried to the heavens, "Why do you hate me?"

"Shut up, you drama queen," Ted snapped with a grin. "Now, unless you want to be washed out to sea, I suggest you get the hell out of bed and put some damn clothes on." Ted took his own advice and pulled on his trusty cargo shorts.

"What, you don't like this all of a sudden?" Bark demanded, hopping up from the bed and standing in front of Ted in all of his naked (and, given the hour, somewhat tumescent) glory, arms and legs spread wide as if caught in the middle of a jumping jack.

Ted looked him up and down, keeping his expression studiously blank. It was hard work, given how the sight of Bark got him in the gut every damn time. "Oh, you are so handsome," he said in a deadpan monotone. "I want to make out with your entire body. Oh please, can I have your babies."

Bark dropped his arms to his sides in a dramatic show of disappointment. "I guess the magic has left this relationship," he moped. "Might as well be swept into the ocean."

"Which is what is going to happen if you don't get moving," Ted practically shouted. He grabbed up his phone and his backpack and stood tapping his foot while Bark meandered to the bathroom.

About five minutes later, Bark was finally ready to evacuate the room, and Ted opened the door. A violent wind shoved him back into the room, and the rain it carried slashed at them as they ran around the pool toward the courtyard. They were completely soaked by the time they arrived at the office door.

"Come in, come in," Winnie cried as he opened the door for them. "Thank goodness you're here. The boys were just about to go after you." He nodded to Paul and Thor, who stood by the registration desk, looking serious.

"It's bad, guys. This stuff?" Thor pointed out the windows. "This is just the leading edge of the leading edge. The real storm won't get here for another couple of hours. Assuming there's still a *here* here by then, of course." He held up his phone; Ted could only see solid green over most of it, but with an advancing band of yellow through the rainbow to deep purple.

"Yikes," Ted said, because what else do you say in the face of a monster storm?

"You'll be happy to know, however," Winnie said, "that the original owners of this property put in an enormous bomb shelter during the Cold War. It was one of the things I loved about it when we were looking for a place to turn into an inn. More storage than I could fill in a lifetime! Come on, let's go get battened down."

He led the way behind the registration desk and down the corridor toward what appeared to be the kitchen. He turned to an unmarked doorway on the left and pushed open the door, revealing a long staircase leading straight down into the gloom. As he stepped on the first stair, lights switched on, showing that the staircase extended several stories down under the inn. Ted couldn't see the end of it.

They stepped quickly down the stairs, and at the bottom, a corridor lined with stone turned to the right and to the right again.

"Built to withstand a nuclear blast," Winnie explained. He led them a few dozen feet down this corridor, until he reached what looked like a bank vault. "And radioactive looters, it seems." He knocked briskly on the metal door, and the locks slid open.

The round door swung out into the corridor, pushed open by Vic, who smiled in greeting at the latecomers. "Glad you could make it," he said. "We hope you will include our luxurious bomb shelter in your Yelp review."

"Best place to ride out Armageddon, five stars!" joked Thor.

Vic laughed and swung the door closed behind them, then spun the wheel in the middle that deployed six bolts into the thick steel of the doorframe. "There we are," he said, as if preparing to survive nuclear war was just another daily innkeeper's chore.

Ted wasn't sure what to expect from a Cold War bomb shelter, but what he saw when he looked around was surprisingly cheery and bright. The room everyone was gathered in was larger than the inn's guest accommodations and filled with sofas and chairs that, while not first-rate, were far better than the furnishings the guys enjoyed in their rented house back home. Light glowed from fixtures recessed into the concrete ceiling, and the smell of fresh coffee wafted through from one of the several doorways that opened off of this central room.

"Wow," Ted said, "this is really nice."

"Why, thank you, dear," Winnie replied with pride evident in his voice. "We haven't had a good storm since we opened the inn, and we're quite excited to share it with guests for the first time."

Vic stepped into the room, carrying a coffeepot. "My parents, may Satan take their souls, were 1970s survivalists. They were certain the apocalypse was coming, and they would not only need to live underground for an extended time but also have to fight hippies for every scrap that remained. They were complete loons, and they eventually grew out of it, but somehow the idea of preparing for the worst always had a kind of romance for me. Plus, I get to bust out the campground skills Winnie will never let me use."

"The great outdoors and I are content to live separate lives in blissful ignorance of each other," Winnie said, laying a delicate hand on his perfectly coiffed hair. "But I do love having a man who knows how to make coffee under duress." He waggled his empty cup at Vic.

Vic poured a steaming stream into Winnie's cup. "We have everything we need to stay down here for weeks, but I doubt it'll come to that. Just make yourselves comfortable, gentlemen, and relax."

"What about if the power goes out?" Thor asked.

Vic smiled. "If we lose electricity, there's an array of marine batteries as backup. You wouldn't even notice the difference. There's also a generator to charge the batteries if the power's out for an extended time. One of the things we added when we bought the place was LED lighting to keep the power consumption down."

"But we'll always have coffee, won't we?" Winnie asked.

"Yes, my dear. There will always be coffee."

"Thank goodness," Donnelly contributed. "That'll keep me from getting blown out to sea while searching the wreckage of the town for caffeine."

"Oh, and I haven't mentioned the facilities," Vic continued. "The bathroom, such as it is, is through that door"—he pointed to a small door at the far end of the room—"and it will put any porta-potty to shame. Now, I'll have breakfast ready for you in a few minutes."

Soon the men were eating the scones Vic had already baked topside, plus eggs and bacon cooked on the induction stove in the shelter. Ted watched Bark eat, seemingly unaware of the emotional roller coaster he'd sent Ted on over the last twenty-four hours. A creeping sadness tugged at Ted's heart, and as much as he hoped their relationship had changed for the better, he couldn't be certain anything was different at all for Bark.

It might be a long, lonely apocalypse for Ted.

Chapter Seven
Decameron

"Now, feel free to wander about our little disaster shelter," Winnie said after breakfast was finished. "Make yourselves at home."

The guys got up and stretched, and then most seemed content to lie back down and get some more sleep on one of the couches. That's what Bark did, of course, once again reminding Ted of how beautiful and peaceful he looked when sleeping. Damn it.

"Winnie, what the hell is this?" Paul called from one of the ancillary rooms. His voice was deep but teasing, so Ted walked over to see what he was talking about.

He stepped through the doorway and found himself in a long room lined with clothes racks, and every single inch was taken up with glittery gowns of all colors and styles. About halfway down the room, there was a mirror and pink pouf chair that sat before a vanity packed with makeup. Paul stood goggling at the extent of the finery.

"Oh, you found my little stash of glamor," cried Winnie.

"I could hardly miss it, since it's the size of a department store," Paul replied, laughing. "Are these all yours?"

"Well, they would hardly belong to Vic, now would they? I've managed to get him into a gown or two over the years." Winnie leaned in conspiratorially. "But just between us girls, he's kind of a drag in drag, so I don't insist on it."

"This is a Smithsonian-level collection," Paul said, brushing his hand along the delicate fabrics. He pulled a gown from the rack and held it up admiringly, then replaced it and pulled out another. "These are beautiful."

Winnie seemed deeply pleased at the interest Paul had taken in his collection. "Let me show you my favorite out of all the many in my gown room." Winnie rushed over to the rack nearest the vanity and pulled out a—well, Ted wasn't sure what it was.

The dress on the special pink padded hanger was a mess. It had one shoulder, but seemed to be meant to have two; the pink spangled fabric was largely intact over the bodice but hung in tatters below the waist. There was a dark smudgy stain down one side of the dress that seemed to be dried blood.

"What the hell happened to this?" Paul asked, his voice hushed.

"That's quite a story," Winnie said, shaking his head at the garment.

"We've got nothing but time," Paul said. "Why don't you tell us?"

The face Winnie made was one Ted had seen only on sweepstakes commercials in which an unassuming housewife is informed that she has won an impossibly vast sum of money.

"Oh, I couldn't," Winnie declaimed disingenuously.

"Come on, it'll be fun." Paul walked back into the main room. "Guys, Winnie's going to tell us a story. This is how humans entertained themselves from the time we climbed down from the trees until the invention of television, so listen up." He sat down in a space he made for himself by shoving the napping Howie upright.

"What?" the aggrieved Howie whined.

"Listen up," Paul ordered. As usual when Paul ordered something, everyone complied.

"Well," Winnie said, standing in the middle of the room holding the tattered gown on its hanger, "I wore this gown for the first and last time one June evening in nineteen hundred and sixty-nine. I had just turned seventeen and had run away from my parents' home for the millionth time. This time I hadn't stopped running until I was all the way in New York City, just a boy with a suitcase full of secondhand ball gowns, some makeup I'd stolen from the cosmetic counter at Woolworth's as I left town, and a dream. I wanted to find a place where I could dress in the finery I felt I deserved, and for which I had been beaten quite badly in high school. Texas today is marginally better than it was then, back when you could get arrested for cross-dressing."

Thor exhaled in disgust. This was what Ted thought of as his "social justice" noise. He made it when people described harassment or exploitation of any kind. It was normally the prelude to an extended and angry disquisition on political or economic inequality. But Winnie, whose train of thought had gathered a head of steam, was not about to let it be shunted to a siding to indulge Thor's need to lecture.

"Yes! It's true. A dear friend of mine was picked up by the sheriff one evening as we made our way home from a social engagement—I luckily was able to hike up my skirt and scale a fence before he got to me—and he was brought up on morals charges because he had dared to walk down a public street in a dress. But that was the case almost everywhere in this fine country of ours back then.

"People who talk about equal rights often focus on things like marriage or even sexual acts, but the truth is if you deny people the ability to dress and behave how they feel most comfortable, the rest of it doesn't even matter.

"So after that experience, I graduated high school early, got on the bus, and found myself enjoying summer in the city. I wasn't old enough to go to bars or anything because the drinking age was eighteen in those days, but I made friends with some of the bouncers and doormen and was able to get into select establishments to work my trade. I was a performer, you see, even at that tender age. I would do a number or two and then dance with the patrons for a couple of bucks stuffed into my bra at the end of the song. I was in heaven, true to myself for the first time in my life.

"At the end of June, I was in the Village with some friends, and we were at one of the only places in the city known openly as a gay bar. I was able to slip in, but my friends—who, alas, were not as fabulously dressed as I was—were stopped at the door." Winnie stroked the glittery fabric of the dress he held in his hands.

"That night the police raided the bar, and I knew I was in trouble. What they would do is bring in policewomen to take the drag queens to the bathroom and check to see what was under the gown. If they found out I was a man, they would have arrested me, and as a minor I could well have been sent back to my horrid parents. Well, I decided I was not going to let that happen. So when the matron came for me, I shook loose of her grip and just tore through the crowd. No fewer than six strapping policemen tackled me, but they didn't suspect they were dealing with a four-time all-county junior steer-wrestling champion. I broke a heel, but I shook four of them off before I hit the door, and I managed to knock the heads of the other two together on the sidewalk outside. I ran down the sidewalk, where people were starting to gather to see the spectacle. I shouted to them about what was going on inside, and the crowd started to get worked up.

"You have to understand the kind of violence we'd been subjected to, day after day after day, not just from bigots but from the police who were supposed to be protecting people. By the time police reinforcements came, they were met by a couple hundred really pissed off drag queens and gay youth and just normal people who were tired of watching us get beaten down. It got a little dicey there for a while," Winnie said, his hands tracing the ragged edges of the gown, "and a dear friend of mine was rather badly injured by a nightstick-wielding maniac in a uniform." He passed his fingers lightly over the bloodstain.

"But when morning came, the burned-out shell of that building stood as a monument to our refusal to be beaten down and abused for being who God made us."

Paul's face was rapt. "Oh my God. You were at Stonewall."

Winnie gasped in surprise. "You know about Stonewall?"

"Of course I know about Stonewall." He turned to the uncomprehending faces of the rest of the college crew. "The raid on the Stonewall Inn was the beginning of the national gay rights movement. Those guys—Winnie and the rest of them—turned the tide."

"I don't get it," Howie said. "How did some drag queens getting arrested accomplish anything?"

Paul shook his head. "You know how I was apparently able to be completely out to all of you and you didn't even realize it?"

Howie nodded, but his queasy expression showed he was still getting used to the idea of Paul as "out."

"Those drag queens paved the way for me to do that. They started a movement that made it possible for people to be gay without having to make a big deal about it. I don't have to march in the streets or sue anybody to be treated just like everyone else, but it wasn't always that way. And the people who started it all were the bravest people the movement has ever known. The ones who put on the dresses and heels and said 'Here we are, and we're not going away. Like it or not, we're citizens too.' You have any idea how brave they had to be to do that? I've never done drag in my life, and still I know the freedom I have today I owe to them for refusing to back down. And that all started at Stonewall." He turned to Winnie. "It's an honor to meet someone who was actually there. Thank you, Winnie. You are an American hero."

Winnie's face was running with tears by the time Paul finished his tribute. He threw his arms around Paul and they hugged for a long moment. Ted noticed Vic standing in the doorway, watching the scene with tears in his eyes as well.

"That was an amazing story," Thor said. "Thank you for telling it."

Ted looked over at Bark. He was transfixed, watching Paul and Winnie hug and murmur in the middle of the room. Ted couldn't tell what that look meant, but he knew Bark had been deeply affected by it.

"Now, there's a story I would like to hear," Winnie said, releasing Paul from their embrace. "Can you tell us, dear, what it's like for someone of your age and"—he squeezed Paul's bulging biceps—"shall we say, masculinity, in today's world?"

Paul looked around at his friends. "Not sure they could take it, Winnie. I apparently only came out to them yesterday. I think they're still getting used to the idea of my being gay."

"Actually, I'd really like to hear that," Thor said. "I feel so bad we went so long not even realizing. It would be good to know what it's like for you."

"You gotta tell us, man," Bark added, to Ted's surprise and delight. "We love you."

"Wait, we don't all love you the way Bark does," Howie cried. "I mean, we love you, but we're not lining up to kiss you like he did."

Winnie's eyebrows shot up, but he didn't say anything.

Paul stood for a moment, his face showing the effort he was devoting to figuring out what he should tell his closest friends about his experience. Then he nodded. "All right. I'll tell you a story."

"OKAY, SO I was pretty much a normal kid in high school," Paul began. "I was a good enough student, though not the best, and I was a pretty good baseball player. Wasn't in the top rank of the popular kids, but I could see them from where I sat during lunch. Didn't have a girlfriend or anything, but I figured that was because I just wasn't in the same league as the girls I liked: the pretty ones, the smart ones, the popular ones. It didn't occur to me I wasn't actually interested in girls because I was a guy, and that's what guys are interested in. I figured it would just take a while for me to develop the urgent need to get a girl that my buddies were always talking about. I didn't know anyone who was gay, so I didn't have any way to know whether my lack of interest in girls was normal.

"Well, in the fall of my sophomore year, I needed some school activity to be able to check off on my sheet. Baseball was in the spring, so that was covered, but my school was all about people being involved in stuff, so I needed something for fall. By the time I got my shit together, all the good stuff had been taken—the Habitat for Humanity, the teach orphans to swim—and all that was left was the bottom-of-the-barrel stuff like picking up litter on weekends and painting the janitor's shed. Then I saw one for building sets for the theatre. They were doing *Our Town*—"

"Ugh," exhaled Winnie.

"I know, right? Anyway, they needed someone to build those tacky modernist things that fly down onto the stage, and I like to build things, so I signed up. That's when I discovered my school actually did have a gay subculture, and they all pretty much lived in the theatre. You've never seen so many ninety-pound emo guys in one place, all hanging out together overdecorating each other's eyes with goth black liner."

"So you finally found your people?" Howie cracked. "Having a hard time picturing you as a goth emo drama kid."

"Yeah, not so much. I viewed them with a deep horror, actually. The only gay role models available on campus and I couldn't stand to be anywhere near them. Not because they were gay, but because all they talked about were anime and foreign films and sneaking off to drag clubs to go dancing. It pretty much convinced me there was no possible way I could be gay, because I certainly wasn't *that*. So I built my sets and worked even harder on digging deep and finding the lust I was supposed to be directing at the girls in my classes.

"But working alongside the drama guys, I got more of a sense of the kind of lives they were leading. One day the guy who designed all the lighting came in with this huge purple black eye. He tried to hide it with makeup, but you could still tell it was there and that it hurt a lot. He laughed it off when his friends asked him about it, but a little later, it was just him and me up in the rigging trying to untangle the ropes that moved one of my flats from the ones that held his lights, and I asked him about what happened. I think it must have taken him a little off guard because he just told me. He kept it from his friends, but to this doofus set-builder, he just lets it all loose. It was his dad. His dad got pissed that his son came home from school wearing makeup, so he just belted him. Punched him right in the face and then made everyone in the family sit down to dinner like nothing happened. And this guy, the ninety-pound emo, gets up the next morning and just puts more makeup on it and gets on with life.

"Here I'd been thinking I was the tough one, but I'd never done anything like that. He gets a beatdown—from his own father—and he just keeps going. Didn't even forget the mascara that day. Guy was alpha as fuck."

Winnie clapped and bounced up and down in his seat, then seemed to notice no one else was applauding. "Sorry, dear. That was just so inspiring. Please, continue."

Paul grinned and did so. "Well, we worked all through that week and got to know each other a little better. Turned out we actually had a lot more in common than I'd thought. So, end of the day Friday, we're trying to get ready for the show to open the next week. Finally, everyone else is pretty much gone, and he turns to me and asks if I want to get something to eat. And I'm like, sure, I could eat, because I could always eat. So we head out and walk to this crappy little diner that's the closest thing to an actual restaurant we can get to because neither of us had a car. We get sandwiches or something and sit in the corner of this dingy dive for a couple of hours, and suddenly I realize—I'm on a date with this guy. And I was having a really great time. So, mind completely blown right there. But I take a deep breath and figure I might as well see where this takes me.

"We finish up, and we start walking, still talking about the movies and the books we both somehow like, though for completely different reasons. Turns out he lives right next to the school, out by the athletic fields. He points to his house, and we stop a few doors down so no one can see us. He says he had a great time and he's really attracted to me, which is really nice to hear because no one's ever said that to me before. Then he leans in for a kiss—"

"Oh, dude," Chad moaned. "Come on!"

Paul fixed him with the same glare a grizzly might direct at a salmon. But before he could reply, Thor spoke up.

"Shut up, Chad," Thor spat. "How many times has Paul—and all of us, for that matter—had to put up with your grotesquely detailed stories of sexual encounters? The day after Valentine's, you treated us to fifteen minutes on exactly how your ball sack celebrated the holiday. While we were eating breakfast. I think you can put up with Paul kissing someone."

"Sorry," Chad said, though without much feeling. "Go ahead, Paul."

"Thank you, asshole." Paul cleared his throat and got back to his story. "Anyway, he leans in for a kiss, and I think, boom. Decision time. Because once you kiss a guy, there's no going back, right? Straight guys don't do that. But we've been having a good time, and there's no one around, so I figure I might as well see what it's like. So I kiss him. And I felt… nothing. Nothing at all. It was just like kissing a girl, which I had managed to do a couple of times despite being a social nobody. His lips were just like a girl's, and they tasted just like a girl's, and the little gaspy breathing noises he made while we kissed were just like a girl would make. Plus all the makeup. Guess I'm straight after all. So I'm trying to figure out how to tell him this is a no-go situation when something lands on me like a ton of bricks. I was knocked completely flat out on the ground, and on top of me is Brian Farber, this jock asshole guy I only knew by reputation. Pretty much king of the jocks. And he's just whaling on me. The emo guy takes off at a run and disappears, which I don't blame him for at all, because this shit is terrifying.

"So I roll out from under the hail of fists that is Brian Farber, and I manage to plant a solid boot right on his kidney. Kind of a lucky shot, but it was all I needed. He seemed shocked I was fighting back at all, and he froze. I just went completely apeshit on him. I mean, I hit him with everything I had. I'd never been in a fight before and haven't since. But I delivered a wrath-of-Zeus beatdown on him and then gave him a little extra dedicated to the dad of my emo friend."

"By the end Brian is just wailing and covering his face with his arms. I'm on top of him, trying to pry his hands away so I can break his nose or something that will show everyone at school I completely owned him, but once I can look him in the face, I see he's scared shitless.

"I got right up in his face and I just growl at him, 'What the fuck you do that for?'"

"'Cuz you're f-f-faggots," he snivels. Now I don't think he realized that when someone has already beaten you half-witless, the thing you don't want to do is call him a faggot. But I got that across with a quick knee to the groin. He yells and then the fight seems to leave him. Suddenly this big football player looks up at me and I can see it—he's giving up. But it's more than that... he's giving it up to me. *Me.* The kid who no one knew and no one cared about. He was putting himself in my hands. God, what a rush that was. So I did the only thing I could think to do with the power that he'd handed me."

Silence fell over the room.

"Please tell me you just kept beating the shit out of him," Howie said, his voice not really hopeful.

Paul shook his head. "I kissed him."

"Fuck," Howie exhaled, dropping his chin to his chest.

"That was the moment I knew who I was and what I wanted. I didn't want a girl, and I didn't want a boy who acted like a girl. I wanted a man, a man like me. Turns out all I needed to be able to see that was to have one pinned under me, struggling a bit while I pressed my knee into his balls. And somehow I could see—like, really see clearly—that he wanted the same thing. We weren't bully and victim in that moment; we weren't jock and loser. We were two guys trying to figure out how to be men and also get their hands on one. I did it by accidentally dating a guy; he did it by jumping me on a dark street corner. I still think my method was the better one, but then again his led me to finally figure this all out, so I can't really hold a grudge there. Anyway, I just grabbed him by the jaw and kissed the fuck out of him. He made like he was going to fight me off, but it was more like he was trying to hold on for dear life. Meanwhile, I'm seeing stars because for the first time in my life I am completely bone hard for the person I have in my arms, and I don't care it's a guy because hallelujah, my junk works, right? Finally when I'm about to pass out from not being able to breathe, I let go of that kiss, and he just kind of blinks at me for a minute and then it seems to hit him what we've been doing.

"'What the fuck you doing?' he asks, like he has no idea. 'Get the fuck offa me.'

"And I'm like 'I'll get the fuck off, but I'm taking you with me.' And I kiss him again and just fucking grind into him like I'm a pole dancer and he's got a wad of hundreds in his drawers. I can feel him getting hard under me, starting to grind back a little, and I know I've got him. 'Where's your car?' I ask him because I know he's gotta live on the fancy side of town and was probably on his way home after football practice when he saw us. Well, he points to a brand-new pickup about twenty yards from where we've been making out on somebody's lawn, and I get up and offer him a hand. He looks at me like he's trying to figure out if he made a break for it, he'd be able to get away and tell everyone I tried to rape him and keep his rep as the straight jock, but he kinda shakes his head and grabs my hand. We get in his truck and drive out to the outskirts of town, to this parking lot by a factory that's closed, and he parks and turns off the engine. He looks at me, and I can tell he's scared out of his mind. And honestly, so am I, because this thing he's suddenly switched on inside of me has got hold of me and won't let go. I slide over to him and kiss him again, and suddenly he's rarin' to go. He whips off his shirt and the dude is stacked—I mean just solid fuckin' muscle. I take my shirt off, and then he's all over me. We get going, and then suddenly he pulls back.

"'I've never done this,' he says, and I could tell by looking into his eyes that he's telling me the truth.

"'Me neither,' I say.

"'No one can find out about this, okay? I would be completely fucked if this gets out,' he says, like I'm going to take out an ad in the student paper that says 'I fucked Brian Farber,' right?

"And I said, 'I think you're going to be completely fucked anyway,' because I wasn't going to let him out of that truck until we both got what we came for.

"I was grounded for two weeks for coming home at three in the morning, but it was completely worth it. Me and Brian Farber fucked the hell out of each other all through high school, and we still get together for old time's sake when I'm home from school. He was my first, and he showed me that you can be a man and still want to fuck a man."

"Wow, Paul, that was amazing," Thor said. "I can't believe we didn't know this side of you before this weekend."

"It's not like I hid it from you," Paul replied. "I just didn't make a big deal of it. Though how you didn't get it from what I did tell you, I'll never know."

"Sometimes you don't see what's right in front of you," Thor said.

"Sounds like there's a story there?" Paul asked, eyebrows raised.

Thor shrugged. Paul stepped away from his spot at the head of the room and made a sweeping gesture, welcoming Thor to the front.

"AS YOU are probably aware, my parents raised me to be active in social and environmental justice issues," Thor began.

"You may have mentioned that once or twice," Howie groaned.

"Look, Howie, when your parents name you after a pioneering activist, you feel the responsibility to carry on his work."

"You're carrying on Thor's work?" Chad said, clearly mystified. "Like fighting Loki and repairing rifts in the fabric of the universe?"

"Thor Heyerdahl. I was named after Thor Heyerdahl, not the comic-book Thor."

"Oh." Chad was silent for a moment. "Who was Thor Heyerdahl?"

"I'll explain later. I have a sixty-three-slide presentation deck on his work I think you'll enjoy."

"Don't count on it," Howie muttered.

"Anyway, I spent last summer on a service trip to Guatemala, working on social justice issues with coffee growing co-ops in the Huehuetenango region."

"Mmm," Donnelly groaned. "Nothing like a good Huehue."

"You are an insufferable coffee geek, and you are interrupting," scolded Brandt.

"No, I totally get it," Thor said eagerly. "They have amazing coffee, and as I always say, amazing coffee brings amazing opportunities for the stewardship of social justice issues."

"Seriously, he has a T-shirt that says that," Howie cracked with a snicker.

"Very enlightened, Howie. Now, as I was saying, I was working in Guatemala with an NGO that sent groups of us into the high country to conduct ethnographic research. A lot of the folks in my group got hit with a nasty stomach bug right when we're supposed to go, so it ends up just being three of us: myself, Ilse, a woman from Norway, and Pedro, a guy from Brazil. We get driven up into the mountains and then dropped off to trek along from plantation to plantation doing our research. It was a lot of hiking, and the plantations are pretty far apart, so we spent a lot of time talking—on the trail, around the campfire, and in the tent at night.

"At one of the workers' co-ops where we spent a day, the foreman offered us some *cusha*, their homemade liquor, as we were leaving. That evening we made camp, and after eating dinner, we broke out the bottle of *cusha*. It was super strong, so we mixed it with some fruit juice and passed the bottle around a few times. Got pretty lit up. Then I notice Ilse has her hand on my leg. I thought that was pretty rude of her to exclude Pedro that way, so I reached over and put my hand on his leg. Just so, you know, he would feel included."

"Oh my God, Thor," Howie said, shaking his head. "Can't a girl just make a pass at you?"

"There were three of us, Howie," Thor replied, as if Howie must have forgotten this vital fact. "And anyway, I figured I had always prided myself on being antihomophobic, so I thought it would be a chance for me to be the change I wanted to see in the world."

"Seriously?" Howie sputtered. "You are so open-minded that you made a pass at a guy just so you could prove it?"

"I didn't make a pass at him, exactly," Thor replied, a bit lamely. "It was more an effort to keep him from being excluded by Ilse's heteronormative stroking of my leg. But looking back on it, I'm inclined to think Pedro saw it more as me making a pass at him. Because the next thing I know, he's kissing me. Like, really kissing me. Hard. Then Ilse gets up and storms away from the fire. So I get up and follow her—after kissing Pedro again, because I didn't want him to feel like I was invalidating his agency in seeking fulfillment of an alternative sexuality—and tell her I wasn't offended by her making a move, but for the good of the group, I thought we should include Pedro. She seemed to understand that—"

"Good, because I don't."

"Fuck off, Howie," Thor said. "Anyway, she came back to the campfire, and Pedro asked me which of them I wanted to have sex with, and I said I thought if two of us were to have sex, it would be really exclusionary of the third person, and that's when they both took their clothes off." Thor fell silent for a moment. "That's when it started to get weird."

Howie was not the only one laughing this time.

"So I took my clothes off as well, since being dressed when others are naked is an expression of patriarchal hegemony. And then we were all sort of standing there naked, and then Ilse kisses Pedro, and Pedro kisses me, and then I kiss Ilse, and then pretty soon we're all kissing at once, which I'd only ever seen on one of those 'Girls Gone Wild' ads on late-night TV, but when you do it in real life, it's kind of awkward. Then Pedro suggests we go into the tent, so we do, and we all lie down, and I guess I kind of had sex with a man. And, you know, a woman. But I'd already done that before, so it isn't the most important part of the story. That's not to say she wasn't nice and all, but...."

"So how was it?" Paul asked, his face showing his disbelief in Thor's narrative.

"Now, I'm not judging your sexuality when I say this, okay?"

"Of course not," Paul replied with an amused chuckle.

"I believe that all sexes have equal value, and that all human bodies are beautiful in their own way. But holy crap, penises are weird."

The entire group burst out laughing.

"Seriously, have you ever taken a good look at one? It's like this floppy one-eyed slug thing, and then when it wakes up, it usually ends up at some weird angle. And don't get me started on foreskin—"

"That's it! I'm done," shouted Howie, who stood up and clapped his hands over his ears.

"Sit down, Howie," growled Paul, whose growl apparently carried as effectively as a shout because Howie sat right back down.

"I kept saying to myself that Pedro was a person just like Ilse, and he deserved to be loved too, and it was only my limitations as a human being that kept me from being able to appreciate his body in the same way as I did her large breasts and her smooth, round buttocks. So I tried my best to overcome my limitations. We did really well when we cooperated on Ilse, and she seemed to enjoy our joint efforts. But I had a hard time honoring his personhood when his penis tasted so bad."

Howie jolted in his chair, but stayed silent.

"I just kept reminding myself he came from a country that had suffered for centuries under oppressive colonial rule. That made it a little easier when he slid it into me."

Howie flopped back in his chair and looked up at the ceiling, perhaps hoping to be struck dead by the storm several floors above.

"Oh my God, Thor, he raped you?" Paul asked, eyes wide.

"No, no, of course not. I told him he could. It seemed the least I could do to make sure everyone's sexuality was completely validated. Plus, one of the purposes of these service trips is to try new things, right? So that's one of the new things I tried during that trip. That and *cusha.*"

"So, you're telling us that you're bisexual?" Chad asked, clearly confused.

"No, I don't think so," Thor replied. "Not that bisexuality isn't a perfectly valid sexual orientation. I wouldn't look down on anyone who expresses that as their affectional practice. But I don't think it's really for me. Pedro was a great guy and all, and I learned a lot from him, but honestly, if I never have semen in my mouth again, I think I'll be fine with that."

"Urgh," groaned Howie, beyond words now.

"I just want to say to you, Paul, that I'm really sorry we were all so ignorant, and therefore unsupportive, of your sexuality. I hope you know now that I speak from experience when I say I didn't do it out of homophobia or an unwillingness to accept non-normative sexual orientation. I feel like we're brothers now because I too have looked another man right in the anus."

"Wow, that's… something," Paul said, taking Thor's extended hand. He frowned thoughtfully as he shook it, as if searching for the right words to honor Thor's bizarre expression of fraternal bonding.

"I think it sounded better when Pedro said it in Portuguese," Thor said with a shrug.

"Okay, I gotta step in here," Howie said, standing. "It's time for a story that doesn't end with buttsex."

Thor nodded. "The floor is yours," he said as they switched places.

"ALL RIGHT, so you guys all know my dad, right?" His college buddies all nodded. He explained for the benefit of those who hadn't met him.

"He's pretty much like me, except he's thirty years older. Though he only looks ten years older."

"He's fucking gorgeous," Paul volunteered.

"Thanks, buddy," Howie snarled. "Anyway, growing up as the only child my parents managed to make before deciding to spend the rest of their lives trying to kill each other, I had pretty much anything I wanted. Dad's business really took off once he didn't have mom and me around all the time and he was able to devote the time to it he needed to. I didn't see him much after that, but he always found ways to show me he loved me. Like buying me a new car every year and always paying my credit card bill. Little things like that.

"So you'd think with a new Beamer and a platinum card I'd have no problem getting all the tail I wanted, right? Well, that's not really the way it worked for me. Sure, I could score with the ugly girls, or the fatties, but the real quality chicks for some reason never wanted to have much to do with me. So my senior year I'm getting kinda nervous about who I'm going to take to prom. I strike out with all of the popular girls, except one. She was this knockout cheerleader who also had a reputation as kind of a kinky chick. I saved her for last because I really didn't think I had a chance. But my dad kept saying I should take a shot, and she would be lucky to go with me, and he was really pumping me up. So I asked her, and she said yes. I kind of thought it was because she wanted to show up in the most expensive car, because she'd never even noticed I was alive until that point. But I wasn't about to question it—I was just stoked to have someone to go with me.

"So prom night comes, and I'm totally decked out. Dad sprung for a Prada tux, and I take her to the most expensive restaurant in the city. We go to the dance, and every girl wants to get with me, every guy wants to be me. It's awesome. I'd arranged to take her back to my dad's apartment rather than to my place because my mom would be a total wet blanket and make us sit in the living room and talk instead of what everyone wants to do after prom, right? So we get to my dad's place, and she and I start getting into it kinda hot and heavy, but then it's one in the morning and she says she has to get home. And I'm like, okay, I'll drive you home, thinking I maybe could still get a handy in the car or something before I drop her off. But my dad stops us in the hallway and says he should take her home because it's so late I shouldn't be driving. Well, fuck that. But he won't budge, and he gets super pissed at me, so I just go back to the guest room and slam the door. Then he's gone for two fuckin' hours. He finally drags his ass back into the apartment, and it's three in the morning, and he comes in to make sure I'm awake, and then he tells me about how they parked down the street from her house and he fucked her in the backseat. Twice.

"He fucking stole my prom date. My one shot at actually closing the deal with a hot chick and my dad cockblocks me and then takes her for a ride himself. That was the end of the line for me in terms of dating in high school, right there."

"That fucking sucks," Bark said. "I can't believe you never told us that story before."

"Wait. It gets worse," Howie intoned morosely.

"How does that get worse?" Bark asked.

"Turns out she and my dad planned the whole thing."

"What?" everyone seemed to gasp in unison.

Howie nodded. "She was a waitress at his country club. He flirted with her for a couple of months before she turned eighteen, right before prom. But they knew her parents would flip the fuck out if she said she was dating a guy old enough to, you know, be her dad, so they plotted the whole prom thing to give them a chance to have their big evening. In the back of his fucking car. All that stuff he told me about how I was just as good as any of the other guys at school, and how she would see what a stud I was, all of that was bullshit he fed me so I would ask his slutty, barely-legal cocktail-waitress crush out to the prom. So I would hand her over to him at the end of the night."

"What an asshole," Bark said.

"What a bitch," Chad chimed in. "I wonder what ever happened to that skank."

"She's my stepmother," Howie replied dismally.

"You are fucking kidding," Paul said, eyes wide.

"Nope. I get to be reminded of how my dad used me every time I see them together. They never even apologized for it."

"I think you need to get them out of your life," Thor said. "That's a completely toxic relationship."

"I would, except I need his money. He makes too much for me to qualify for any decent college loans, and his lawyers made sure my mom ended up with no money in the divorce. So if he stopped paying my tuition, I wouldn't be able to finish. But tuition is pretty much all he's paying these days, which is why I have to rent a rundown ghetto house with you losers—that's all I can afford with the money I make in the summers."

"How are you paying for this trip, then?" Ted asked. Howie had covered the entire cost of spring break for all the guys.

"Oh, he's happy to give me the credit card for things like this. He wants to show off his fortune by giving me a credit card everyone knows I couldn't have if I had to pay it myself. He says he wants me to have a good time and treat my buddies because that will make them loyal to me. I would tell him to fuck off and that my friends would be my friends even if I didn't have his fucking credit card, but then I wouldn't be able to fly you guys down here and spend a metric shit-ton of his cash. So that's the lameass way I get revenge on him for what he did to me. I spend his money on a clothing-optional gay resort for a week in the sun with my buddies. It's all working out great, don't you think?" He looked around the bomb shelter. "I'm fucking pathetic."

"We don't think of you as pathetic," Chad offered.

"No, we think of you as a rich asshole," Paul said with a grin. "But at least we know now why you're that way, and I for one think you can be as big an asshole as you want because you've earned it."

"C'mere, big guy," Thor said, getting up and walking over to Howie with his arms wide. "Hug it out."

Howie looked panicked as Thor embraced him. "Dude, is that Brazilian dong I smell on your breath?"

Thor just held on tighter. "Fuck off, Howie," he murmured sweetly as he rubbed his cheek against Howie's.

Finally, Howie put his arms around Thor, as everyone knew Thor wouldn't let a hug go unless it was returned.

"Well, that was horrifying," Howie said once Thor had let him go. "Who's next in our parade of sexual dysfunction?"

"I'm sure you're all waiting for the Chadster's big sexy adventures, right?" Chad asked as he stood.

"Are there any you haven't told us?" groaned Howie as he took Chad's seat, though he looked relieved to relinquish the spotlight.

"WELL, THERE is something I've never told you guys. It's not a story so much as a kind of confession."

"Vic," Winnie blurted in a stage whisper. "Go make some popcorn. This just keeps getting better!"

Chad smiled at this outburst and kept going. "Getting into modeling wasn't my idea. My dad had been laid off, and my mom was working really hard to keep everything going. I was working a ton of hours as a lifeguard at the country club in town during the summer, trying to contribute what I could to keeping the lights on at home. One day I rotate off the pool for my fifteen-minute break, and there's this guy waiting at the lifeguard station to talk to me. He's like, do you model? And I'm all, hell no. And he's like, you should think about it, and he gives me his business card. He's a photographer, and he says he's got all kinds of connections that could get me super noticed by people in the industry. I tell him I'm not really interested because I never really thought I had the… look, or whatever, for modeling, but I take the card to be polite and I stick it in my locker and don't think about it again for a while.

"Then the next month my mom loses her job, and we're completely fucked. Me and my mom and dad and my four brothers and sisters and no money coming in except what I make as a lifeguard and a couple of my sisters mowing lawns around the neighborhood. And no sign of anything more coming, either. I saved this fat stockbroker guy from drowning one day, and he tipped me like fifty bucks. As if I'd brought him a special martini or something. I would have been insulted except that fifty kept us from getting kicked out for missing the rent again. But since rich dudes weren't exactly drowning right and left, the whole 'getting tipped for CPR' thing isn't going to make me much coin. So I dig down in my locker, and under my spare tube of zinc, I find the guy's card. I text him, and he texts back like five seconds later. We arrange to meet up after my shift ends, at his place. And before you ask, Thor, yes I did tell a friend where I was going and when I would check in. You don't have to lecture me on stranger danger.

"The guy lived in a tract house on the edge of town, and he'd converted his basement into a studio. It was a pretty cool setup, and he took some really great shots he said would get some attention at agencies, which sounded great to me. I thanked him for helping me out, and then he's like, now would you like to help me out?"

"Uh-oh," Thor murmured, unable to keep silent any longer.

"Yeah, okay, I wasn't making the best choices right then, since he had gotten me all excited about possibly making the modeling thing work. He asked if I would take some photos in my lifeguard outfit, which I said I didn't have with me, and he's like, I just happen to have some stuff here. So he pulls out this tiny—and I mean tiny—little red Speedo, and he's all you can go into the bathroom to put that on.

"I look at this little scrap of spandex, and I start to think real hard about how much I really wanted to break into modeling. But I don't know any other way to go about it, and he's promised to help, so I go ahead and put on the little suit and go back out there. He's changed the lights so it's a lot darker in the studio, and he's got a screen going with some porn on it. Way to set the mood, right? But I figure I'm just going to do this thing, and I pose for him. It's going well for the first few minutes, but then I catch sight of the porn he's showing and I'm like boing! Which would be awkward anywhere, but since I was wearing that tiny little Speedo, I really have a problem. I'm like completely busting out of that thing and trying to turn away from the camera. But he's like, all over the place, and finally my nuts were so squished that I just... kinda... pulled the stupid thing off. Well, that was basically the end of the shoot right there. I was afraid he'd want me to... do stuff, but he didn't. He just took a few more pictures and then he's like, thanks that was great, and I'll let you know what I hear about the pictures. And I'm all, you're not going to show those last ones to anyone are you, and he's like, no, those are just for me. And then he hands me two hundred-dollar bills, just casual-like, as if I'd shown up to wave my dick at him and now he's like, job well done, buddy. But I figure as long as he didn't tie me up and fuck me, we're all good.

"So I go back to my job, and it takes a while for it to sink in that I made more from ten minutes standing around in a Speedo in his studio than I did standing around in stupid baggy trunks for an entire week at my regular job. And I start to put two and two together and see that maybe I can sex it up a little by the pool and see if that doesn't open some new doors for me. So I get myself one of those little red Speedos, and I start wearing that to work. And just like magic the rich old wrinklies at the club start forgetting how to tread water and suddenly I'm diving in to "save" people like six times a day. They're always real appreciative, and they find ways to slip Benjamins into the waistband of my little red Speedo—the old dudes tipping better than the old ladies, by the way. Suddenly I'm making three, four hundred a day saving people from not drowning. I'm thinking this is a pretty cool gig, and I didn't even have to get naked for it.

"Out of the blue about two weeks later, the photographer guy texts me and says there's an agent who wants to meet me. So I go and meet the guy at his office. And he has a photographer there who takes some shots, and he says he'll call me. The next day my photographer friend-slash-pimp texts me again and says he's got two more lined up, and I go meet with them too. And the thing is that all of them are dudes, which I kind of wasn't expecting, because wouldn't it make more sense to have a woman find the male models? Anyway, all of them say they'll call me soon, so I just go back to the pool and wait.

"Then one of the bigwigs at the club comes up to me at the end of my shift and asks if I'd be interested in making a little extra money. I'm like, yeah, I'm all about extra money. She says she's planning a private party for some friends at the club, and they need a lifeguard to work the party. They do that kind of stuff all the time, so I'm like sure, let me check with the head lifeguard to get on the schedule for it, and she says no, it's a *private* party, and the club will be closed when they do it. So I'm like, sure, I'll do it, and she says to come back to the club the next day after it closes.

"I show up the next night, and she meets me at the door and lets me in. She says she has something special for me to wear for the evening, and it's in the locker room. So I go in, and there I find four other guys who work at the club—two bartenders, a waiter, and the guy who parks the cars. And they're like, hey, she said there'd be something for us to wear in here, but all there is is this pile of red bow ties. So I turn around and go out and she's like, didn't you find your outfit? And I'm like, it was just a pile of bow ties and she's like yeah, that's what we want you to wear. And I'm like, just that? And she's like, yeah. So I go back into the locker room and I'm like, guys, that's what she wants us to wear. And they're all fine with it, which seemed kind of weird to me, but they just strip off and put the bow ties thingies around their necks and walk out to the pool area completely naked except for the ties. So, decision time again. On the one hand, I don't really want to walk naked around a bunch of old ladies, but then I figure if they're doing this, they are probably paying really well so we don't tell anyone what's going on. So I do it. I walk out with just my bow tie and my dick swinging, and then I realize no one's in the pool. They don't need a fucking lifeguard: they just wanted to see me naked.

"How awesome is that?" Chad beamed at the memory. "But then things got weird."

"God, the fucked-up stuff we've been through," muttered Howie. This time no one told him to fuck off.

"So they have us serving them drinks and these little appetizer thingies, and then some of them start to get a little handsy. Just a little touch here or there, but then they start to get a little more aggressive, and I'm trying to stay away from them because most of them are as old as my mother, and who wants some old crone pawing at the goods, right? They seem to take the hint, but then other shit starts going down. One of them holds up a fucking roll of twenties and says she'll give one to each of us if we kiss. Like, kiss each other. I'm like, no fucking way, but the other guys just go for it. Like, really go for it. Kinda seemed like it wasn't the first time any of them had kissed another guy for money. I'm like, no thanks, I'm good, and while the others are starting to like straight-up make out for money, I kinda hang back by the bar to wait out the weirdness. Well, all of them get super wasted on whatever they're drinking, and then they throw us wads of cash and stumble out to their cars and somehow manage to drive out of the parking lot. Then it's just me and the guys, and they're like, well now we're completely horned up, so how about it? And I'm like, how about what? And they're all, we're going to wash the old lady stank off us in the shower. I'm up for that because the whole thing was really gross, so we're in the showers, and the guys totally pair up and start making out again, only this time for free. And they're like, get in here, and I'm all no thanks because I'm not gay, and then one of them—the one who parks cars—is like, you are completely gay just get over yourself.

"Now, I really had nothing against gay people, I just knew I wasn't one. So I tell him that, and he's like, there is no way a straight guy looks like you do. And I told him I work out and stuff, but it's not like I'm doing anything else, and he starts pointing out my hair—which my sister cut, by the way—and my allover tan—courtesy of genetics—

and my six pack, which I worked damn hard for. He says no one looks like that unless they want to get guys.

"And that's when it hits me. The whole modeling thing—it's all about guys. All of the agents I met were guys, and all of the photographers. I had some friends who worked at the mall, and they said that most of the buyers for the stores are men, and most of the designers are men. So in order for a male model to make it in the business, he needs to look good enough that a male photographer wants to shoot him, and a male designer wants him to wear the clothes he's making so that a male buyer for a department store will buy his stuff, most of which will probably be bought by gay customers because what straight guy is going to spend butt loads of money on the designer stuff? The valet dude was right: it's all about guys. If I'm going to be successful in the business, I need to make guys want to look at me. Now, since I'm straight, this is kind of awkward. I'm not going to pretend to be gay so I can make it because that's not how my mama raised me. So that's when I got a fake name I thought sounded straight—though now I find out even Howie thinks it sounds gay—and, well…."

"What?" Thor asked, hanging on every word.

"That's when I started being a slut," Chad said. "I'm not proud of it. Before I started modeling, I had only ever dated one person, and she was awesome. But she wasn't the kind of person who puts on couture and hits the parties where models snort coke and bitch about having to lose more weight. In order to keep getting work I needed to travel in that circle, but I couldn't go without a woman on my arm because then all the guys would be all over me, so I started, basically, being a complete slut. It's not what I wanted, but it was the only way I could defend my heterosexuality. And then it kind of became a habit. And now I'm the kind of person who hands out boxes of underwear with my picture on them. I never wanted to be that guy. I wanted to make money for my family and go to school. But now I'm not sure I know how to stop."

Chad looked around the room. "Hi, I'm Chad, and I'm a sex addict."

Howie looked dumbfounded. "Wait. You are, by my count, the only one of us who has a normal sex life, and you're telling me there's something wrong with you too? Holy shit, what a freak show we turned out to be."

"Fuck normal," Paul spat.

"Howie, there's nothing normal about compulsively throwing myself at women," Chad replied. "You know I haven't slept with a single woman more than once? Ever?"

"But you're living the dream, man," Howie retorted. "You're what every other man in the world wants to be."

"Every other man in the world is so scared someone will think he's gay that he will sleep with any woman he can get his hands on? Never having any kind of relationship? Telling his friends every sick detail of his sex life to make it more real to himself? That's what every man wants?"

"Yes. I mean... no, not... ah, shit," Howie sputtered. "Sorry, man. I didn't know it was like that."

"Well, it has been like that, but I don't want it to be anymore. This shit stops right now. I'm not going to sleep with any more women just to prove I'm not gay. I'm going to only date women I can talk to and respect and spend actual time with. Dammit, I'm going to beat this thing."

Ted wasn't sure who started it, but the room broke out in applause. Actual, nonironic applause. Chad beamed, looking as if the world had been lifted off his chest. On his way to his seat, he cast a glance at Ted and Bark. "You're up," he said, to either or both.

Much to Ted's relief—the only sex stories he had were about Bark, after all—Bark stood to take his turn.

"YOU KNOW that guy in high school who is fat and doesn't seem to know it? He kinda lumps around campus like a big doofus, but still goes out for sports and works his fat ass off to make the team, even though no one thinks he'll survive another practice, much less the next game?"

The guys all nodded. There was one, apparently, at every high school.

"I was that guy."

A collective gasp filled the shelter.

"I'd always been big. My mom showed her love with baking, and I ate up every bit of the love she gave. My dad said I needed to be big to take on the world and get what was coming to me. He said life was a battle, and he wanted to be sure I was big enough to take on anyone. I don't think he ever really understood the difference between being big and strong and just being a lardass who eats all the time and doesn't get enough exercise. Anyway. By the time I got to high school, I was about two fifty, two sixty, and could barely walk down the block to get on the bus. But my dad kept pushing me to go out for a sport, and so I chose the one that was the most likely to reject me: lacrosse. You have to run and stuff in other sports, but in lax you are running all the fucking time, and I knew I wouldn't last two minutes at the tryout.

"What I didn't know is the coach for the team didn't like the elitist rep lacrosse had and thought everyone should have a chance to play no matter how ridiculous they look panting around the field. Just my luck, right? So I run as hard as I can, till I'm soaked with sweat and can barely breathe, and he tells me I should come back tomorrow and try it for another five minutes. Doesn't cut me, just keeps me hanging on. And then calls my dad and gives him an Oscar-worthy speech about great athletic potential and the value of sticking with it and how he should support me as much as possible. So by the time I get home that day, Dad's waiting in the garage with a whole home gym setup, and Mom's standing there just beaming at me. And I see it in their eyes, in the hope they have on their faces. They want to change me. They want me to live up to the perfect image of the perfect son they had in their minds when I was born a big fat baby. But I had stayed a big fat baby, and goddammit if I was going to change for them. I felt like a big fat fuck, but I was ready to own being a big fat fuck so a big fat fuck I was going to stay.

"I went back to the lacrosse field the next day, and I was able to keep moving for ten whole minutes before dropping to my knees and giving up what the lunch ladies fed me. The next day I did fifteen, and the salisbury steak stayed put. Pretty soon I was able to do a full practice, and I didn't drop a pound. I just kept what I had and changed some of it into muscle. Not a lot of it, but some of it.

"I was determined to be a lacrosse player without changing into a lacrosse player. Didn't get to play much, in terms of game time, but that was fine with me. I stayed on the side and helped the coach with strategy and analyzing the players, the way they moved and how they could improve. I learned the game inside and out, and the guys accepted me as the big fat fuck who knew a lot about lacrosse.

"My freshman year, the team wasn't very strong, but it got better over the season. Then second year we had a winning record for the first time in years. In my junior year, we almost took the regional title. A couple of stupid mistakes in the final game was all it took. But some of our best guys were seniors, and the team was looking to be pretty weak the following year. So I decided I was actually going to try to play the game for real.

"I talked to the coach, and did a ton of research about nutrition and working out, and we came up with a plan. I started telling Mom I knew she loved me even if I didn't eat a dozen of her cookies when I got home from school, and I bought a couple of big tubs of protein powder with some birthday money I hadn't spent on comic books and console games. And I started sneaking down to the basement to use the gym equipment Dad had chucked down there after I refused to use it.

"I busted my ass all summer long, and by the end of it, I really had busted my ass—down to about half its original size. When I got back to school in the fall, no one even knew who I was. I had to introduce myself to my teachers, and even some of my friends didn't recognize me at first. That spring when we hit the lacrosse field, I kicked some major ass, and we not only took regional, we took the entire state. Gave me my choice of universities, because any school with a lax team wanted me on it."

"So, let me get this straight," Howie interrupted. "We all tell stories about varying degrees of sexual humiliation, and you stand up and give us a behind-the-scenes look at why you are a lacrosse god? Seriously, Bark, Thor got drunk on Guatemalan moonshine and took it up the ass from a guy he barely knew. This is what you give us in return?"

Bark just shook his head slowly, not rising to Howie's bait. "You'll have your humiliation before my story is through. May I continue?"

Howie shrugged and made a "whatever" motion with his hands.

"Thank you. Now, once I got to college, I was suddenly in a place where no one knew my story. No one there had ever called me Fat Boy, or remembered me trying to pull my boxers out of my ass after a nuclear wedgie on the quad. To them—to all of you, actually—I had always been… well, this," he said, pointing to his chest. "You would think that would make me really happy, but it didn't. Because inside I still weigh nearly three hundred pounds. When I look in the mirror, I still expect to see myself buried under rolls of fat and triple chins. I still don't think I'm… good-looking."

"You?" blurted Ted. "You, not good-looking? What the fuck? You get naked any chance you get. You talk all the time about how people come to games just to watch you move. You've hardly had clothes on the entire time we've been here." He realized immediately that his outburst had surprised the others, but he was too shocked to care. "I can't believe you don't know how beautiful you are."

That last bit seemed to hit Bark like a crop across the face. "Beautiful? Why would you say that?"

"Sorry… I meant… handsome," Ted replied, fumbling.

Bark shook his head as if clearing it of what had just been said, but he struggled to regain the rhythm of his story. "Anyway… so halfway through freshman year, my parents decide to take our annual trip to the mountains during the university's winter break so I can go with them. My dad and his brothers have a couple of cabins way up in the middle of nowhere, and we go with family to ski and snowshoe and basically roll around in the snow for a week at a time. So we're up there, my mom and dad in our big cabin, and my aunt and uncle and cousins over in their little cabin about a hundred yards away across a creek that runs all winter because it's fed by a spring. And one day everyone decides they want to take **this** long-ass ski out to a place where you can look out over this whole big valley and marvel at the wonders of nature or whatever, and I'm totally not into it. I barely made it through Calc I, and so I dragged my books up there to refresh before starting Calc II spring semester.

"I decide I'm not going, and my cousin's girlfriend, who's back from college too, she doesn't ski. So everyone else takes off first thing in the morning, and I go over to my aunt and uncle's cabin to hang with my cousin's girlfriend so we only have to keep the smaller place heated during the day, and when they get back we'll all head over for dinner at our place. I spend the day studying, and she spends the day reading whatever girls are reading these days.

"About midmorning she says I should look out the window. I do, and all I can see is snow. It's a complete whiteout. Can't see a thing outside. And it keeps it up all through the day. Must have dropped like two, three feet in the space of a few hours.

"It's pretty clear my family's not going to be making it back for a while. There's a shelter out by the overlook where they were heading, so I'm not too worried about them, but I know they're not coming back today or maybe even tomorrow. So I figure I'll see if we can get to the other cabin, because that's where the food and our emergency beacon and stuff is. Takes me like an hour to push the snow out of the way just so I can climb out, and I can't see a thing when I look over toward our cabin. We can't just set out walking because we'll probably get lost, and if we don't we'd likely end up falling into the creek. So we hunker down and wait it out with no food, only the water we can make by melting snow on the wood stove, and only enough wood to either keep the place warm for a few hours or at a survivable temperature for a day or two. The sun goes down, and with it any chance of seeing anyone return, so we basically pile up all of the blankets in the place into the bed closest to the fire, and we strip off and climb under them to try to keep ourselves from freezing to death."

"Hold the phone there, cowboy," Paul says. "You say 'strip off' like it isn't a throwaway line from a bad porno."

"I'm getting to that. You all sat patiently through everyone else's story, but you're pretty quick to jump on mine. Chill out, and I'll explain as much of it as I can."

"Why can't you explain it all?" Howie chimed in. "It's your story."

"I'll explain that too, for fuck's sake," Bark cried. "Now shut up and listen. So I remembered something from a survival skills class my dad had made us all take when we bought the cabin. The guy running the class said that to share warmth you should be covered with as many blankets as possible but wearing as few clothes as possible. But when I thought about it later, the guy running the class was this old hippie ranger dude who probably just wanted to get everyone naked. But that doesn't really matter, because I suggested it to her, and for whatever reason she was totally into it. Just kinda threw everything off. I mean, everything. It wasn't until that moment I realized she was kind of hot."

"Wait, you just noticed it? You were stuck in a cabin all day with someone else's girlfriend, and you only notice she's hot once she strips off?" Chad asked incredulously.

"Look, Chaddy, I'm going to explain something that will seem really foreign to you. Not everyone has your self-esteem. Not everyone wakes up in the morning knowing they are the hottest man in the room. It's like I've been trying to tell you, in my mind I was still a fat loser. And the way fat losers deal with the world is we stop seeing the beauty in anyone because it's something we can never have. What good would it do me to spend an entire day obsessing about her tight ass or her, um… boobs or whatever, when there was no way in hell I was ever going to get close to them? So, no, I hadn't really noticed she was hot because I had spent a lot of years not noticing those things. And taking my clothes off wasn't that easy, either."

"Now I know you're shitting us," Howie shouted. "You get naked quicker than anyone else I know."

"When it doesn't matter, yeah, I do."

"What does that mean, when it doesn't matter?" Howie asked.

"When it's just people looking, that's one thing. The only reason I am so quick to drop my drawers is that I need to see people looking at me. I've never… I've never told anyone this." His voice dropped, almost to a whisper. "Having people look at my body is the only way I know it's real. That the image I see in the mirror isn't a trick my fat, lardy brain is playing on me. That people think I'm"—he looked right at Ted—"beautiful. I don't believe it any other way. But that's just people looking. I was about to be in close proximity to another human being, and that's a different thing altogether. Again, I never dreamed anyone would want to lay a finger on me, much less have sex with me. I barely wanted to have sex with myself when I was big.

"But the cabin's getting colder, so I suck it up and slide under the covers and then slip off my clothes and stuff them at the foot of the bed so she can't actually see me. So that's how we spent the night. I chucked another piece of wood into the stove every hour or so, trying to pace the fuel so the fire would last all night, and she lay there trying to keep me talking. It was like she actually wanted to get to know me better, and I've never had anyone be that way with me. And I never imagined people did that in bed—you know, talked to each other. And suddenly she's like twice as hot. I was really lucky she drifted off to sleep before she could accidentally find out I was getting totally boned up just being there next to her in the bed. So I lay there and watched her sleep. All night long. I tried to memorize every inch of her body, at least the parts I could see, and I watched her as she dreamed. Over that night she became my ideal—she was so nice and so smart and so beautiful, I just knew I'd never be able to find anyone as amazing as she was."

"And you didn't make a move?" Chad asked.

Bark shook his head. "No. I didn't want to ruin it. I didn't want to risk doing something stupid and making her hate me. We still had a long night, and who knows how much longer than that, and there was no way we could get out of there. If I made a move, and she wasn't into it, would she feel forced into it because we were trapped alone? Plus, what would my family say? It's not like she was available or anything. So I didn't do anything more than just stare at her and feel my boner ache all night long. In the morning my dad woke us up by banging on the door like the place was on fire, and we pulled our clothes back on before anyone saw what we'd been doing. The really fucked-up part of the whole deal is that we never talked about it. Not once, ever. She had no idea I completely fell in love with her that night. And that every woman I've ever slept with since has been a distant runner-up to her.

"I managed to arrive at college a virgin, on account of being a tremendous fat fuck, so I decided when I got back to campus after winter break I would get my shit worked out and find a woman who would set my head back on straight. Since then, I've been with a lot of women. But every single one of them—every last one—has only made me realize I left my first and true love back at that cabin. No one has ever meant anything to me the way she did then."

"Dude, you're not sleeping with the right women," Chad counseled.

"It's not about the women I sleep with. It's how that first person made me feel. About myself. She showed me I was worthy of her attention, and she showed it not by sucking my dick or letting me stick it in, but by talking to me and asking me questions and really listening to the answers. She made me feel like my body didn't matter, which is ironic since when I was with her was the only time in my life I actually felt like I was in my body. Do you guys know what I mean?"

Howie cleared his throat. "Bark, I think I speak for all of us when I say we have no idea what the fuck you are talking about."

"I'm not sure how to explain this. I know I have a reputation for getting naked and fucking anything that moves. But all of that, everything you think you know about me, is wrong. Just wrong. If I could go back to that night in the cabin three years ago, I would. Everything I've done since then has been an effort to undo that."

"What would you do?" Thor asked.

"I would… find a way to let her know. How much she did for me. How much she changed me. But you know what I've realized? If I had the chance, if somehow I managed to find her and be with her, I would fuck it up completely. Like I wouldn't even be able to say anything. Like I would just break down and never even be able to let her know…." Bark could no longer hold back the tears that had been forming in his eyes.

The awkward silence that followed the trailing off of Bark's story was oppressive, and it was broken only by Ted bolting suddenly to his feet and walking into the room that held Winnie's gowns. He walked along the rows of dresses until he came to the makeup mirror. He studied his reflection, trying to convince himself no one else would know just from looking at his face what he was feeling. He closed his eyes, preferring not to see at all.

"Ted?" Donnelly's voice was soft and gentle from behind him. "Are you all right?"

Ted didn't dare speak for fear his voice would break and he would let out the sob he could feel building inside his chest. He looked at Donnelly's reflection in the glass and shook his head miserably.

Donnelly put his hand on Ted's shoulder. "Pretty hard to hear Bark tell that story, wasn't it?"

Ted nodded as the sobs began to force their way to the surface.

"Did you get a chance to talk with him? About what we talked about yesterday on the beach?"

Ted shook his head again.

"Well, maybe that's for the best now."

Ted continued to shake his head. He cleared his throat, and tried to calm the surging pain that was making it hard for him to draw breath.

"Bark…," he began. "His story was…."

"Yes?" Donnelly nodded encouragingly.

"His story was about… me."

Donnelly blinked and shook his head, clearly confused. "What do you mean, it was about you?"

"Bark wasn't stuck in a cabin in a blizzard with his cousin's girlfriend. It was me. We're the ones who were bundled up under all those covers all night. When he told that story, he was talking about me."

Donnelly's mouth dropped open. "Are you sure?"

Ted nodded. "Yes, of course I'm sure. I was there. What I didn't know about was what he felt about that night. I had no idea he watched me sleep, and I certainly had no inkling he felt the way he says he does. And then last night, when I tried to talk with him, well, we ended up soaking wet and so we got into the shower and I tried to tell him how I feel and he just sort of came unglued and he said he was scared and he cried and I held him, just held him, and then he collapsed and we haven't talked about it except for a few minutes ago when he told me— well, he told everyone, but I'm the only one who knows what he was talking about—he told me everything he couldn't last night. At least I hope that's what it all means. I have no idea anymore. I really don't."

"You need to talk to him," Donnelly said. "If you are right about how this all worked, then you have to talk with him right away. He seemed to be in such pain. He really needs to hear from you that you're okay with all of this, and with him."

"How am I going to do that?"

"How about you tell him a story?"

"IT PROBABLY won't shock anyone if I tell you right off the bat my story isn't going to have much in the way of sex. In fact, my entire life hasn't had much in the way of sex. All through high school, I was the kind of guy who will look at someone attractive, obsess about them, and never ever let on I've even noticed them. Not that I'm a creeper or anything, really, it's just that I spin out such a story in my head about anyone I'm attracted to I can never get the courage up to actually talk to them. So I follow them around and try to be their friend, and nothing more can ever develop because I won't make a move of any kind.

"I really wanted college to be different. I was going to come in and start making my moves and finally letting girls know when I thought they were nice-looking, and maybe even date some of them. You know, the stuff everyone else learned to do in high school. But as soon as I set foot on campus, my entire plan went out the window. Because the first person I met, literally the first person, was just... fucking gorgeous. Like, everything I ever wanted but wouldn't let myself even hope I might find. And all I had to do was show up, and there it all is. I was so stunned, and so shocked at my reaction, I was right back in high school before I'd even really started college. There was no way I could ever say anything, because I wasn't even in the same league—shouldn't have even been allowed in the same room.

"But because I am apparently a glutton for punishment, we became friends. All through the first semester of freshman year, I was a total love-struck puppy dog. I would do anything, say anything, be anything to be close to the person I knew I could never have. And all the while, I knew I couldn't say anything, or be caught looking at anything, because then our friendship would end. I knew that, for a certainty.

"So here's why my story sucks. Because it's been almost four years, and I've never moved on. I just sit and watch and dream and am scared to death I'll be found out. There was a time, actually pretty recently, when I tried to say something. We'd been caught in the rain, and we were cold and soaking wet and I couldn't hold back anymore and I tried to say what I was feeling, but it all kind of came out wrong and I didn't understand what... well, I just didn't see what was in front of me, that's all."

Ted fell silent.

"Is it just me," Howie said, "or do Ted and Bark have basically the same issue?"

"Yeah," Chad added. "Wouldn't it be funny if they were both talking about the same person?"

"That would be something, wouldn't it, Ted?" said Bark, his voice low and even.

"Yes, it would," replied Ted, meeting Bark's gaze and nodding slowly.

"Well, thank you for that story," Winnie said, clearly trying to keep the mood light. "Now Vic has prepared lunch, and—"

The lights flickered, but came right back on.

"Power's out," Vic called from the kitchen. "The backup battery is fully charged, so we're fine."

Howie consulted his phone. "It's here," he said simply. "Shit's about to get real." He held up his phone and showed the group a radar image covered in lurid red.

CHAPTER EIGHT
SHELTERING

OVER VIC'S lunch of stew and biscuits (Winnie called it "apocalypse cuisine"), Brandt and Donnelly told the group the story of how they had come to be together. Winnie renewed his plea for Brandt to reveal his *nom de porn*, but he again demurred.

Throughout the lunch, Ted and Bark sat opposite each other and didn't speak—they barely looked at one another.

When the meal had been cleared away, Donnelly turned to Winnie. "You know that thing you needed help with? I think Ted and Bark and I could probably take care of it for you right now."

Winnie looked baffled, but then seemed to remember what Donnelly was referring to. "Oh, yes, of course. How nice of the three of you to take care of… that. For me. Thank you."

"Ted, Bark, can you come with me?"

The young men rose from their seats and followed Donnelly into the Gown Room. Once there, they turned and looked expectantly at Donnelly.

"Great. Thanks. Now, there's just one more thing I need to do before we get started. I'm going to go out and shut the door and let no one in until you're finished. Okay? No one will come in until you open this door. Okay?"

"Um, okay?" Ted said. He had no idea what was going on.

Donnelly turned and left the room, closing the door firmly behind him.

Ted looked at Bark. Bark looked at Ted. Eventually, the weight of the unsaid overwhelmed him and he had to speak.

"So I guess we should—"

"Did you mean what you said, in your story?" Bark asked quietly.

Ted stared hard at his friend, trying to see what was going on behind those green eyes. He nodded. "Did you in yours?"

Bark stared back, just as hard. Finally, he nodded.

"Why didn't you tell me?" Ted asked.

Bark shrugged helplessly. "I was scared."

"Of me? Seriously? Who's scared of me?"

"Not of you, necessarily, but…."

"But now you know I feel the same way," Ted said. "There's nothing to be scared of."

Bark turned and paced around the room, slowly and aimlessly. "I don't know how…. I'm afraid I'll find out you don't exist."

Ted tried to parse this nonsense and got nowhere. "What?"

Bark stopped his pacing, but spoke to the wall, not Ted. "Everyone I've ever known has been in my life because of my body. When I was fat, the only friends I had were either as fat as I was, or for whatever reason liked being around fat people. Then when I started working out, the whole cast of characters changed, and everyone around me only wanted to be around me because of the way I looked. I traded one set for another, but neither cared that much about the person inside the body. Except you." He turned to Ted, his eyes reddened. "That night in the cabin, you talked to me, and you listened, and you made me feel like a person, not just a body. It's like you were the only person on the whole fucking planet who didn't see me, but saw what was inside me. I didn't think anyone would ever do that, and I'd given up even looking for it. Then I found you."

"But you think I don't exist?"

"I just can't believe you'd want me."

Ted stepped closer to Bark. "I've wanted you from the moment I saw you. Didn't understand it at first, and honestly I thought I was kind of losing it. I mean, you were amazing to look at, but in my experience, beautiful people tend to be shallow and kind of dumb. But as I got to know you, I started to see you were this amazing person who just happened to be wrapped in a godlike body. It was the first time in my life I actually felt lucky."

"Lucky? How?"

"Lucky I had drawn you in the roommate lottery. Lucky I had found the one guy who was not only smart and funny but whose body makes my chest pound."

"But, Teddy," Bark said, his expression pained, "I'm not gay."

Ted stared at him for a long moment. "Honestly, after the stories Thor and Paul and even Chad told, I'm not sure I even know what gay means anymore."

Bark huffed out a frustrated breath. "I think it means you don't want to have sex with women, but you do want to have sex with men. I'm pretty sure that's a definition most people would agree with."

"So what's the problem?"

"I'm also pretty sure I've been having sex with women on a regular basis. Like two or three times a week."

"Okay…," Ted replied, brow furrowed.

"Okay, so I think the natural conclusion to draw is that the odds are pretty good I'll continue to have sex with women. Like straight people do."

Ted nodded. "But I've been having sex with no one on a regular basis. Like every night. Does that mean I should want to continue to have sex with no one for the rest of my life?"

"No," Bark replied, but then seemed lost in thought. "Look, it's like this. You are the only person I can imagine spending my life with, and that you're a guy, well, it's all fucked-up."

Ted could hardly catch his breath. "Spending your life with?"

Bark nodded miserably. "I know it sounds stupid, but honest to God, Ted, you are the only person who makes me feel human. You get me, and I'm better when I'm with you than at any other time, no matter who I'm with or what I'm doing. I just cannot imagine life without you, but I'm going to have to start living it in a couple of months. Once we graduate there's no reason for us to still live together, or even see each other as much as we do now. And that's killing me."

"And that's why you did it?" Ted asked, putting his hand on his chest.

Bark nodded, glancing down to Ted's chest and then back up again. "I was empty inside. No matter how many women I sleep with, there's a hole in my heart. I wanted to find out if touching you would make me whole." He blinked hard. "Having you there, touching you, it made me feel… complete. Like for the first time in my life the physical part of sex and the emotional part of it were there all at once. For the first time, sex didn't just make me feel good, it made me… happy. I want that again, more than anything in the world I want that every day."

"That's what I want too," Ted said, taking Bark's hand and pressing it to that place on his chest. "Why can't we have that?"

Bark paused awhile, his lips moving as if trying out unspoken ways to explain. "Because I don't know if I can."

Ted puzzled over this for a moment. "That's why you kissed Paul, isn't it?"

Bark startled, but then a weary smile appeared. "It shouldn't surprise me anymore, but when you read my mind like that…." He shook his head and took his hand back from Ted's chest. "I did it because I had to know whether I could kiss a guy."

"It didn't seem like it killed you."

Bark chuckled under his breath. "No, it didn't. I love Paul, and he's an amazing kisser, but it just wasn't the life-changing Prince Charming kiss I was hoping for."

"Like once he kissed you, you would be gay?"

Bark shrugged. "It was worth a try, right?"

"Why didn't you try with me?"

"I didn't know how you felt. And what if I tried it and it didn't work? I mean, if it turns out I'm not really able to… do that… with a guy?"

"It's not about doing it with a guy, it's about doing it with me," Ted said, entirely unsure how to go about making his feelings clear. But all he could do was try. "I have never thought of you as just another guy. I fell in love with you, and the fact that you're a guy, well… that's just the way it happened."

"I want to be able to see it that way, I really do. I just don't know if I'm… wired that way."

They were hard words for Ted to hear. He simply shrugged—he really didn't have any idea what to say—and then started to open the door. But Bark stopped him before he had opened it more than a couple of inches.

"Wait," he whispered. He leaned in and kissed Ted.

It was a quick, chaste kiss, but it seared Ted to his core. Without a word, Bark pulled the door fully open and slipped out, leaving Ted completely confused.

"WELL, THAT was a lovely dinner, Vic," Winnie said, gathering up plates. "I'm fairly certain it contained enough calories to keep us going through repopulating the entire planet, should that be required."

"And assuming at least a couple of women survived," Howie groused.

"Hey, maybe then some of them will sleep with you," Chad said brightly. "You know, last guy on earth and all."

"In terms of the competition for available women, even then I wouldn't be first choice. There's you and Bark, and against you, I'll die without reproducing. Thor wouldn't want to burden any woman with his seed, so I'm good there. I may stand a chance against Ted."

"Fuck off, Howie," Ted replied lazily. He had been quietly watching Bark throughout the rest of the day, trying to gain any sense at all as to why Bark had suddenly, after saying it was something he didn't think he could do, kissed him. So far he had nothing.

"According to the radio," Vic announced, "the eye of the storm should be passing over us in the next couple of hours. Then the trailing edge will make landfall overnight, and by morning we should be able to head on up and take a look at the damage. I wish we could guarantee you the inn will be able to resume normal operations, but we have to assume there has been some damage that will need to be cleaned up. We hope you understand."

"We'll be happy to help however we can," volunteered Thor. "Right, guys?"

They all signaled their assent, grudgingly in the case of Howie and with a graceful smile on the part of the others.

"Now, we have air mattresses and sleeping bags for everyone," Winnie said, "although...." He knitted his brow as he sorted through the bin he'd brought out from the storage room. "Once again I'm afraid we have found ourselves ill-equipped for a guest roster of straight young men. Most of these bags are doubles." He shrugged apologetically to the group.

"We've been sleeping in the same bed already. What's the big deal with a double sleeping bag?" Paul asked the group.

"If there's a single in there, I'm taking it," Howie said definitively.

"Works for me," Paul replied. "I'll spoon with anyone who doesn't have Howie's stunted self-development."

Winnie handed Howie a small sleeping bag without comment.

Thor turned to Chad. "You okay with a double?"

"Hell yeah," Chad laughed. "I'm kinda figuring I can leverage your white liberal guilt into a blowjob."

Thor squinted at him. "On the one hand, I'm heartened to see you are able to set your homophobia aside and make that kind of joke. On the other hand, the only shot you have is being the actual last man on earth. Then maybe you'll get a handy. Maybe."

Winnie hauled a large bag out of the bin and handed it to Thor.

"Well, Bark, what do you say?" Paul asked. "Gonna make good on that kiss and curl up with me?"

The blood pounded in Ted's ears as he tried to decipher the look on Bark's face. If Bark rejected him now, after their confusing conversation and that bizarre kiss, he didn't know if he could survive.

"Thanks, buddy," Bark said.

Ted closed his eyes and bit his lip in an effort to keep from crying out.

"But I'm gonna dance with the one what brung me," Bark continued. "If you feel up to it, Ted."

Ted nodded, unable to do any more on account of the emotional whiplash he'd just suffered.

"Though I have to warn you," Bark said, "after striking out last night, and spending tonight underground with this sausage fest, this is the longest dry spell I've had in years. Things might get bumpy." He winked at Ted, and it was like the old Bark was back, the one Ted knew before things got so weird and intense between them.

"I think I'm up for it," Ted replied, desperately trying to sound suave and playful and everything except what he was actually feeling, which was panicked and thrilled and possibly nearly passing out.

Winnie handed Bark a large sleeping bag.

"Well, shit," Paul said with a grin. "Looks like the gay bro is out of luck."

"I'm sure we can work you in somewhere," Winnie replied. His double entendre could mean only one thing.

Thor looked up from where he and Chad had laid out their large sleeping bag. "We'd be happy to have you pile in with us. But you'll need to stay on my side, since Chad's got issues."

"You sure you trust yourself around me?" Paul teased. "I might roll over in the night and give you a Guatemalan flashback."

"Sounds like something you need to add to Urban Dictionary," Chad said with a laugh. "I can hardly wait to see the definition of that one."

"It's a chance I'm willing to take," Thor said to Paul with a wink.

"Is it hot in here, or is it just you?" Winnie joked. He handed a sleeping bag to Brandt. "Now, Ethan, you and Gabriel should take the gown room, which will give you a little privacy." He looked around to make sure everyone had gotten settled. "This is probably a lot earlier than you normally get to sleep, though we may have a big day ahead of us tomorrow. How about a little nightcap to pass around?" Vic handed a large square green bottle to Paul. "I trust college parties still run on Jaeger?"

Paul tipped up the bottle and took a healthy swallow. "If there's a proof number on the bottle, I'm in." He passed the bottle to Thor.

Winnie and Vic retired to the kitchen to make their bed on the floor.

After the green jug had made its way around the room two, or perhaps three, times, Brandt and Donnelly rose a little unsteadily and made their way to the gown room. "Good night, guys," Brandt said as he shut the door behind them.

"Hey, Howie, get the lights," Paul called across the room.

Howie reached up and turned off all but the dim lights over the doorways leading off the main room. In the mostly dark room, the guys sat on their sleeping bags and passed the bottle around until it was empty.

"What do you think it's going to look like up there?" Chad asked.

"We have to assume it's going to be pretty bad," Thor answered. "I haven't been able to get an updated radar picture for several hours because I think the cell towers lost power—or they were blown over. It could be nasty."

"Strange being down here and not even hearing the wind or anything," Ted said. "It's like it's not even happening."

"Winnie and Vic have taken damn good care of us," Paul said. "We owe them a lot for all they've done."

"Absolutely," Thor replied. "If we need to spend some time helping them get back up and running, we should. We're all in this together."

"Great," Howie grumbled. "Spring break turns into Habitat for Humanity. Gay humanity."

"Fuck off, Howie," Bark replied. "Just get your beauty sleep and try to be a better human tomorrow."

The room was filled for a moment with the soft shuffling of all six men making themselves as comfortable as possible under the circumstances, and then quiet descended over them.

Thor's whisper broke the silence. "Paul, is that your—"

"Yep, sorry. I'll turn over." More shuffling. "It's been like that since I woke up this morning. I guess it thought you were interested."

"I take it as a compliment," Thor replied. "It's probably the most action I'll get this whole trip."

"The night is still young," Paul rejoined, his voice full of insinuation.

"Will you two put a sock in it?" Howie blurted.

"Or a cock in it," Chad offered with a chuckle. "Not gonna judge."

Ted zipped open his side of the sleeping bag and slipped in. Bark did the same on his side, leaving what seemed to Ted to be an insurmountably large no-man's-land between them. Then he felt the sleeping bag shift a bit, and the gap seemed to narrow. Bark was still for a moment, and then Ted felt it: Bark's hand was moving across the divide, reaching out for him. He held his breath without knowing why as it approached. Bark's fingers brushed his shoulder, then moved suddenly down, along his ribcage, until they reached the hem of the shirt Ted had worn to bed. Slipping nimbly under the fabric, the hand glided back up, this time electrifying Ted's skin with random skittering touches until it came to rest on that spot right above his heart he had already consecrated as Bark's alone. Warm and soft, the hand nestled into its now-familiar place, and Ted breathed again.

What it meant, what Bark meant by it, he had no idea. It was a gesture that made no demand but to be accepted, and Ted accepted it gladly.

He reached up and laid his hand on top of Bark's, and they stayed that way all night.

THERE WERE no bands of sunrise light streaming across the bed this morning. They were awakened instead by the sound of Winnie and Vic whispering softly as they moved about the kitchen preparing breakfast.

Even before Ted opened his eyes, he was aware of Bark's hand, still in its place above Ted's heart. What thrilled him even more than the warmth of contact was the effort it must have taken Bark to keep it there all night long, never turning away or moving his arm from that position. Ted lay under the sweet heaviness of that hand for a long while.

Eventually the others began to stir. Ted heard Chad's distinctive yawn and stretch as he woke and sat up. Ted opened his eyes but didn't stir for fear of waking Bark and losing touch with him.

"Get a room, you two," Chad said to Thor and Paul. "You're spooned up like sweethearts."

"I don't think I ever want to sleep anywhere else," Thor's sleepy voice replied from somewhere near Chad. "I slept like a baby."

"A baby monkey," Paul replied with a chortle. "You didn't let go of me all night."

"Ugh," groaned Chad, who got to his feet and walked off toward the bathroom.

"Well, that was awful," Howie opined, sitting up in his sleeping bag.

"Disappointed no one spooned with you?" Thor asked teasingly.

Howie's response was a growl and a wadded up shirt thrown at Thor's head.

The door to the gown vault opened slowly, and Donnelly peeked out. "Everyone decent?"

"All except Howie," Thor answered, "who has never behaved decently in his life."

Howie growled again but apparently had nothing else to throw.

"I'll just see if I can help in the kitchen," Donnelly said as he tiptoed nimbly through the piles of sleeping bags.

Ted looked up as he passed, and Donnelly winked at him, tipping his head almost invisibly at Bark. Ted smiled at the sudden reality of gay telepathy. He shrugged slightly but kept smiling, and Donnelly seemed to take his meaning.

Ted felt Bark's hand begin to twitch as he stirred, sighing in the liminal space between sleep and waking. Then he shifted suddenly toward Ted, and his hand pressed even harder into Ted's chest.

"Morning," he whispered softly.

Ted snuggled farther down into the sleeping bag with him. "Morning," he said, feeling like his face would crack from the width of his smile.

Bark's green eyes were bright this morning. "Thank you," he murmured.

"For what?"

"For being patient with me," Bark replied. "I don't know how to do this, and you're letting me figure it out. Thank you."

"There's no wrong way to do this," Ted said, putting his hand once again atop Bark's. "Anything you do is okay with me."

Bark beamed at him but could only shake his head with a complex expression of both yearning to communicate and relief he didn't have to in order to be understood.

Ted simply nodded. "I know," he said reassuringly.

They lay there, wordless, for a long while.

"Breakfast is ready, gentlemen," Vic announced. "Then I believe it's safe for us to venture to the surface to check out the damage. Power's not on yet, but the news on the radio is that the storm is in its final hour or two."

"Any word on the amount of damage?" Thor asked as he took a plate from Vic and passed it to Paul. "Anyone hurt?"

Vic sighed and shook his head. "There's a lot they don't know yet, mainly because with so many spring breakers crammed into every hotel room it's hard to get an accurate count. But the town was hit pretty hard, and there are several dozen people unaccounted for. There were two fatalities that they know about. Townies, older folks who waited until the last minute to lock their shutters and take cover. One got hit by a falling tree, and another dropped with a heart attack. We haven't seen a storm like this since we've been here, and it sounds like it caught a lot of people by surprise. They're calling it the storm of the century, but I think that's mostly just for drama."

"People do *so* love their drama, don't they?" warbled Winnie, who bustled into the camp room wearing his bright floral dressing gown, handing plates of breakfast to Howie and Chad.

Donnelly brought a couple of plates over to Ted and Bark, and knelt down next to their sleeping bag. "Gentlemen, I trust you passed a pleasant evening?"

The young men sat up and took the plates from Donnelly.

"We did, thanks," Ted replied, blushing deeply. He knew Donnelly would understand why.

"I crashed pretty hard," Bark said. "I hope Teddy wasn't looking for too much excitement." He grinned and nudged Ted with his shoulder.

"It was all the excitement I needed, thanks," Ted replied, overjoyed at rediscovering the easy rhythm of his early friendship with Bark, before his attraction complicated things.

"Good," Donnelly said with a smile and a pat on Ted's knee through the sleeping bag. He returned to the kitchen and came back with two more plates on a tray with two cups of steaming liquid. "Now to wake the beast," he said with a dramatic horror-movie voice. He pushed open the door to the gown room and stepped in.

"Those guys are pretty great," Bark said, chewing thoughtfully. "I tell ya, after meeting them, and finding out about Paul, I'm starting to think I don't know anything about sex."

Ted looked at him skeptically. "Seriously? You forget we lived practically on top of each other for two years. I heard a lot of things, but never a complaint. Seemed to me you knew what you were doing."

Bark smirked. "That should creep me out, but for some reason, it doesn't. Huh." He shook his head and consulted the middle distance for a moment. "Anyway, what I meant was that if those two cops are gay, and Paul is gay, then I have no idea what being gay means."

"I think it means they have sex with other gay people."

"Shut up." Bark smacked him on the back of the head, laughing. "I just meant they don't act the way you always see gay people acting. You know, like Winnie."

"I don't know that there's anyone else like Winnie," Ted said, cracking up.

"What are you two lovebirds whispering about over there?" Paul demanded. "Sweet nothings, or something you'd like to share with the group?"

"You know a gentleman never tells," Bark scolded, then started laughing again.

Ted felt a huge weight lifted from his chest, seeing Bark so happy and free from the gloom that had enveloped him yesterday. For the first time, he let himself begin to hope they would find their way through this.

They finished their breakfast, and the guys rolled up their sleeping bags and air mattresses, then got themselves dressed in what they hoped would be their final set of pool-boy hand-me-downs. After a last check of the radio news to be sure the storm was on the wane, Vic spun the wheel in the center of the bank-vault door and pushed it open. Instantly the shelter was filled with the sounds of wind and rain.

"Sounds like it's still pretty wild up there," Winnie said. "Perhaps we should wait another couple of hours?"

But Vic's head was tipped in an odd way as he stood with one foot on either side of the rounded threshold. He shook his head, then listened again. "It sounds like someone's up there," he said in a low voice.

"Perhaps they're going around making sure everyone's okay?"

"Maybe. I'm going to check it out," Vic said.

"I'm coming too," Paul said, striding purposefully to the door. "You shouldn't go up there alone."

Vic nodded. "Thanks, Paul. I appreciate it." He turned to the others. "We'll go make sure it's safe to come up, and then we can all get out of here."

"Be safe, love," Winnie said, kissing Vic on the cheek.

Paul turned back to Thor and tapped his cheek expectantly.

"Ugh," groaned Howie.

But Thor just smiled and walked over to Paul. He kissed him on the cheek daintily, and Paul clapped a vigorous hand onto Thor's ass. Thor smacked him on the shoulder.

"Stop it, you," Thor scolded, but his voice was playful.

Vic and Paul stepped out of the shelter and disappeared around the corner of the corridor.

"Men," sighed Winnie with a sisterly glance at Thor.

Thor simply smiled and put a hand on Winnie's arm. "They'll be fine."

"I'm sure you're right."

But they stayed by the doorway, listening to the tread of manly soles on the stairs up to the surface.

The first shout was Vic's. Ted couldn't hear what he said, but it wasn't a friendly greeting. Then Paul's voice rang out—not the playfully gruff voice he used when issuing commands to his friends, but one that meant trouble.

"Guys?" Thor said, not taking his eyes from the corridor. "I think something's wrong."

Ted got up and ran to the doorway. He could hear more voices now, and they sounded as angry as Vic and Paul's had. He turned back and went to the door of the gown room. The troopers would know what to do.

BRANDT OPENED the door immediately in response to the urgent knocking. On the other side, he found Ted, looking frantic.

"Vic and Paul went to the surface, and there's something wrong."

Brandt's back stiffened instinctively. "What happened?"

He listened, but his body was on autopilot. He grabbed for his pack, from which he pulled his gun and badge, locked together in a sleek metal case. He tossed Donnelly's to him, and they both pressed their fingers to the biometric locks. The cases popped open, and they withdrew their firearms, checked them for ammo and proper operation, and slipped them into their waistbands. Badges went on chains around their necks. All of this happened in the blur of no more than ten seconds, as they had so often practiced.

"Vic was going to head up, but he heard noises. Paul went with him. As soon as they got up there we heard voices—theirs, but also others. They sound angry."

Brandt strode into the main room, taking charge. "Everyone stay down here. Shut and lock the door behind us. If we have a situation up there, we don't want you to get involved." He glanced at Donnelly, who signaled that he was ready to move. They stepped through the doorway, and Brandt shoved the door back into place. As it closed, he called to Winnie, "Lock it, and don't open it unless you hear my voice. Got it?"

"Yes." Winnie's reply was shaky, but he did what Brandt told him to do.

In the corridor, Brandt could hear voices above. The sounds of an angry confrontation filtered down to them. "I make our two and at least three others?"

Donnelly nodded. "Standard approach?"

Brandt gave a quick nod and they started up the stairs to the surface. Their footsteps were silent, Brandt taking the lead and Donnelly following close behind. They stopped every few steps to listen, but they quickly reached the door at the top of the stairs. Here Brandt paused, ear cocked.

"Looks like the storm damaged your computers too," a husky voice said with saccharine sympathy. Then a crashing noise erupted from around the corner, as if someone had taken a mighty swing at the check-in counter with a sledgehammer. "It's going to be a long while before your precious little faghouse can open again, after this act of God. Maybe you should just close down for good and go back to San Francisco or whatever Sodom you came from."

"Stop it!" yelled Vic, and there were sounds of struggle.

Brandt stepped through the doorway, intent on getting the situation under control. What he found as he entered the inn's front office was total chaos. Paul lay on the floor, bleeding from a wound on the side of his head, his eyes glassy and dazed. Donnelly knelt next to him, checking him for signs of consciousness. Vic was trying to wrestle an axe out of the hands of a burly man while two others landed punches on whatever part of Vic's body they could reach. He was struggling heroically, but he was clearly overmatched. In the corner lay an unconscious thug, bleeding from a wound that matched Paul's.

"Stop! Police!" shouted Brandt in his crowd-control voice. It was not one he used often, and its ferocity had been noted in several gang-related incident reports.

The man wielding the axe froze for a second, but then took advantage of the others being startled by Brandt's arrival to wrench the axe from Vic's grasp and take another mighty swing at the front desk. With a crash the counter buckled and the remains of the computer and other equipment clattered to the ground.

"I said stop!" Brandt shouted, and advanced on the man, holding his badge up. The other three men stepped back, allowing Vic to slump to the floor.

The burly man with the axe rounded on Brandt with a vicious gleam in his eye. "Oh, is it a costume party?" he jeered. "I thought you fags were better at dress-up than that. Look, cocksucker, waving around a fake badge doesn't make you a cop. I suggest you bug the fuck out of here before you get your manicure chipped." He hefted the axe, clearly intent on leveling the remaining furnishings in the office.

A crash from out on the pool deck, visible through the window behind the desk, distracted Brandt for a moment. He could see another group of men outside, taking turns smashing the tables and chairs around the pool.

Brandt held up his badge so the big man could see it clearly. "This is not a fake badge," he replied angrily. "I am a state police officer, and I order you to put the axe down. Now!"

The man squinted at Brandt's badge. "I don't know who you stole that from, you ass bandit, but even if it is real, you have no jurisdiction here."

"I am authorized as a state police officer to detain you until local law enforcement arrives. So put the axe down and call off the rest of your crew."

"Like hell I will," the burly man snarled. "Local law enforcement is already here."

Brandt instinctively looked around for signs of the arrival of the police.

Vic, still catching his breath from the beatdown he'd already suffered, managed to speak. "Officer Brandt, this is the sheriff."

Brandt was instantly furious. This was not the fake anger of the commanding persona he had been trained to adopt for crowd control; this was real fury, and it coursed through his body with a searing intensity. He leapt at the sheriff, catching him around his considerable middle and smashing him back against the wall next to the remains of the front desk. Before the sheriff knew what hit him, Brandt flipped him over onto his belly on the floor and wrenched his arm behind his back. He cried out in pain; the satisfaction Brandt felt at hearing his cry shocked him, but he would look into that later.

"Get the fuck off him!" One of the other men who had been watching the drama unfold shouted at Brandt.

Brandt was too occupied trying to keep the struggling sheriff pinned down to even turn to look.

"Gun!" Donnelly sprang to his feet. "Police! Drop the gun!" he roared. "Drop it now! Now!"

Donnelly's own gun was drawn, and he aimed it directly at the man standing behind Brandt. For a moment, all was frozen as each man waited for one of the others to move.

"Get down!" The other man dropped to the floor immediately. Donnelly advanced. "Drop your weapon," he said with deadly calm. "I will shoot if you do not comply."

Brandt, knowing now there was a gun pointed at his back, pulled up on the sheriff's arm a little more. "Tell him to drop it," he snarled at the prone man, whose sharp intake of breath told Brandt all he needed to about how much pain he was causing.

The sheriff's voice was labored. "Drop the gun," he managed. "Do it, deputy."

The other man lowered his weapon to the floor.

Donnelly reached down and retrieved it, tucking it into his waistband. "Either of you have weapons, hand them to me right now." Neither man made a move. "Clear, Brandt."

Brandt removed his knee from the sheriff's back and released his arm. He picked up the axe and handed it to Vic.

The sheriff struggled to his feet and brushed splinters of the front desk off his shirt.

"Call off the others," Brandt ordered, nodding his head to the pool deck where the destruction continued.

The sheriff nodded grudgingly to his deputy, who went out to the pool deck.

"How's Paul?" Brandt asked.

"I'm fine, thanks." Paul got to his feet and blotted at the bleeding wound on the side of his head. He jerked a thumb at the henchman passed out by the door. "Skeeter there is a brave man when he's got an axe in his hand and the other guy doesn't see it coming. But I managed to get a few in before going down."

"See if you can get dispatch?" Brandt asked Donnelly, who nodded and pulled out his phone.

"Now, 'Sheriff,' want to tell us what the hell you were doing here?"

The big man hefted up his sagging pants and attempted to pull himself up to a dignified full height. "I don't owe you an explanation, especially if you are an inmate of this asylum for degenerates."

Brandt closed the distance between himself and the sheriff's nose in a fraction of a second. "Look, asshole," he hissed, "you thought you could smash this place up under cover of a storm, instead of being out there helping the people of your community. You were wrong. You are a disgrace to whatever uniform you can wedge your fat, bigoted body into, and I will make it my job to be sure you face charges for this."

"Got state police," Donnelly reported, gesturing at his phone. He stepped away to talk.

This clearly alarmed the sheriff, whose eyes bugged out a bit. "You think you can just mince into my town and cause trouble? Well, fuck you," he spat at Brandt.

"No, I think you're the one who's fucked," Brandt retorted, and then he turned to Donnelly. "Are they sending someone?"

"Oh yes," Donnelly said, hanging up his phone. "The officer I talked to seemed to know exactly whom I meant when I said we had an out-of-control sheriff on our hands. They'll be sending a team here as soon as they can."

"Oh my God!" Winnie's shocked voice startled everyone in the office.

Vic turned to his partner. "It's okay, hon. All under control now."

Winnie surveyed the damage to his front desk, hands clasped to his mouth. Then he caught sight of the sheriff. "Oh. It's you."

"Fuck off," the sheriff growled and looked away.

"Our dear friend here has been a thorn in our sides from the very beginning," Winnie said, turning to Brandt and Donnelly. "In addition to being the sheriff, he's the president of the chamber of commerce, such as it is in our little town. He's worked tirelessly to drive us out of business. First it was the church league, until they decided he was being a little un-Christian in his bigotry. Then he joined up with the innkeepers' association, but they were only interested in making sure we didn't flood the market with new rooms, and since we are so small, they lost interest. He worked on drumming up a boycott on moral grounds, but in a spring-break town that's always a little dicey." He turned to look at the sheriff with obvious distaste. "Guess he tried to take matters into his own hands." He wrinkled his nose imperiously. "Asshole."

The rest of the college crew walked tentatively into the office. Thor cried out and took Paul's face in his hands. "Oh my God," he whispered. "Come on, let's get you cleaned up." He led Paul by the hand down the hall toward the bathroom.

Howie watched them go, shaking his head. "Those two. Who would have thought?"

"Fuck off, Howie," Bark muttered.

"You guys okay?" Ted asked, looking at the destruction.

"We're fine," Donnelly replied. "Paul got the worst of it."

"Fags like cockroaches, running out from underground," the sheriff muttered.

Brandt leaned in and put his lips directly on the fat man's ear. "I would be careful if I were you," he hissed. "The stairs can be a dangerous place for a fall. Now shut the fuck up and you may be able to keep your footing."

The sheriff looked venomously at him but kept quiet.

The lights flickered on, and the computer, which lay in pieces on the floor, buzzed and clicked as it attempted to come back online.

"Well, let's go see what damage the storm did, and what our local bigot crew contributed," Vic said, holding out his arm for Winnie.

The two exited the office and walked through the courtyard where the wreckage of the fountain lay on the ground. Winnie faltered, distraught, as they stepped over the pieces, but he squared his shoulders and they carried on with a dignity that impressed Brandt.

"Why don't you gather up the other vandals," Brandt said to Donnelly, "and we'll wait in here for the state police."

Donnelly nodded and stepped out to the courtyard.

"You guys want to see if you can help Vic and Winnie clean up? Looks from here like the inn has sustained some damage in addition to what the smash-up crew was able to accomplish."

"Yes, sir," Ted said. He and Bark headed out behind Donnelly, followed by Howie and Chad.

"Now, Sheriff, I guess we'll just kick back and have a little wait for actual law enforcement to arrive. Feel free to remain silent, as anything you say may be used against you, right now, by me. And no one would ever know it wasn't an accident."

Chapter Nine
Cleanup

THE RAIN was finally waning as Ted and the other guys walked out onto the pool deck, passing Donnelly and a half-dozen sullen thugs as they walked. Out over the sea, the clouds were still lowering ominously, but the wind had calmed.

A palm tree lay in the swimming pool, though whence it had come was not immediately clear; there had been no palm trees on the property. All of the tables by the pool had been smashed, the chairs as well, though some of the loungers seem to have survived; the six that remained had been blown against the wall outside Ted and Bark's room. Many of the bright blue shutters had been torn from the building, though a few still clung to the window frames. It was a sad scene, but it was not one of utter destruction.

Ted and the others were soon joined by Paul and Thor. Paul wore a professional-looking bandage on his left temple, and Thor was standing protectively near him.

"Well, this place got fucked up," Paul said. But rather than mope about it, he started in picking up pieces of furniture and shutter and was joined by Thor (who seemed not to want to be more than three feet from Paul).

"Let's gather the debris over here so it's out of the way," Thor ordered. "Once we get the deck clear, we can tackle the tree. If we can rig some rope around the trunk, we can pull on both sides of the pool and lift it up to the water line. Then we can work it over to the side. We swing the ropes from the other side and if we all pull we should be able to roll it right out." The group seemed stunned into silence by Thor's comprehensive instructions. Thor looked around. "What?"

"Well, usually Paul orders us around," Bark replied. "And how do you know so much about getting trees out of swimming pools?"

"I'm certain Paul will be back up to full Leonidas strength soon," Thor said with a smile. "But surely you guys have studied how native peoples logged forests before mechanization?" More blank looks. "I spent a summer in high school with a Tlingit clan, and I got to participate in some totem rituals. You guys need to get out more." He shook his head and got to work clearing debris.

"Looks like some of Paul's command authority slipped into Thor during the Guatemalan Flashback last night," Chad quipped. The entire gang laughed and then set to work.

Within a couple of hours, Bark and Ted had the deck swept of debris and removed the tree from the pool. They pushed it over the edge of the terrace where it joined a host of downed trees that had accumulated on the slope toward the beach. The shutters simply needed to be reunited with their hinge mounts, and Paul took care of the ones at ground level in short order.

Late in the afternoon, Winnie came out to the pool deck with lemonade and sandwiches. He had been occupied with cleaning up the front office and had not noticed the progress the guys had made. "Oh my heavens," he said, stunned by the state of repair. "It looks like the storm just came through and freshened things up a bit."

Ted considered this to be a rather rosy view as Winnie was standing where his teak tables used to be, before they had been reduced to splinters by sledgehammer-wielding ruffians. But then he figured that to make it through what he had in his lifetime, perhaps a rosy view is required.

Paul and Vic stood on the roof, shirtless, hoisting the last shutter back into place on the upper suite occupied by Brandt and Donnelly. The troopers themselves had gone with the state police when they took the sheriff and his deputy, along with the other thugs, into custody. Given that the chaos of the storm's aftermath had surely stretched emergency services thin, they weren't expected back for some time yet.

"I've heard on the radio most of the hotels in town have been badly damaged," Winnie said, coming to stand where Ted and Bark were skimming the last of the debris out of the pool. "They're sending people home and closing up for a while."

"Gonna be pretty quiet for the rest of spring break," Bark said as he fished yet another pair of underwear out of the pool. "This rogue gust of wind must have torn through a whole line of sorority girl rooms. I've never seen so many pink thongs outside of a Victoria's Secret."

"And how familiar are you with the *inside* of a Victoria's Secret?" Ted teased.

"Yes, do tell," Winnie said, nudging the thong pile distractedly with the toe of his sandal.

"It's just sometimes the boys need to be wrapped in something softer than boxers, you know? And by boys I mean testicles," Bark said with mock seriousness. "Nothing like a dainty pair of panties with some, you know, lace and shit." Unable to keep a straight face, he burst out laughing.

"Yeah, like you wear underwear at all," scoffed Ted. "Taking them off would add precious seconds every time you got naked. Can't slow down the magic, right?"

Bark beamed. "I'm glad we understand each other, my good man. Now, Winnie, we've gotten the pool and tub as clean as we can with the sweeper and the pool vacuum. Want to switch on the filter pump and we'll see if it's all good?"

"Oh! Thank you both so much," Winnie said excitedly. "What a nice change to have pool boys who know more about pools than just how to look sexy next to them—though you still have that covered." He winked broadly at them, then walked around the corner of the inn to where the pool equipment was located. The pump groaned to life, and currents erupted on the surface of the water.

"Looks good," Bark called. He stepped over to the hot tub and pushed the button to start the jets. Bubbles roiled the water, and he dipped his hand in. "Gonna take a bit to warm up. By the time night falls, this is going to feel so good."

"Everyone's been working really hard," Ted said. "Even Howie. I saw him in the office trying to put the computer back together. He and Chad were working on it for hours."

"Where did Thor go?" Bark asked, finishing his glass of lemonade.

"He went with a couple of people who came by asking for help evacuating an animal shelter. Apparently most of it ended up underwater, and they need to move the animals to higher ground."

"Right up Thor's alley, helping the downtrodden." Bark smiled. "I have a new respect for our old buddy."

"I know, right?" Ted replied. "All along I had him pegged as a clueless hippie, but it turns out he's a pretty great guy."

"Funny about him and Paul," Bark said. "I never figured those two would get so close."

"It's like they're brothers or something. I think it's really sweet."

Bark grinned and nodded. "I think it's good for both of them. Soften Paul up a little, and help Thor recover from his Guatemalan Flashback."

"So...," Ted began. He was not sure how to say what the lump in his throat was driving him to say. "How are... we?"

Bark nodded as if he'd been pondering the same question. "Honestly, man, I don't know. I don't mean I don't know about you—you, I'm sure of—but I don't know about me." He cleared his throat and looked out over the ocean. "I'm not making sense, am I?"

"Actually, it makes perfect sense to me," Ted replied. "We'll get it figured out somehow."

Bark fixed him with a stare that startled him. "I hope so," he said quietly.

Ted nodded with what he hoped looked like confidence. That was not at all what he felt inside on the subject of himself and Bark.

The troopers returned as darkness was falling, and the rest of the men finished up their work and retired to the kitchen for dinner.

"Vic likes to do impromptu cooking demonstrations here," Winnie said, showing the guys into the large space with stainless steel counters and a high table with stools around it. "Some of our older clientele like to gather for a glass of wine or two and watch my man cook." Pride was evident in the way Winnie beamed at Vic. "The view is as fine as the cuisine."

Vic waved his hand at Winnie in a "pshaw" motion but smiled as he went about his work. He served up plate after plate of food, laying them before the men around the high table and waiting each time for their delighted reaction.

"How did it go with the assholes who busted the place up?" Howie asked Brandt between dishes.

"Let's just say this was not the first time the sheriff has been caught imposing his own brand of perverted justice," Brandt answered. "This time, though, there's apparently a new review board in place at the state level, and the sheriff and his deputy have been suspended indefinitely while they gather evidence and figure out what charges to bring."

"The rest of them were just muscle," Donnelly added. "Seems the sheriff uses the county work release program as his personal militia. They didn't even know why they were smashing stuff—they just did it because the sheriff told them to."

Vic shook his head. "He kept expecting us to get scared and run out of town with our tails between our legs."

"I've had a lot of things between my legs, but never once my own tail," Winnie said with a whiff of high-drag dudgeon. "When one wears heels, one accepts that running is no longer an option."

After a long, delicious dinner, everyone seemed ready to turn in for the night. Brandt and Donnelly retreated to the comfort of their penthouse suite, while Vic and Winnie stayed in the kitchen to tidy up before bed. The college crew walked out onto the pool deck.

"Well, I'm beat," Howie said, stretching and yawning noisily. "The airline says our luggage should finally be on the flight tomorrow morning, so we'll have clothes again. Not that there's anywhere to go anymore with the town beat all to hell."

"Good thing," Chad replied with a laugh. "I'm almost out of underwear."

"Hey, Chad?" Thor asked quietly.

"Yeah?"

"Would you mind if we switched the room arrangements tonight?"

Chad squinted at him uncertainly.

"That is," Thor continued, "if Paul's up for it." He turned to Paul with a hint of a smile playing on his lips.

Paul looked at Thor for a moment, and then a smile broke out on his face as well. "Thor, are you courting me?"

Thor shrugged. "Sleeping next to you last night was… nice. I just thought maybe we could do it again."

"Yeah, you can def have my place," Chad said, shaking his head. "If Thor's feeling grabby, better you than me." He nodded to Howie. "Can I bunk with you? We can call it the No Homo Suite."

"Oh great. You're out of underwear and now you're going to be in bed with me? I must have been some kinda serial killer in a past life to deserve this." Then he smiled tiredly at Chad. "Come on over, Chaddy. We'll put a line of pillows down the middle of the bed just to be sure it's all kosher."

Paul walked over and put his powerful arm around Thor's shoulders. "I'd be glad to share a bed with you, buddy. You're a real grown-up, unlike those two textbook cases of repression over there," he said, jerking a thumb at Howie and Chad. "No pillows in the way for us." He kissed Thor on the head and ruffled his hair.

Thor beamed. "Night, everyone. Don't hold breakfast." They walked into Thor's room and shut the door.

"Ugh," spat Howie as he and Chad retreated to Howie's room.

Bark and Ted stood on the pool deck for a moment, the silence stretching out into the realm of awkward pause.

"So," Ted ventured.

"Yeah," answered Bark.

They stood a little while longer, studying the ocean and sky, undifferentiated in the distance.

"Well," Ted lamely murmured.

"Look," Bark said, his voice definite for the first time. "We don't have to be weird about this. You're you, and I'm me, and we're best friends, right?"

Ted nodded, his mouth suddenly dry.

"So let's try to be more like Thor and less like Howie and be open to new things."

Ted smiled. This was the side of Bark he hadn't seen for a while—the one that took life by the horns and rode it wherever it took him. Ted walked over to the hot tub and put his hand in. "It's hot—feel like getting in?"

"Oh fuck yeah," Bark replied with a grin. He pulled his shirt off and dropped his shorts in quick succession. "See? No boring underwear to cause a delay." He hopped over the tub's side and settled into the water. "You coming?"

Ted took a breath. Normally, he would turn around and get the fuck out of there before Bark could notice his erection, the one caused by seeing Bark's naked body for a grand total of a second and a half as he vaulted into the tub. But he remembered what Bark had said: they needed to be more open to new things. So he pulled his shirt off and then unbuttoned the cargo shorts he put on who knows how many days ago. They slid to his feet, and he stepped out of them. He looked up at Bark who, to Ted's surprise, was watching him intently. But Ted set his jaw and slipped his thumbs into the waistband of the lost-and-found briefs he wore.

Bark didn't look away.

Ted swallowed hard and slid the briefs down. He kicked them off, then stood, naked, his every exposed inch of skin feeling the weight of Bark's unblinking attention. He was open, he was calm, he was already semierect. He stepped over the edge of the hot tub and slowly lowered himself into the water. His instinct was to sit on the far side of the tub from Bark, but this was another impulse he fought against; he sat down a few feet away. Once he was settled, Bark smiled and tipped his head back against the edge of the tub.

"Beautiful," he murmured.

"What?"

"The sky," Bark said. "All those stars. So beautiful."

Ted looked up as well. "Amazing to think what damage the sky did yesterday. Now it looks so peaceful."

"Things aren't always what they seem," Bark mused. He brought his head back upright. "This has been an amazing trip."

Ted nodded. "Not exactly your standard-issue spring break."

Bark chuckled. "Yeah, no. I actually cannot think of a single thing that's happened to us that was in any way normal."

Ted tipped his head at his friend. "Well, you did manage to seduce a woman within a couple of hours of being here. I'd have to call that normal."

Bark looked down at the water. "I feel bad about that," he said quietly.

"Why? You do it all the time at home."

"It was pretty scummy of me to involve her in something that wasn't really about her."

"You lost me."

"That night was about… you." Bark looked out to the ocean as if the sight of Ted was too much for him to risk.

Ted felt his stomach flip, his chest tighten. "That night is the reason why I can't go back to the way things were."

"How were things? For you?"

Ted tried to find the words. "For the last four years I've been… a prisoner."

"What?" Bark's voice was suddenly pained.

"It's not your fault. It was mine." Ted took a deep breath and looked out over the water. "Ever since I saw you that first time in the dorm, you've been my image of perfection. I kinda figured I was gay before I got to school, but seeing you… well, that made it all fall into place for me. You're the one who showed me what I am, and I will always be grateful to you for that."

"What did you mean about being a prisoner, though?"

Ted sighed. "I just meant with you in my life I couldn't go out and explore who I was, because I knew all I wanted was you."

"Oh, Ted…." Bark's voice was increasingly agonized.

"Don't. Just don't." Ted looked into Bark's eyes, trying to make him see the meaning. "Being with you, even if I could never let you know what I was feeling, was the best thing in the world for me. The closer we became as friends, the better it got, and the worse it got because everything you did just made me want you more."

"I had no idea," Bark said simply, pain still evident in every word.

"That means I was doing it right. I never intended for you to know. I couldn't think of anything worse than having you find out I was completely in love with you."

Bark closed his eyes and shook his head. "You have no idea what it feels like to hear you say that."

Ted said nothing but scooted a little closer to Bark.

If Bark noticed Ted's proximity, he gave no sign. "That night, up at the cabin… that just about sent me to the loony bin. It was like nothing I'd ever experienced, or imagined, or even thought possible."

"It was like that for me too," Ted said.

"But it was completely out of the blue for me," Bark said, his voice a little stronger now. "It was the most amazing time I've ever had in bed." A wry smile tugged at the corner of his mouth. "I never wanted it to end."

"So we're even," Ted said. "You were clueless that I loved you, and I had no idea you felt that way about that night. About me."

"At least you had words for your experience. 'I'm gay, and I fell for my straight roommate' seems like it's probably more common than 'I'm straight, but I never wanted to get out of bed with my best friend.' Not that yours is any easier to handle, but honest to God, Teddy." Bark huffed out a couple of breaths. "I never wanted to get out of that bed. With you." He fidgeted, as if facing this truth made him physically uncomfortable. "Think about what that means for a straight guy."

"It's not like we had sex, Bark. We just lay there and tried to keep from freezing to death. Our bodies hardly even touched."

"We didn't just lay there," Bark blurted. "We talked. Like all night. I told you things I had never told anyone. Things I hadn't even said to myself. And you listened, you really listened to me. I felt so… complete. For the first time in my life I felt like a whole person."

Tears filled Ted's eyes in an instant. He felt like he had been punched in the stomach.

"Ted, what is it? Did I say the wrong—"

"No, no, you—" Ted swallowed. "—you're fine. You're perfect. I mean, I just had no idea. Even when you told the guys about that night I just didn't get it… how much you… oh, fuck." Ted's voice trailed away helplessly.

"What's wrong? I've never seen you like this."

Ted took a deep breath and tried to calm himself down. Then two more breaths, and still calm eluded him. "Bark, I came on this trip to tell you something."

Bark nodded. "I think I know what it is."

"I… I came here to say… good-bye."

Even in the dim, watery light of the hot tub, Bark visibly paled. His expression was one of raw bereavement. "What?" His voice was thin and high.

"I came to say good-bye." Ted sniffed. "We can't keep doing this—I can't. This has to end. I can't keep mooning after you, and you will eventually find a woman you want to sleep with more than a couple of times, and life will go on. Even if I can't imagine life without you, the fact is I have to figure out how to live it. I don't want to, I don't want to...." Ted sobbed, unable to hold it back any longer. "I don't want to, but I have to. Or die trying. And you... well, you will pick one of the many beautiful women who throw themselves at you on a regular basis and settle down and make beautiful children and live a long and beautiful life. And I... well, to quote the great American poet Dolly Parton, I will always love you. But I can't have you, and it's not fair to either of us to keep doing this. So I came on this trip because I thought maybe in a different place I would have the courage to say good-bye. Well, I still don't, because nothing here has worked out the way it was supposed to, but I am so physically exhausted and so emotionally wiped out I can't do anything but tell you the truth. And that truth is the hardest thing I've ever had to tell anyone. I have to tell you good-bye." Ted collapsed against the side of the hot tub and covered his eyes with his hands, crying freely.

They sat in silence for a long time, Ted's sniffling eventually giving way to the sound of the water lapping gently.

"Why would you do that to me?" Bark's voice was hollow, lost.

"I don't have a choice, can't you see that?"

"But what do you *want* to do?"

"This isn't about what I want. It doesn't matter what I want. I can't have what I want, so it doesn't make sense for me to go on wanting it, does it?"

Bark grunted. "If we could choose what we want, and only want the things we can actually have, believe me, I would have done it a long time ago. We don't get to choose. At a certain point you have to accept that we want what we want. We may not get it, but we can't change the fact that we want it."

"I accept that I want... you. I want you. I want you to be gay, and I want you to be in love with me, and I want us to graduate and get married and buy a little house and raise a family and grow old together. But none of that is going to happen. That's what I have to accept."

"Don't do this. Please don't do this."

Teddy looked hard at Bark's face, trying to see what emotion was behind his plea. "I don't understand. You know nothing can happen between us."

"Something already has," Bark said quietly. He reached out and put his hand on Ted's chest, right on that spot. He looked Ted in the eyes. "This. This has happened between us."

"Bark, that's—"

"Shh. No. Let me talk." Bark took a deep breath. "Do you know why I did this? Back before the world ended and we were in bed, the three of us? Do you know why I did it?"

Ted shook his head. He had asked himself this question a million-and-a-half times over the past couple of days. He had no answers.

"I did it because I didn't know what else to do. I know I'm going to lose you. I know the end is coming. I know you're going to leave me, and I'll have to try to figure out how to be a complete person without you. But I don't want it to end. I don't want to lose you. And I will try anything to hold on to you, Ted. Anything."

"Hold on to what, Bark? What do we have, between us? What do you call it—in your head—when you think about it?"

"I don't think there's a word for it, besides… love. It's beyond friendship; it's beyond brotherhood. It's the feeling I get when I come home at the end of the day and I know you'll be there. How many times in every single day does something happen to me, or someone tells me something, and all I can think is, I can hardly wait to get home and see what Ted thinks about *that*? Or when life kicks me in the balls one more fucking time, I know if I get home to you, you'll make it all better. Because you know me so well, and you never judge me. Never. There's no one else in my life like you, not even my family, and they're supposed to love me no matter what. They don't, but you do." Bark wiped his nose with an impatient brush of his other hand. "And now you're telling me good-bye? You're going to sit there and tell me the best person in my life, the one I love more than anyone or anything, is leaving? Just leaving. I don't… I just can't…. Shit." Bark closed his eyes for a long moment and then, shaking his head all the while, stared down into the water.

Tears streaked down Ted's cheeks as, in his confusion, he simply stared at Bark and shook his head. He had no idea what any of this meant.

Bark took a breath and continued. "If you were a woman, I would know what to do. It would be easy because we would just do what people do when they mean to each other what you mean to me."

"What is that?"

"Hold on to you and never let go." Bark looked at his hand, the one that was still pressing on Ted's chest. "I would never let you go."

"But you aren't—"

"I know. I'm not gay. I have never looked at another man and thought 'Hmm, I'd sure like to jam that down my throat.' I guess I'm just limited as a person."

"Being gay isn't just about jamming things down your throat," Ted replied. "I'm no expert, being that I've never done anything with anyone, but I think being gay is mostly just like this." He placed his hand atop Bark's and pressed both of their hands into his chest. "It's about connecting with another person with absolute honesty, and truth, and love. And that other person happens to be a guy. I honestly think that's all there is to it."

"But you've heard the guys talk about it, right? The way everyone kind of had a little freak-out about Paul? And how no one is really sure what to make of Thor and his bizarre three-way thing in the jungle? You make it sound so simple, but from where I sit, it's about the most complicated thing in the world."

"Here's how simple it is," Ted said, and before his better judgment could stop him, he stood up. His cock, erect as always from simply being within a hundred feet of Bark, pointed directly at him, steam rising from its entire length. "This. This is what happens to me every time I am near you. This is how I know being with you is what I want more than anything in the world, and it's what I cannot have. I don't care what Paul and Thor do, though I honestly hope they are making sweet, sweet love to each other right now. I don't care what freaks Chad out or what makes Howie say stupid, bigoted things. I care about you. I care about you more than anyone or anything else in the world. Every single other person on the planet could go fuck themselves if you would just say we can make it work. If we can find a way to be together, nothing else matters to me."

He fell silent, somehow finding the courage to stand up before Bark and stand by his own emotions, something he had never done before.

Bark looked up at him. "Can you give me a little time? This has come at me so suddenly, and it's a lot to take in. Please, Teddy," he said, taking Ted's hand in his, "please don't say good-bye. Not yet. Give me a chance to sort things out. Please?"

Ted, having finally summoned the courage to tell Bark the truth, was reluctant to slide back into their old pattern of unrequited longing. But if there was a chance things could change….

"Okay," he said finally. "You know where I stand. It's up to you to figure out where you do."

Bark smiled for the first time, a full and happy grin that made Ted's heart light.

"Thank you," Bark said. "You won't regret it."

Ted returned his smile. "I hope not." He felt a chill in the breeze. "I think I'm going to take a shower and get to bed. We'll pencil in another angst-filled session for tomorrow?"

"Wouldn't miss it," Bark said with a laugh. He sat back against the edge of the tub. "I'm gonna count the stars for a while, okay? I'll see you in the morning."

"Good night, then," Ted said, stepping out of the tub.

"Teddy?" Bark called as Ted walked toward their room.

"Yeah, Bark?"

"I love you."

Ted looked at the silhouette of his friend. "I love you too," he whispered.

CHAPTER TEN
THE CAVE

WAKING UP in an empty bed was not a new experience for Ted; that he had been sleeping with Bark during this trip represented a significant departure from the normal course of his life. But today the bed felt particularly empty.

After leaving Bark in the hot tub, Ted had quickly showered and crawled into bed; it had been a long day. He must have been sound asleep by the time Bark joined him, which was probably just as well. Proximity would only complicate things for them right now. He stretched and yawned and stood and did the first two three more times and then gathered up his clothes from the floor where he had tossed them. Opening the door, he found the morning getting underway: the sun bathed the pool deck in its early light, and Vic and Winnie were setting up breakfast. The only other sound was the regular splash-splash of Bark's easy freestyle stroke, back and forth in the pool. Ted stepped out of the room and stood by the side of the pool.

Against the deep blue of the pool, Bark's ginger-white body was a brilliant vision. He swam gracefully and powerfully, executing a smooth flip turn at each end. Ted was mesmerized by his strong shoulders and the way his buttocks rose out of the water at the end of each lap as he somersaulted effortlessly before pushing off the wall— well, that just took Ted's breath away. He could watch this all day.

"Morning, Ted," called Donnelly from one of the folding tables set up to replace the teak umbrella tables that had been "storm damaged."

Ted walked over to the table to greet the troopers.

"Morning, Officers," he said, nodding respectfully. "Sleep well?"

"Our room lacks the particular ambience created by the close proximity of a half-dozen guys in sleeping bags," Brandt answered with a grin, "but it was good enough for us."

"How was your evening?" Donnelly asked, suddenly serious.

"It was okay," Ted replied, knowing Donnelly would be able to read the complicated situation with his trademark insight. "We did have a chance to talk, though I'm not sure it got us anywhere."

Donnelly nodded. "Well, talking is a good start."

Ted shrugged. "I honestly don't know what's next. I told him how I feel about him, and he told me how he feels about me. What's stupid is that we both can't stand the idea of leaving each other after graduation, so we pretty much agree on that. But that doesn't really matter unless we're both...." He shrugged again.

"Here's what I've learned about straight men," Donnelly said, flashing a quick look at Brandt. "Some of them are straight because they've considered all the possibilities, perhaps even tried some things outside of what people think of as straight. Having approached it with an open mind, they decide that straight is what they really truly are. I think your friend Thor is probably one of the few who falls into that camp."

"Yeah, we'll see about that," Ted interrupted with a laugh. "Last night Thor asked Chad to switch with Paul so they could spend the night together."

"Okay," Donnelly chuckled. "We'll set Thor aside. But the vast majority of straight guys think of themselves as straight because that's what everyone expects them to be and how they've been raised to see themselves. Some of those—I tend to think most of those—would be open to having a relationship with another guy if the right opportunity presented itself, as long as they didn't feel their masculinity was going to be compromised. Then there are the guys who will defend their straightness from every challenge, and will not even admit the possibility that they might not be 100 percent straight. You can tell those from their reflexive angry reaction when anyone mentions anything even vaguely gay in their presence. I present to you Exhibit A, Howie."

Ted looked out over the pool, where Bark pulled an even wake behind his smooth stroke. "I wonder where he fits."

"Ted, I know it's hard to look at this objectively. But he told you, and everybody else in the room, that you are the only one he's ever known who made him feel like a whole person. I saw his hand on your chest yesterday, in the sleeping bag, and he seemed so happy to be there with you. Up until now he's thought of himself as completely straight, and that means he needs you to go slow and honor his experience. No straight guy wants to be told he's been living a lie and he's been gay all along; plus, I don't think that's true. What he needs is for you to show him having a relationship with you will be exactly like being your best friend, but with some additional intimacy he will come very quickly to appreciate. Get him to think of it as an enhancement, not a departure, and certainly not as a monstrous eruption of repressed sexuality." Donnelly smiled. "Because that shit freaks straight dudes out."

"Hell yeah, it does," muttered Brandt as he lifted his coffee mug.

Ted turned this over in his head, and it made sense to him in ways he hadn't considered before. "Thanks, Gabriel. That's really helpful."

Donnelly beamed. "Now, shall we get some breakfast?"

As they walked to the buffet table, the door of Howie's room opened, and he and Chad stumbled sleepily into the sunlight.

"Did the great wall of pillows hold all night, gentlemen?" Ted teased.

"I am pleased to report that our virtue survived the night intact," Howie said.

"Oh, that's too bad," Winnie tutted sympathetically. "Better luck next time, dear."

Howie just rolled his eyes and picked up a plate.

"Let's keep this line moving!" commanded Paul's deep voice from behind them. "Some of us men worked hard yesterday."

"And probably all night," muttered Howie.

"Where's Thor?" Chad asked, looking around the pool deck for his old roommate.

"He got a text hours ago from Abby and Ryan, the people he was helping at the animal shelter yesterday. I guess the power hasn't yet been restored at the free clinic in town, and they needed help getting medicine and supplies in to replace what was damaged in the storm. They swung by to pick him up before dawn."

"You must have gone easy on him if he was able to walk this morning," Chad joked.

Paul was suddenly serious. "Look, Thor is a great guy, and if we have fun being together, then we should be together. It's not like we're engaged or anything—we're just guys having some fun."

"And did he have any fun, or did he just take the fun from you all night long?" asked Howie.

"Fuck off, Howie," Paul said, no venom in his voice. "What Thor and I do is not only none of your business, it's nothing I could explain to you because you don't have any way to understand it. You would have no idea what grown-ups do in bed."

"You go," Ted murmured to Paul with a wink before returning to the table with Brandt and Donnelly. He carried two plates, and once he set them on the table, he went to the side of the pool. He picked up Bark's towel and then knelt by the pool's edge.

When Bark finished his lap, Ted called to him. "Breakfast is ready."

Bark wiped the water from his eyes and grinned up at Ted. "Morning, good sir."

"A fine morning it is, sir," Ted replied. "Now haul your naked ass out of the pool and come eat."

Bark effortlessly lifted himself out of the pool, and Ted wrapped the towel around his shoulders. He rubbed himself vigorously with it, then wrapped it around his waist and walked to the table.

"You got breakfast for me?" Bark asked, seeing a plate already on the table.

"Yeah, is it okay?" Ted replied.

"It's perfect," Bark said with a smile. "Thank you."

Ted beamed.

They ate their breakfast and chatted with the troopers, Donnelly replenishing everyone's coffee with repeated trips to the kitchen. On the last of these, he returned to the table with a leather-and-canvas backpack, which he set on the pool deck next to Ted.

"What's that?" Ted asked.

Donnelly smiled. "Winnie was telling me while we were in the dungeon about some caves near the beach he says are really cool. Of course, while we were underground, the idea of exploring caves seemed a little redundant, but it's much nicer today, and with the town basically emptied out, you would have the place to yourselves. I asked Vic if he would make you two a picnic lunch so you can go spend some time away from the inn. I threw in a bottle of wine and everything. Consider it a gift from some old folks who remember being your age."

Ted was so struck with this kindness he could hardly speak. "Thank you," he managed.

"That's really awesome of you guys," Bark said, clearly as touched as Ted was. "Sound like a fun way to spend the day, buddy?"

Ted nodded.

"I'll go shower up, and we'll get going," Bark said, jumping to his feet. The towel he was wearing caught on his folding chair and tore away from his body as he did so. "Oops." He tugged at the towel, but was unable to work it free. He shrugged in surrender. "Back in a few." He turned and walked to the door of his and Ted's room, the eyes of all three men on his undulating buttocks.

"See?" Donnelly said to Brandt.

Brandt nodded. "I get it now." He reached a fist over the table to Ted, who bumped it with his. "Go get him, tiger," he said with a grin.

Ted, who had never imagined having such support in his life, at first could only nod. Then, after a long moment, he found the words. "You two are a miracle," he said. "I'll never be able to make you understand how much you've helped me."

Donnelly laid a hand on Ted's arm. "We've been there, Ted. We made it through, and so will you."

"Thank you," Ted said, his voice thick with the emotion he was trying to keep tamped down in his chest.

About an hour later, he and Bark were on their way, walking down the beach in accordance with Winnie's painstaking directions. The tides had taken care of a lot of the debris the storm had deposited on the lower part of the beach, but further up the dunes there were trees and pieces of structure that had been blown there by the hurricane-force winds. They walked barefoot, feeling the sand made cool and wet with each lap of the waves. Bark had insisted on carrying the backpack, and it bumped against his smooth, powerful back as he walked.

"Beautiful, isn't it?" he asked. "Even the wreckage is arranged in kinda cool patterns."

Ted turned his face up to the sun, reveling in its warmth. "Beats the hell out of spending the day in a bomb shelter, that's for sure."

They walked along for a while, the screech of storm-addled gulls the only sound that rose above the waves.

"Can I tell you something?" Bark said, not looking up from the sand as he walked.

"Of course," Ted answered. That was what they were here for, after all.

"It's kind of creepy."

"You can tell me anything, you know that."

"I watched you sleep last night." Bark turned and looked at him. "See? Creepy."

Ted smiled.

"What?" Bark asked. "Why are you smiling?"

"If you only knew how many nights I spent watching you sleep." Ted smiled even wider at the memory; he hadn't thought of those nights in the dorm for a long time. "Do you remember that night-light you brought with you?"

Bark laughed. "The blue canary? God, I loved that thing."

"It was ridiculous. But it made the most beautiful cool glow, and that was the light I would watch you by. You would sleep and breathe and dream, and I would lie there imagining what it would be like to be next to you, feeling the rise and fall of your chest, basking in the heat of your body." Ted was lost in his memory for a few paces. Then he shook his head and returned to the present. "I think as creeping goes, I'm gonna have you beat no matter what."

Bark smiled. "It's not you watching me that creeps me out. It's how you always describe exactly what I'm feeling before I even have the words for it myself." He stooped to pick up a shell from the sand. "I got into bed, and the light from the pool cast this blue streak across the bed, lighting up your face. You looked so peaceful. After that kind of intense conversation we had in the hot tub, I was so relieved to see you looking so calm and... happy, I guess. I just lay there, watching you, wondering how I was going to be able to live without you in my life. And you know what I came up with?"

Ted shook his head.

"I can't. And I don't want to. I don't know how we'll make it work, but we have to find a way. I thought and thought about it for a couple of hours, watching you sleep, and I couldn't figure it out. So I just put my hand back where it belongs—right on your heart—and I gave up trying. And I fell asleep next to you, feeling you breathe, warmed by your body, and I knew. That's where I belong."

"Bark, are you saying—"

"I'm saying I know where I belong. How I get there—how we get there—I have no idea. But I want you to save the place next to you, because that's where I belong."

"That's about the sweetest thing I've ever heard," Ted said, his voice thick.

"That's nothing. I'm just getting started," Bark replied with a smile that nonetheless quickly faded. "It's not going to be simple, though." He shook his head, a gesture tinged with a sadness Ted understood all too well.

"We'll figure it out," Ted said, hoping there was hope in his voice. He wasn't sure he felt any of it inside. "We have all day, right?"

Bark laughed, and they quickened their pace along the beach. They had work to do.

About a half hour's walk from the inn, they finally arrived at the caves. Winnie had told Ted they were the result of a tragic mishap at a concrete factory that had dominated this part of the coast early in the last century. The ungainly formations of cement and stone had then been eroded by several decades of oceanic aggression, and then sometime in the nineties a location scout for some long-forgotten pirate epic had happened upon them. They had been coated with a black slag to resemble a volcanic formation, and the effect had far outlasted the film.

"Winnie said there's a tidal pool in through this cave that we have to see," Ted said, pointing to an entrance in the rock. "Because the rock is dark, it absorbs heat from the sun and the water is really warm. Come on." He climbed up and ducked through the opening, followed closely by Bark.

They crouched low and followed the passage for a couple of minutes until the tunnel suddenly jogged left and opened onto a domed cave lit from above by an opening at the peak. It was about forty feet across and as high; there was a wide ledge around the inland edge of the pool, while on the sea side there were a number of small openings that admitted ocean water in a gently rising and falling rhythm.

Ted dipped a toe in. "Wow, it's really nice. Not as warm as the hot tub, but a whole lot warmer than the ocean. Winnie said this was some kind of cistern, so it's super deep."

"Care for a swim?"

"Thought you'd never ask," Ted said. He pulled his shirt off over his head and unbuttoned his shorts.

"Holy shit," Bark blurted.

"Yeah, I figured they would just slow me down." Ted laughed as he kicked off his shorts and launched, naked, into the water.

Bark shucked off his clothes and followed with a great splash. This began an all-out splash war, which they fought to a draw after an exhausting frenzy. Still laughing, they hauled themselves out onto the ledge and lay, panting and staring at the dome over them.

"I could do this forever," Bark said as their rapid breathing slowed.

"Swim in the abandoned ruins of a concrete factory? Sounds like a dream."

"No, I mean this. Just being together, not giving a fuck what we're doing, or where we're going. Just being."

Ted turned and looked at Bark. "Then why don't we? Do this forever, I mean."

Bark's brow furrowed as he considered this. "What would we be, then?"

"Hmm. Great question. How about this: I'll be Ted, and you be Bark. Sound like something we might want to try?"

"I meant what would we be to each other?"

"Bark, I don't know how to break this to you, but two guys can spend their lives together. They can even get married and have a family, and have midlife crises and go to marriage counseling and then rediscover why they fell in love in the first place, and then go to their kids' college graduation and have their hair fall out and retire to someplace probably less than a mile from where we are right now and descend into senility looking into each other's eyes. You know, normal life stuff."

"You know I love it when you rant," Bark said. "But I'm being serious. I don't want to lose you, but we can't keep doing what we're doing. In a couple of months, we're not going to be students anymore. We can't keep being roommates, because grown-ups don't do that. So what do we do?"

Ted nodded. "You have no idea how many scenarios I've run trying to find a way through that very question."

Bark rolled over onto his side, propping his head on his elbow. "Tell me."

"Well," Ted said, surprisingly relieved to finally be able to give voice to what had been his most secret thought. "First, we can move into an apartment together, just to save money as we start our careers. We should be able to get a few years out of that, until you finally give in to family pressure and get married. Then you move into wedded bliss, and I take in a string of sketchy boarders, one of whom will kill me in my sleep to get his hands on my collection of *Star Wars* memorabilia."

"Oh, that turned dark at the end."

"Yeah, kinda. But I don't have any *Star Wars* memorabilia, so I'm probably safe."

"Okay, give me another one."

"In this one we both get jobs with the same company, and they send us overseas for a few years to gain experience. We live in snug apartments in Seoul, Mumbai, and Cape Town, until we get promoted and move back to the States. Then, after years of exotic locales, you marry an all-American girl from down the street. I stay in the old apartment, which I fill with cats. I spend all my spare time writing angry screeds on *Star Wars* fan-fiction discussion boards."

"I'm sensing a theme here," Bark said with a laugh.

"Wait, I'm not done yet," Ted cried. "In the next one, we're in a terrible accident, which results in us ending up with only one functioning kidney between us. We have to share it, which means we have to live together forever so we can swap out the organ on a daily basis. You never get married because no girl wants a guy without a functioning kidney. We grow embittered by our codependent relationship and each plot to steal the kidney. In a hilarious slow-motion montage, we struggle over it until it pops out of our grip and flies through the air, where it's picked up by a passing crow who takes it to his nest and eats it. Our last breaths are consumed by strangling each other. Then more crows get to eat."

"These scenarios are not getting cheerier."

"Nope," Ted replied, looking him in the eye. "Bark, honest to God, in reality there are only two ways this works out."

Bark nodded. "I'm ready. Go."

"We graduate, we hug it out in our caps and gowns, we promise to keep in touch, and for the first few months we do. Then it turns into an e-mail every few months, then once a year, and finally we trade Christmas cards. Then one Christmas I get a card from you that shows you hugging the love of your life on a beach or in front of the Grand Canyon, and I stick it in the corner of the frame around my diploma, to remind me of a time in my life when I thought it possible that I'd be happy."

"Shit. Option number two has got to be better than that."

Ted swallowed hard. This was a story he had always figured he would take to his grave. "I don't think I can."

"Teddy, you can tell me anything. Do you really think I'm going to get mad after all we've been through?"

He took a deep breath, and then Ted started into the story he'd told himself so many times it was like an alternate timeline, a life he had already lived and now remembered. "After graduation, we ditch our families and take a drive out to the lake. We sit on that old pier out past the cabins and dangle our feet in the water and drink beer and talk about what our lives are going to be like. Then, completely out of the blue, you look at me, and you say you can't bear the thought of living without me. And before I know what's happening, you kiss me, and it's like no one has ever kissed anyone in the history of the world before that moment. And under the stars, on that pier, we… make love." Ted took a moment to catch his breath, as the effort of forcing out these secret words cost him dearly. "You tell me you love me. And I tell you I loved you from the first moment I saw you. Suddenly we are able to find all of the ways our bodies fit together that we never even dreamed of, and we go at it hard enough to shake the heavens and scare the ducks. We watch the sun rise, still wrapped in each other's arms, and then, after making love one more time, we get back in the car and drive home. We sit our families down and tell them we're in love, and my mom cries and your dad says something homophobic, but it doesn't matter because we have each other. And on that day, we take our first steps into the future, not sure what it holds but sure of each other, knowing as long as we never let go, there is nothing we can't do. And we are happy." When he had started crying, Ted had no idea, but he closed his eyes and felt the cold progress of the tears down his cheeks.

There was a long silence.

"That was beautiful," Bark said. "I want that one."

Ted opened his eyes and studied the face of his best friend. "You do? All of it?"

Bark smiled. "I've already told you I can't bear the thought of life without you. So we can check that one off. Now, what's next? Oh, right, the kiss." He leaned down to Ted, and his eyes fluttered closed as he neared. His lips brushed Ted's, tentatively at first, and then more confidently.

It was the kiss Ted had waited for all his life. It soothed and inflamed him in equal measure. It stopped his heart and started it beating in a new rhythm. He never wanted it to end.

Finally, Bark pulled back. He looked Ted in the eyes with a startling intensity. "Like no one's ever kissed anyone in the history of the world." He sighed. "Fuck, that was amazing."

Ted beamed. "Really?"

Bark nodded. "I've never felt anything like it."

"Even when you kissed Paul?"

Bark laughed. "Well, first, Paul is scratchy because of that stubble he pretends is naturally occurring but that he actually spends at least fifteen minutes a day trimming to a precise length so it looks like he doesn't care how it looks. And second, I haven't been in love with Paul for the last three years."

"You're teasing me now," Ted said. "There's no way—"

"I have loved you ever since that night at the cabin. I didn't know it was love I was feeling because I had no words to describe that experience. All I knew was it's not something that's supposed to happen between guys. And yet, there it was. Now I know what to call it. It was me falling in love with you. And I've been in love ever since."

Ted was touched, but he took a deep breath and set his jaw. It needed to be said. "But you're straight. That's still kind of an obstacle to the completion of my scenario, isn't it?"

Bark shrugged. "Only if we let it be. I mean, seriously, are we going to let something as stupid as a label keep us from getting what we want?"

"But that still leaves out a pretty important part of my lakeside vignette."

A sly smile crept across Bark's face. "You mean the part about making sweet, sweet love all night long?"

Ted could feel his cheeks burn. "That's the part I mean. As you can no doubt divine from the fact that I'm still a virgin, I'm not used to being assertive when it comes to sex. But this is the one time in my life when I'm going to put my foot down and say I cannot spend my life with someone who won't have sex with me."

"Then there's something we need to do before we go any further," Bark said.

"What's that?"

"We need to figure out how two guys make sweet, sweet love. All night long. And scare ducks."

"And the thought of that doesn't send you running away?"

"Hell no," Bark said. "Scares the crap out of me, but I'm not going anywhere. You?"

"Terrified," Ted replied. "But I would be terrified to do it the first time anyway. I don't have your years of experience slutting it up with any woman who passes you on the sidewalk."

"Gotta be honest, Teddy. I have fucked a lot of women. A lot a lot. But I would be lying if I told you the time with Darlene a couple of days ago was the first time I'd thought about you while doing it."

"You have got to be fucking kidding me," Ted said with a gasp.

Bark shook his head. "As fucked up as it sounds, there are times when I closed my eyes and thought of Theodore."

"Oh my God," whispered Ted. "Of course, every single time I've had sex, I thought of you. But I was the only one in the room, so it wasn't like I was being rude or anything."

"Wait, you were cheating on yourself with me?" Bark asked with a laugh. "I'm honored."

Ted laughed too, since everything about this was ridiculous, and yet more important to him than anything else in his life. "So," he finally summoned the courage to say, "now what?"

Bark looked suddenly serious. "Kiss me."

"What?"

"Kiss me. I've kissed you twice, and now it's your turn." He cocked an eyebrow in challenge. "Give it to me, and make me feel it."

Ted sat up, scared and thrilled by Bark's command. He had never—ever—made a move on anyone, and now Bark was demanding he do it.

Bark rolled over onto his back, waiting.

Ted leaned down, taking in every detail of the face he knew so well but had until now only been able to study from oblique angles. Now he had the luxury of really looking, seeing it in all its glory. "You're beautiful," he whispered.

The corners of Bark's mouth twitched, but he didn't make a sound.

Ted drew closer, and closer still, until the gap between their lips was narrow enough to bend light. Then, the first whisper of contact, a delicate brushing of his bottom lip against Bark's, and a spark shot down his spine, a feeling of being alive to sensations he had never felt before. He pressed his mouth to Bark's, reveling in this most frank contact. The surge of blood to his head, the sudden intake of breath, it all electrified him, and he was in frenzied motion. He kissed Bark's bottom lip, and then his top; he tasted them with his tongue. Every time he pulled back, even a little, Bark raised his head to follow, pursuing him, never letting the kiss end. In the place where their lips met they created a new reality, one in which two best friends who fell in love could invent a life together that was beyond definition.

Having bent reality to their liking, they released their hold on each other.

"Oh fuck," Ted huffed, drained from the intensity of their contact.

"Yeah," Bark answered. He took a deep breath. "Well, that solves one of our issues."

Ted looked at him questioningly.

Bark glanced down. Ted turned his head and saw what Bark was talking about. The object of Ted's most secretive creeping, Bark's essential manhood, stretched up to him. It was larger than Ted had ever seen it, and was so hard it didn't even touch Bark's belly but throbbed up at Ted, demanding his attention.

Ted looked back up at Bark, who shrugged and gave a goofy grin.

"I'm going to ask you something," Ted said quietly.

"I think we've reached the point of absolute honesty, buddy. Ask me anything."

"Did I do that"—Ted nodded downward—"or is that just something that happens to you because you're you?"

Bark's response was to crane his neck up and kiss Ted again.

"No one," he said once he lay back on the ledge, "no one has ever done that to me."

Ted jolted. He felt the walls closing in on him, and it was hard to breathe. Without a word he turned and threw himself into the water. He plunged down far enough that darkness started to settle over him. He floated, not moving, trying to decide whether to come back up. Then Bark's arm looped through his and they were on their way to the surface.

"What," panted Bark, once they were bobbing on the surface of the water, "was that?"

Ted wiped his eyes and looked up at the top of the stone dome for a moment. "I just... I don't want to change you."

"What does that mean?"

"When you said no one has ever done that to you before, I kind of freaked out. I... I love you the way you are. I love you because of who you are. And if you can't be the way with me you have been with other people, then I don't want that. I want—I need—you to be you."

Bark smiled and nodded as he reached out and put his arms around Ted, continuing to kick with his powerful legs to stay above water. "Teddy, the only thing that's changed for me is that for the first time in my life, I got a boner from someone kissing me. That's the thing that has never happened before. I'm not a super romantic guy, apparently. Kissing doesn't do a thing for me. Never has before, anyway. But it turns out I wasn't kissing the right person. The right... guy. I wasn't kissing you, and that was my problem." He kissed Ted quickly on the lips before Ted knew it was coming. "I haven't changed, I've come home."

Ted smiled at the words that were beyond his imagining, far beyond anything he had dared hope he would hear. He kissed Bark, his best friend, and knew that he, too, had come home.

Chapter Eleven
Picnic

BARK AND Ted sat on the ledge, feet dangling in the water, eating the lunch Vic had packed for them and drinking the wine Donnelly had provided.

"Fuck, this is the life, right?" Bark said, sitting back against the smooth rock wall behind him.

"It's amazing. Every single day has been amazing—for good or bad. I can hardly imagine going back home after this."

"Do we have to?" Bark whined. "I like it better here." He looked around the cavern. "So how about we look for jobs somewhere warm like this? I've had enough winters to last me a long, long time."

Ted beamed.

"What?" Bark asked.

"You said 'we.'"

"First-person plural pronoun. Used to speak on behalf of oneself and others. Or, in this case, an other."

"I just never thought I'd hear that and know it meant you and me."

"You and me," Bark repeated. "Yes." He nodded decisively and then took a drink of wine. He looked at the bottle. "This stuff could make me reconsider my relationship with beer."

"I think it's a pretty good bottle. I've seen this label in my dad's 'touch that and feel my wrath' collection. He brought some out for Thanksgiving one year, when my rich uncle was over for the holiday."

"Those troopers sure are nice. I don't think I've ever met anyone who was so easy to talk to and yet could also go all wrath-of-God on the criminal element."

"They encouraged me to be honest with you, and I have to say that's worked out pretty well."

"Very well indeed." Bark popped one of Vic's ginger cookies into his mouth and chewed thoughtfully. "We came awfully close to fucking this up, my friend."

"Really?"

"We were a couple months away from letting it go without even giving it a chance. I would have carried that loss with me for the rest of my life."

Ted smiled at him. "You say you're not a romantic, but then you spit out stuff like that. Makes me blush and gets me boned up at the same time."

"Boned up? My goodness, Theodore, the way you talk!" Bark did a pretty much dead-on Winnie impression, with his hand fluttering at his throat. "I think I'm rubbing off on you."

"I wish you would," Ted replied playfully.

Bark turned to face Ted, his expression one of delight. "This is a whole new side of you. I had no idea there was a sexy Teddy in there alongside the smart Teddy and the sensitive Teddy."

"I guess I hadn't really given him much of a chance to come out," Ted said with a sheepish shrug, "since before today the chances of him being happy were pretty much nil."

Bark smiled broadly. "What you have before you is a sure thing," he said. "I am up for any kind of action you might want to try."

"Seeing as I had never even kissed anyone before today, I don't want you to get your hopes up about the 'action' I might be capable of."

Bark scooted closer to Ted. "I will be happy if we just talk. I will be happy if we just kiss. I will be happy if we just touch each other. I will be happy no matter what we do because you're here with me." He put his arms around Ted and nuzzled his neck. "Here with me," he murmured, as if saying the words again made it more real.

Ted seized Bark's head with his hands and held him, face-to-face. He kissed Bark softly, then planted delicate kisses all over his face. Bark groaned softly and closed his eyes.

"Here with me," Ted whispered.

They kissed, wrapped tightly in each other's arms, for a long while. Then, suddenly, boldly, Ted laid his hand between Bark's legs. For the first time his fingers touched a penis other than his own.

Bark gasped, eyes wide, but then kissed Ted with renewed vigor and more insistent groaning. "Mmm," he purred when he broke their kiss, "I like sexy Teddy."

Ted ran his fingertips along Bark's considerable erection, from base to tip and back again, several times, while a chorus of voices inside his head cried out "You're touching another man! You're touching his penis!" These were the same voices that had told him to ignore his feelings for Bark and to suffer in silence. For the first time in his life, Ted told those voices to fuck off.

Touching Bark, and seeing his reaction to being touched, was the best thing in the world, and Ted intended to enjoy it fully. He stroked, feeling the heat and heft of Bark's cock, reveling in the shock of the new and scandalous thing they were doing. He watched Bark's eyes and saw the thrill registered there. It was the first time Ted had ever made anyone feel physical pleasure, and it gave him a rush of joy so pure he thought he would burst.

"Lie back," he whispered, pressing with his fingers on Bark's chest.

Bark kissed him one more time and did as he asked. He lay back, stretching his muscular frame out languidly, giving Ted another visceral visual thrill. Ted crept forward and laid his body atop Bark's, feeling its solidity in a new way. Coming into full contact with his best friend was a feeling so safe and so erotic at the same time that Ted was a little dizzy from the friction. But he looked into Bark's bright green eyes and found his center again. They kissed.

"Have I told you," Ted said when he took a break from licking delicately at Bark's upper lip, "that I love you?"

"I always knew," Bark said, shaking his head and smiling sweetly. "I just wasn't ready to admit it. Just like I wasn't ready to admit that I love you."

"Can I," Ted began, looking a bit sideways at Bark, "do something I've always dreamed of doing?"

"Anything you do—anything—I will love."

Ted smiled, and then kissed Bark's chin, and his throat, and finally his strong but prominent collarbone.

"Oh, yeah," Bark sighed. "I love that."

Ted felt a rush of excitement from Bark's words, and they spurred him on. He kissed the strong, rounded muscle of Bark's pectorals, and arrived, delightedly, at his nipples. They were already pointed imploringly, and Ted planted a delicate kiss on each one. Bark's back arched, and his hands scrabbled along the rough surface of the rocky ledge as if he were afraid of being swept away. Ted sucked and nibbled at Bark's nipples, ultimately scraping gently with his teeth.

"Oh fuck," groaned Bark.

"Like that?" Ted asked teasingly.

"You know me, Ted. You know everything about me. Anything you do is everything I want."

Ted shivered with excitement and continued to kiss his way down Bark's perfect body. He gently nuzzled each of the six distinct ingots of abdominal muscle and was fascinated by finally getting to see them up close, how they came into and out of relief with each breath. He had caught glimpses of them over the years, but the luxury of being able to actually experience them so immediately was overwhelming. He pressed his cheek, his lips, to those precious bundles of strength.

But he had more territory to explore, and so he headed south once more. Bark's erection reached beyond his navel, but Ted wanted to save that for last. He slid down until he felt Bark's rough pubic hair tickle his lips. He knew Bark manscaped on a regular basis—"the ladies expect it," he had said a few months ago—but from a distance of a couple of inches, Ted realized how artfully Bark managed his personal grooming. Symmetrical and even, it was like a ginger welcome mat laid out for "the ladies." And now, Ted.

Ted slid back up to get a closer look at the most prominent feature of Bark's tackle. He wrapped his hand around the rock-hard cock, marveling at the smooth, firm, perfect flesh. He loved it, as he loved Bark, but he had no idea what to do with it. He knew, of course, the general procedure involved, but exactly how he could perform the requisite acts he wasn't sure. But then he remembered: they were in this together.

"Bark?"

"Yeah," Bark gasped. He had clearly been driven to distraction by Ted's explorations.

"Tell me what to do?"

Bark looked down at him. "I told you, Teddy. You can't do anything wrong."

"I know, but you have experience in this area, and I don't. I want you to tell me what to do." He smiled up at Bark and stroked the length of his cock several times.

Bark smirked, a look that Ted suspected had resulted in panties hitting the floor on a regular basis. "Lick it."

Ted grinned and then leaned in until his lips were millimeters from the tip of Bark's penis. He extended his tongue and it made contact with the hot and salty glans. Bark groaned and tipped his head back. Ted flicked his tongue about, taking in the new and complex tastes.

"Get it wet," moaned Bark.

Ted made his tongue broad, and swirled it around the head of Bark's penis, working up as much saliva as he could. It soon glistened, and spit was starting to drip down the shaft.

"Now kiss it," Bark said, his breath short.

This is what Ted wanted to do more than anything, and he was thrilled that Bark wanted it too. He pressed his lips to the hot flesh, then felt it lift in response to his gentle suctioning kiss. He found the slit at the tip with his tongue, and kissed it as if it were a smaller version of Bark's mouth. When his tongue probed the opening, Bark gasped and sighed.

"Now, please," Bark huffed, desperation in every word, "in the name of all that is hot and dirty in the world, please take me in your mouth."

Ted opened his mouth and felt, for the first time, another man enter him. He had captured between his lips the essence of the man he loved, and he would never let him go. Moist with saliva, the head slipped easily through his lips and over his tongue, but he very quickly realized the importance of moving slowly; as much as he wanted to take the entirety of Bark's considerable manhood in at once, his tonsils represented an obstacle that would need to be overcome. They had a lifetime to practice, Ted thought happily.

"Oh fuck, that's amazing," Bark moaned. "I really am home."

Ted worked his tongue around the sizable intruder in his mouth, slicking it up and beginning a bobbing motion that he hoped would bring Bark even greater pleasure. In this he was not disappointed.

Keeping his fist wrapped around the base of Bark's cock, he slid as much as he could into and out of his mouth, building up a rhythmic friction that soon had Bark writhing. With his other hand, he felt the muscles of Bark's torso rising and falling as his breathing sped up and his back arched, revealing his yearning for release. Never had the body Ted loved seemed so perfectly suited to its motion; lacrosse may have been Bark's sport, but this, this was his body's true calling.

"Teddy, I'm close, I'm close," Bark whispered.

Delighted, Ted gripped harder and sped his motions, sliding his fist up and down in time with his mouth.

"I'm gonna… I'm gonna…," Bark moaned, his voice rising.

Ted knew Bark was warning him, in case he wanted to pull off and finish him with his hand. But there was no way that Ted, having dreamt of this moment for years, was going to let Bark out of his mouth.

Suddenly Bark's body twitched and every muscle locked. His abdominal muscles strained and quivered beneath Ted's hand, and his buttocks tensed, attempting to fulfill the task they had evolved to perform—implanting seed as deeply as possible. Bark's cock throbbed, and Ted's mouth was filled with hot, slippery, salty fluid. Bark growled, and his hands intertwined in Ted's hair for a moment before flailing wildly under the influence of orgasm.

Ted felt his dream come true. Ted wanted to scream in joy. Ted had to swallow.

Throb after throb, Bark filled Ted's mouth to overflowing; he tried to swallow it all, but it overwhelmed him and some flowed back out, down Bark's shaft. Ted hung on, and as Bark's spasms subsided, he began to lick up the excess. He wanted Bark to know he loved him completely, and that this first time had fulfilled him in a way he hadn't thought possible.

"That was…," Bark murmured, "amazing. Come up here."

Ted beamed as he slid up Bark's body, kissing all the objects of his long-repressed desire along the way: the bulging muscles, the sweat-glossed flesh, the nipples that remained erect even as Bark's hard-on began to subside. Finally, Ted reached Bark's face, and he looked into those green eyes, unable to stop smiling.

"I love you so fucking much," Bark said and kissed Ted so vigorously all he could do was hang on and be violated by Bark's tongue. Then Bark's head tipped back to the surface of the ledge. "Be honest with me, Ted. You've done that before."

Ted's grin grew even wider. "Not once. But luckily I had a good coach."

"Well, you are very, very good at it. I've never come that quickly with anyone. In fact, I usually can't come that way at all. Only two or three women have been able to do that, and none of them were even close to you in terms of sheer... power, I guess you'd call it? You are a natural."

"I feel like the luckiest man in the world," Ted said, laying his head on Bark's chest.

"If you think giving me an amazing blowjob makes you lucky, then I just won the fuckin' lottery," Bark said, running his hand up and down Ted's back.

"Come on, I'll bet you've had much more creative handling than I was able to deliver."

"No one's done it like you did," Bark said. "But I would be happy to show you some of the tricks I've learned along the way, if you'd like."

"Barclay Burnett, are you offering me sexual favors?" Ted asked in a shocked voice.

"Not so much offering as telling you to hang on tight, because I'm about to lose my bro-virginity."

"You don't have to," Ted said. He had a hard time believing anyone, especially someone as built as Bark, would want to take a run at his body. He was fit enough, he thought, but he wasn't the bulging athlete Bark was.

"Teddy, there is nothing you can say or do that would keep me from having my way with you, right here, right now. I love you, and until you paint me with your spooge, my life will not be complete. I want you on your back, and I want you there now." He sat up and patted the ledge where he had lain.

Butterflies were zooming frenetically in Ted's belly, but he did what Bark told him to do. Lying there, stretched out naked before him, Ted felt more naked and exposed than he ever had been in his life. But it wasn't a feeling of violation; it was a feeling of giving himself up, body and soul, to the man he loved. It gave him a delicious shiver down the spine to open himself up this way.

Bark straddled him, pinning him to the rock with his bulk and force. Wrapping a hand around the back of Ted's neck, cradling his head in a strong grip, he leaned in and kissed him so gently that Ted marveled such delicacy could come from a body so powerful. Ted ran his hands up and down the corded muscles of Bark's arms, feeling how the muscles articulated to the bones, an anatomy lesson in one slow sweeping movement. That those muscles, that power, was completely dedicated to holding him, loving him, was beyond his comprehension.

Bark nuzzled Ted's ear. "You are so fucking beautiful," he whispered.

The tickle from Bark's hot rush of breath ran deliciously down Ted's body. He reached up and swept his fingers along Bark's strong shoulders and then down his torso. Soon Ted found Bark's hips, which he gripped strongly and pulled harder into him.

Bark chuckled. "All right, all right, I'm going!" He kissed his way down Ted's jawline, then down his throat, and finally to his chest. He flicked his thumbs over Ted's nipples, which was something Ted not only had never had done to him, he didn't recall ever touching himself there before. If he had known it felt like this, he certainly would have started years ago. He gasped and writhed under Bark's aggressive manipulation.

Bark looked up at Ted's face and smiled wickedly. He dove down and sucked Ted's right nipple into his mouth, then grazed it with his teeth. Ted moaned at the loving violation, giving himself to it with an abandon that surprised him. But Bark was moving quickly now, and he lifted himself off Ted and put first one and then the other leg between Ted's, settling himself where they met. Ted, who had rarely even been naked in the presence of another person, was more completely exposed and vulnerable than he had ever imagined being; he couldn't cover his nudity even if wanted to. He didn't want to.

"So beautiful," Bark sighed as he ran his hands down Ted's torso. They met at the base of Ted's achingly hard erection, where Bark gripped the muscle and sinew in a powerful, soothing massage.

Ted felt warmth spread throughout his groin, and he looked down at the sight he never thought he would see: his essential manhood in the hands of another man. His man. His cock, achingly hard now for so long, dripped a crystalline thread of precum onto his belly. Ted leaned back and looked to the sky through the hole in the top of the dome and felt all of the anxiety of the last four years drain from his body. All of that was okay because it had led to this moment.

Bark bent forward, and Ted felt the warm and cool flow of breath at the base of his cock. He arched his pelvis forward, his penis yearning for contact, but it did not come. Instead, he felt Bark's lips brush along the loose skin of his scrotum. And then, suddenly, he felt Bark's mouth close around both of his balls, sucking them into his mouth in one great swoop.

"Unh," Ted groaned, lost in the whirl of sensation as Bark tugged and suckled at his testicles. Ted knew what balls did but never dreamed of how they could feel. His felt very, very good.

Bark made playful slurping noises as he worked Ted's balls over, and when he finally let them slip out from between his lips they made a wet *plop* as they fell back into place.

"Oh God, that was awesome," he moaned, amazed at what Bark knew how to do.

"I'm just getting started." Bark put his hands behind Ted's kneecaps and pushed up, folding Ted double and exposing his ass obscenely.

"What are you—"

"Just wait. You are going to love this." Bark bent forward again.

Ted couldn't believe what he was feeling. Was that Bark's tongue? Did people really do this? The wet, slurpy kiss Bark laid on his ass answered his every question. Ted had never even seen his own asshole, much less thought of it as a sex organ. But when Bark's tongue poked at his opening, and then ventured inside, he knew it was what he wanted.

"Oof. Fuck," he grunted, trying to adjust to the intrusion.

Bark pressed harder into the gap between Ted's buttocks, thrust his tongue deeper, and moved it about with impressive vigor. Ted writhed under the onslaught, desperately trying to adjust to the presence of Bark's tongue, desperate for it to continue. He wanted this with a passion that shocked him.

With a great, suctiony smack, Bark pulled off his asshole and grinned up at him. "Right?" he asked with a wink.

"Oh fuck yeah," Ted answered.

"The first time a chick did that to me, I just about hit the ceiling," Bark said, chuckling. "But when I came back down I asked her to get right back on it. I'm glad you like it too."

"My new favorite thing in the whole world."

"Well, I hope that won't be true in a minute, because I've got more tricks to show you," Bark said with a raised eyebrow.

"Yes," Ted cried, and lay back to prepare for even greater violations.

Bark licked his way all the way up, lancing Ted's tight ass once more before tracing his tongue up to his balls and slurping them in one more time. Then he kissed the base of Ted's cock, and then lips and tongue alternated in slow adoration up to the tip.

"You're a drooler," Bark said in delight. He lapped up the small pool of clear fluid, dragging a long strand up as he lifted his head to wink at Ted. Then he closed his eyes and licked his lips. "God, you are so sweet."

Ted moaned, overwhelmed at dream after dream coming true. The next thing he felt, though, he had never even dreamed because he had no idea it existed. Bark simply opened his mouth and inhaled fully half of Ted's cock. Ted bolted up, unable to control the frenzied action of his muscles in response to overstimulation. He looked down at his friend, whose head was making slow transits up and down, fitting more of Ted's cock in every time.

"Oh fucking fuck," Ted breathed.

Then, just as he began to feel the stirrings of orgasm building, Bark pulled off of him. A whimper emanated from his throat, a sound Ted had no idea he could make. His body was in this for its own purposes, and it protested when the stimulation it craved was removed.

Bark slid up Ted's torso, kissing his way along. He looked into Ted's eyes, smiling, and kissed him.

"Please don't tell me you started in and then suddenly turned back into a straight guy," Ted begged.

"Oh fuck no," Bark said with a grin. "Those days are over. But since you're basically about to lose your virginity, I wanted to see you do it. Everyone deserves to have someone look them in the eye and say 'I love you' when they share their body for the first time."

"So what are you going to—"

"I found something at the bottom of the backpack," Bark said, reaching over and digging deep into the pack. He pulled out a small baggie and showed it to Ted. It contained a small bottle and some condoms. "He wrote on the bag. It says, 'Be safe. Love, Gabriel.' How cool is that? It's like we have our own guardian angel."

Ted's eyes widened as he looked at the package. "You're not going to use that on me, are you?"

Bark laughed. "No, I'm not plotting to spring buttsex on you. At least not yet," he said with a wink. "But I do want to use this." He pulled out the bottle and popped the lid open; then he reached down and squirted a zig-zaggy line of lube along the length of Ted's erection.

Ted gasped as the cool liquid ran down both sides of his cock. Then Bark's hand returned, smoothing the gel up and down. He gripped it more tightly, and the lube crackled, echoing around the dome.

"Oh God, that's—"

"I know," Bark whispered. "It feels different when it's not your own hand, doesn't it?"

Ted could only nod and bite his lip. He wouldn't last long under this kind of attention.

Bark slowed his pace and looked deeply into Ted's eyes. "I love you," he whispered. "I have loved you for so long I can hardly remember a time before I fell in love. You are beautiful, and you are perfect, and you will be mine forever."

Ted felt his old, reserved, dismal self crushed in the vise of physical pleasure and romantic elation; Bark was destroying the dark future he had imagined for himself and forging a new bright vision of love and fulfillment. "I love you," he moaned.

"I love you," Bark murmured. "I love you so much. Now come for me. Give me what you have never given anyone else. Give it to me and I will treasure it forever. Come for me, Ted. Come for me." His strokes quickened as Ted began to thrash. "Here with me," he whispered.

Sparkling lights erupted at the edges of Ted's vision, and he clamped his eyes shut. The dome echoed with his yelps of ecstasy. His balls pulled up tight, and the surge came. His body went rigid, and hot liquid streaks burned across his torso. Bark kept at him, stroking him long after Ted would have stopped, squeezing the last drops out of him.

Finally, he began to shake from overstimulation, and he rolled toward Bark, burying his face in the warm, firm muscle of his chest.

He breathed heavily for a minute, clutching tight, until equilibrium was restored and he began to unclench. Exhausted, he flopped back to the ledge and looked up at Bark.

"Why are you crying?" Ted asked him, startled.

Bark wiped the tears from his cheeks and smiled. "Because that was the most beautiful thing I've ever seen. You looked so happy and so surprised by the whole thing—it was like watching someone discover a new world. And I am the only person who will ever get to experience that, because it will never happen again." He kissed Ted, then looked at him wonderingly. "I am the luckiest man in the world."

"Second luckiest," Ted replied. "You will never be able to convince me I'm not the luckiest."

Bark looked down at Ted's torso. "We should get you cleaned up before this gets all sticky."

"I have a better idea," Ted said. He lunged up at Bark and hugged him, pressing their bodies together from neck to knee. He even wiggled a little to be sure Bark was completely frosted with his semen. "There, that's almost clean, right?"

Bark scowled at him, but then a sly grin crept in. "Almost," he growled, then slid his hands under Ted and flipped him easily into the water. Bark cannonballed in after him, and in the splash and spray they finished tidying themselves up.

They swam and splashed and gamboled for a while, then hauled back out of the water and lay together on the ledge. They spent a heady hour or so kissing and cuddling and letting themselves get used to the idea of being together this way.

"So," Bark said, tickling down the front of Ted's torso with his fingertips, "are you ready to try something?"

Ted looked at him with a wry grin. "Let's see. I've already made out with a guy for the first time, lost my virginity to my best friend, and given my first blowjob. I think I've proven myself ready to try things. What did you have in that oversexed mind of yours?"

Bark reached for the packet with lube and condoms. "Now, I know this is moving pretty quickly...." He fell silent for a moment in a thoughtful pose. "I never in my life imagined saying this to anyone, but here goes. Ted, will you fuck me?"

"Wow. You really went for it." Ted studied Bark's face. "Are you sure you're ready for that? I have to think it would be… uncomfortable, at least at first."

Bark grinned. "Let me tell you a little story."

"Ooh! Story time. I love story time. Especially because this is likely to be a very dirty story."

Bark laughed. "You got that right. Do you remember that writing class we had junior year?"

"With the dragon lady?"

Bark nodded.

"She was crazy," Ted continued. "I mean, most college profs are crazy, but she was crazy crazy. All of the other classes just got to write lab reports and stuff, and we had to read *The Great Gatsby*. Shit was weird. I wonder what happened to her—I don't think she teaches in the department anymore."

"You may also recall I didn't do all that well on the papers."

"Yes, because I also recall you didn't do all that much reading."

"Whatever. Don't try to sidetrack my story. Anyway, I went to talk to her after the semester was over, about my grade. Turns out she'd been fired for failing a student who was about to do a full year internship at some big German engineering firm. When they saw the *F* on his transcript, they yanked the internship and told him he needed to take the class again. So the dean fired her and changed the grade."

"Huh. Didn't know that happened."

"Yeah, it's the kind of stuff academics get all worked up about, but who cares. Anyway, I went to talk to her, and she was packing up her office. So we went to get coffee and talked, and it turns out she was pretty cool. We ended up getting dinner, and then I walked her back to her apartment."

"Shit, Bark," Ted cried. "You dated a teacher?"

"We didn't date," Bark said, rather unconvincingly. "We just went up to her apartment, and she poured us something to drink, and then one thing kind of led to another, and we ended up in bed."

Ted's eyes were wide, but he didn't want to interrupt the story.

"Then things got a little weird."

Ted laughed. "They always seem to in these little stories we tell, don't they?"

"You got that right. Anyway, she like, pounces on me, and she just goes nuts on me. Pawing at me, scratching me up, thrashing me pretty good. Then she like flips me over and kicks my legs apart. Well, you know I'm down for butt stuff, so I just twerk it up for her and she goes to town. Then she's got her finger in there, and she knows what the fuck she's doing. I hardly noticed it when she slipped a second one in there, because her fingers were kinda small. But she starts working a third finger, and I notice that. I turn and look back over my shoulder, and she's just grinning at me while she sticks another one in. So she's got two fingers of each hand right up my ass, and it feels full but... nice, you know?"

"I can honestly say I don't, but please continue."

"She looks at me and says she's never had a guy who could take four fingers without screaming, and she's as turned on as she's ever been. She works my ass for a while, then she straddles my leg and basically rubs herself off on my thigh, which I have to say was kind of hot. Then once she's come like, a dozen times, she starts hitting this spot in my ass with her fingers, really jabbing at me, and it's amazing. I had like, one massive never-ending orgasm until I had to beg her to stop. Which she did, thankfully. Then she made me a sandwich."

Ted wrinkled up his nose. "I hope she washed her hands first."

"Shut up. We ate sandwiches and talked after, and I kinda got to know her. Turns out she wasn't crazy, she was just going crazy trying to teach literature at a polytech. Then she asks if I had fun, and I'm like, hell yeah, and she asks if I've ever had anything up my butt before, and I'm like, hell no, and then she tells me I demonstrated the most 'precocious anality' she's ever encountered. I thanked her and then looked it up later. I think she meant I could take it up the butt pretty good, which I'll be honest, I wasn't sure I really thought was a good thing, but now... well, now I am delighted to be able to place my precocious anality at your disposal, good sir."

"But Bark, I've never...."

"Never what?" Bark asked playfully.

"I've never... fucked anyone."

"Until today." Bark reached down and wrapped his hand around Ted's erection. "Feels to me like you might be into it."

"I told you, the dirty stories do it to me every time. And you getting reamed by crazy teacher lady was pretty hot."

"I'll take care of everything else." Bark reached over for the packet of lube and condoms. He put a little lube on the head of Ted's prick. "Makes it slippery inside the condom," he said, waggling his eyebrows at Ted, "for his pleasure."

"Very thoughtful of you," Ted replied.

"Now, we place the condom like so, and then we roll it smoothly down," Bark narrated as he worked, "making sure to leave room at the tip for all of that stuff you hosed us down with earlier. Then just a little more of the slick stuff." He drizzled a generous helping of lube all over Ted's rigid cock and then sat back with a grin, clearly pleased with his handiwork.

"What do I do now?" Ted asked a little nervously.

"Just lie there and watch me lose the last bit of virginity I possess," Bark said with a sexy grin. He straddled Ted, then backed up a bit to align the equipment.

Ted felt the head of his cock touch Bark's buttocks, then slide between them (that playing lacrosse builds considerable gluteal mass was a fact with which he was well acquainted) until it nudged something solid. He couldn't believe he was going in there.

He looked up at Bark, who smiled as if the pressure was more than bearable—it was welcome. He rocked back and forth a bit, and furrowed his brow. Then he pushed back more purposefully, and Ted felt the previously solid obstacle begin to yield. Bark gasped and froze.

"You okay?" Ted asked, fearful he'd somehow caused pain.

Bark's smile returned, wide and easy. "Just getting used to it. You're a bit bigger than the dragon lady's fingers."

"Please stop if it hurts you," Ted said.

Bark shook his head slowly. "Only one way this ends, mister." He took a deep breath and pushed back a little more. His eyebrows lifted and a small "oh" escaped his lips.

The head of Ted's penis was now inside, and he felt a distinct second ring of pressure, as if he were passing through another muscle. Asses were more complex than he had imagined. Then he reflected that he was now the kind of person who had opinions about assholes, and he marveled at how his life had changed so suddenly.

Bark froze again as Ted's cock passed through this second pressure, and the smile returned, though there was sweat starting to bead on his brow. "Okay, okay," he murmured, his eyes rolling back in his head. Then he suddenly looked down at Ted. "Ready?"

"Ready for what?" Ted asked.

"This," Bark replied with a sexy curl of his lip. He pushed down on Ted and slid him all the way in. They were united.

"Oh, fuck, fuck, fuck, fuck," Ted moaned. "That is so… oh fuck, fuck, fuck." He turned his head side to side, trying to take in all the sensations crashing down on him and erupting in him. He took a steadying breath and looked up at Bark.

Bark's eyes were closed, and he was either at peace or about to implode. Then that smile returned, and he opened his deep green eyes, and all was right with the world. "Ohhhh," he moaned. "That's the stuff." He stayed settled on Ted's hips for another minute and then began to rock gently back and forth.

The space inside Bark that Ted now occupied had been designed, it seemed to Ted, specifically for him. His penis was surrounded tightly on all sides by hot pressure; as Bark shifted his hips forward and back in a sultry dance of passion, the pressure varied but never relented.

Suddenly Bark pitched forward and landed atop Ted, gripping his shoulders and holding him tight. "God, this is amazing," he panted. "You're hitting every button I have in my precocious ass, and it's incredible."

"I had no idea it could feel like this," Ted answered. "What the fuck was I thinking not doing this before?"

"We should have started freshman year," Bark agreed. "Oh, this is…." He slid forward, giving up a couple of inches of Ted, and then rocked back, reclaiming them as his own. "Oh yeah."

"Do that two more times and this show is gonna be over," Ted warned with a grin.

Bark stopped. He took Ted's head in his hands, held him tightly. "This show will never be over. I will always be here," he whispered, leaning close to Ted's ear. "Here with you."

Ted had never been happier in his life than at this moment. He tipped his pelvis up, gently and slowly, and reveled in the sound of Bark's contented sigh at the welcome intrusion. They rocked and kissed and whispered until finally the pressure built and Ted could hold it back no longer. He pushed Bark upright, wanting to see him, all of his beauty, at the moment they truly became one. As Bark bounced and moaned, Ted took hold of his penis and began to stroke it gently, using the precum that had been steadily dripping from it as lubrication. Bark sighed and rocked his hips forward and back as Ted pushed up and down, and in this spontaneous symphony of motion, they reached for orgasm together.

Ted felt a hardness at the base of his cock he had never known before, and then the spasms began. He roared and shook, and his hand was a blur of motion on Bark's jutting erection. Bark stiffened in turn, and his thighs squeezed tightly around Ted's hips. Then, as Ted climaxed within him, Bark's cock blasted out a jet of semen that splashed onto Ted's chin. More followed, each slashing heat accompanied by a tightening around his penis as Bark's ass contracted vigorously in the effort to paint the wall with his sperm. Ted felt the hot fluid lace across his face and throat, just as he felt his own surround his erection as it filled the condom deep inside Bark.

Bark fell forward again, panting rapidly into Ted's ear. "I fucking, *fucking* love you," he sighed.

"I fucking love fucking you," Ted answered.

Bark laughed and hugged him tightly. "Sexy Teddy is fun. Let's keep him around." He beamed at Ted, his smile one of pure contentment.

They lay together and looked at the top of the cavern, listening to the waves beat against the rocks, until the light began to fade.

"We should probably get going, back to the inn," Bark said, between kisses on the side of Ted's head.

"What happens when we get there?" Ted asked.

"I imagine Winnie will rush around pouring everyone wine, Howie will complain that he's not going to get laid—again—and Chad will scowl while Paul and Thor paw at each other. You know, the usual."

"But what about us? Do we tell them?"

"How can we not?" Bark asked. "My whole life has changed in the last twenty-four hours. I can't really go back and pretend it hasn't happened."

"If you're ready for it, I certainly am. No one's going to bat an eye if the guy who hasn't ever had sex with a woman turns out to be gay. But you are kind of going to blow everyone's mind, since you've been such a manwhore."

Bark grinned and kissed him. "But I'm your manwhore now, you lucky guy."

"I've always wanted one of those. Just another dream you've made come true." They kissed again. "I guess it's time for our big public debut."

Bark frowned jokingly. "I have to wear clothes, don't I?"

"Nah, let's not change everything at once," Ted replied with a laugh.

As they dressed and packed up, Bark turned more serious. "This is going to be okay, right?"

Ted was struck by the plaintive note in his voice. It reminded him of that night in the shower, when Bark had said he was scared and simply held Ted as they stood in the water. "Of course it will, Bark. Everything's going to be fine."

Bark nodded, then hefted the backpack and led the way out of the cavern. Ted followed, wondering how their new relationship would fare in the light of day.

Chapter Twelve
Ocean's Six

"Our wanderers have come home," called Donnelly from the pool deck when he caught sight of Ted and Bark on the beach walking toward the inn.

They waved, and Ted gave a subtle thumbs-up sign to convey their good news. Donnelly smiled so brightly Ted had to laugh. It was nice to finally have someone in his life who was there pulling for him as he sorted all of this stuff with Bark out.

Bark and Ted walked up the beach steps and through the courtyard where the fountain once splashed. Just before they stepped out onto the pool deck, however, Ted took Bark's hand and pulled him back.

"So, how do we do this?" he asked.

"I say we go subtle. Like walk in, cool and casual, and then find a way to bring the conversation around to buttsex. And then I can just sort of toss out there, 'funny you should mention sodomy. My good man Ted here railed me vigorously this very afternoon.' And then everyone will chuckle gaily and sip their martinis."

Ted's response was a swift smack to Bark's forehead. "Seriously, that's what you use your brain for? Good God, man, what a waste."

"Too subtle?" Bark grinned.

Ted shook his head. "I don't think we have to make an announcement. We can just act natural, and if it seems appropriate to tell them anything, we will. We have nothing to be ashamed of."

"Ted, you may not have noticed, but our friends are a pretty solid bunch. Well, except for Howie—he can be an asshole. But the rest of them are going to be fine with this, and they've probably been expecting it for a long time, given how gorgeous I am and how you had so clearly fallen in love with me."

Ted's response was to kiss him. Then smack him on the forehead again. "Let's go, buddy. What's the worst that could happen?"

"As long as we never let go there is nothing we can't do," Bark said lightly, but Ted could see he really meant it. It was that kind of wide-eyed optimism, combined with a body that took his breath away, that Ted loved in Bark.

"I love you," Ted said in a low and serious voice.

"I love you," Bark replied, just as seriously.

They stepped through the courtyard and onto the pool deck.

"There they are," Donnelly called, smiling broadly and coming to greet Ted and Bark. He pulled Ted into a hug and whispered in his ear. "Everything okay?"

"More than okay," Ted whispered back. "We're... really good."

Donnelly doubled the force of his hug. "Awesome," he said.

Then, releasing Ted, he held his arms open for Bark, who smiled and threw his arms around the trooper.

"Thank you," Bark whispered into Donnelly's ear. "You are our guardian angel."

"It was an honor."

"And thanks for the lube and condoms," Bark added. "Teddy kinda went to town on me."

Donnelly pulled back, eyes wide, looking from Bark to Ted and back again. Both young men beamed at him and started to laugh, and he joined in. "Well, why waste any more time, right?"

"Bark, Ted, get over here," Paul's deep voice beckoned. "Strategy session."

Bark and Ted exchanged a confused look, but Paul's tone brooked no hesitation. They walked over to a table around which was gathered the rest of their group.

"Gentlemen," Paul said, his voice worthy of a gruff five-star general in an action movie, "our mission tonight is one that many have said is impossible. They called me insane for even suggesting it. But it is our duty, and failure is simply not. An. Option." He punctuated these words with his fist on the table for emphasis.

"Give it to us straight, chief," Bark said with deadly seriousness. "What's the mission?"

Ted beamed at Bark, utterly charmed by his ability to pick up Paul's tone and play along so effortlessly.

Paul walked halfway around the table to where Howie stood. He clapped his hands on Howie's shoulders from behind. "He is one of ours. A good man. And tonight, he gets laid."

"Nooooo!" cried Thor, hands extended to heaven. "It's suicide— suicide, I tell you!"

Howie rolled his eyes, shaking his head ruefully.

"You better have a damn good plan," Chad said with a theatrical snarl. "I don't want a repeat of the Applebee's campaign. We lost some good men that day." He was clearly practicing for his eventual transition from model to B-movie actor. It was the kind of earnest overacting that would likely set him up for a career in made-for-TV romance.

"I call it Operation Honeypot," Paul snarled.

"Ew," Thor opined. "Do we have to call it that?"

Paul snapped his head toward Thor. "It's a reference to catching more flies with honey."

"Oh, that's fine then. I thought you were referring to the women as honeypots, which seemed kind of—"

"Moving on," Paul broke in. "We have discovered that one of the hotels in town has remained open. Staying at this particular hotel is a large number of young women from a university several hundred miles away. They rode chartered buses here, and the buses haven't been able to make it through to take them home because of road closures after the storm. The nightclub on the ground floor will be opening this evening for a last hurrah before the buses get here in the morning to take the ladies home. This is a target-rich environment, men, and into it we will insert our comrade."

Howie groaned, but Ted noticed he didn't protest beyond that.

"What's our strategy?" Bark asked.

"Each of us will leverage our particular skill set. Bark, you will take the lead. You enter first, with Ted. The combination of your muscular charm and Ted's witty conversation will attract a circle of admirers. Once you have pulled all of the women interested in lacrosse-y hotness and intellectual conversation, Thor and I will take up station at the bar. We will make eye contact with at least three ladies each, and then we will begin to make out. With each other."

"Excuse me?" Thor asked, though his voice showed him to be in no way offended.

"It's a classic move. Start the seduction, then become immediately unavailable. Plus, two hot guys kissing will reel in a few more, because some women get turned on by that kind of thing."

"Seriously?" Ted asked.

"Seriously," Paul replied. "Some of them even read romance novels about it."

"Huh," Ted grunted.

"So now we come to the pivot point of the operation. Chad, you and Howie enter together. You cruise through the room, casually making eye contact with all prospects. Chad, you focus on looking gorgeous, like always; Howie, you just keep your mouth shut. Then, you two take up station down the bar from myself and Thor, and once you have built an audience, you make the big move. Chad, you make eye contact with me, and I give you the nod."

"The nod?" Chad asked.

"Yes, the nod. This one." Paul arranged his face in a sexy smirk, raised an eyebrow, and give his head a quick jerk upward. Then he set his expression on "full smolder" and fixed Chad with a smoky stare.

"Fuck," Thor exhaled.

"You have *got* to teach me that," Chad said, his voice as admiring as Thor's.

"Then you come over to join Thor and me, and we make a gay little threesome. Now, for those of you keeping score at home, here's the game: Howie is now the best thing on the market, because his model friend has come to the dark side. The crowd closes in on him. Once he has made his selection, Chad starts to have second thoughts about his sexuality, and finds a woman who is willing to do anything to show him the glories of hetero fucking. Two down. Bark, once you have helped Ted secure a sweet, gentle woman who will take good care of him, you are free to give yourself to the woman or women of your choice. Four down. Then, Thor, the floor is yours. Chad will leave at least a handful of disappointed women who are eager to turn the gay guy, and you can have your pick. By this time the bartender will have called every concierge and personal trainer left in town to tell them that there's a real man in the bar who needs attention, and I'll have Y-chromosomes all over me. Six and done." He stepped back, arms wide. "You may now express your admiration."

The guys looked at him, stunned.

"Questions?"

Thor raised his hand.

"Yes, Thor?"

"Can you do the nod again?"

Paul sighed and looked heavenward, but then dropped his stare on Thor and repeated his smoldering look.

"Yeah, I don't think I'm going home with anyone else tonight. Any concierge tries to get between us, I will fuck him up."

There was a collective gasp around the table. Ted had never heard Thor talk this way. But then Paul did something Ted had never seen him do: blush. A smile slowly insinuated itself on his bearded face. "Is it erect in here, or is it just me?"

"It's not just you," Thor said quietly.

"Good God, ladies," Howie grumbled. "Can we just get going?"

"One more question," Bark said, raising his hand.

"What is it, Bark?" Paul asked.

"Is it okay if Ted and I do our part and then, once Howie has his companion for the night, we just leave together?"

"Uh, sure, I guess," Paul stumbled, clearly puzzled. "Not up for sexy times tonight?"

"Didn't say that. I just said Ted and I were leaving together."

A silence fell over the group. Ted felt the heat rising in his cheeks. All eyes turned to him, and he couldn't help it. He smiled and burst out laughing.

Thor gasped. "You two…?" He pointed from Bark to Ted and back again.

They both nodded, and then Bark took Ted's hand and held it to his lips.

"You have got to be fucking kidding me with this," Howie groaned and pushed back his chair. He got to his feet and stalked away.

"Finally," Chad said, smiling at the two of them.

"What does that mean?" Ted asked.

"I was wondering if you'd ever find the nerve to tell him."

Ted was mystified. He shook his head and shrugged, waiting for Chad to continue.

"I spend a lot of my time around people who like spending time around models. I know every look, and I know what it looks like when people don't want to look like they're looking. You've had it bad for Bark since I met you." He extended a fist to Ted to bump. "Good for you, man." Then he turned to Bark. "This guy…." He pointed to Ted. "You are a lucky man. And if you hurt him, I'm coming after you." He bumped fists with Bark as well.

"That was beautiful, Chaddy," Thor said.

"You crying?" Paul asked, manly scorn in his voice.

"It's just so… perfect."

Paul put his arm around Thor and squeezed him, letting his silence speak for him.

"Fucking fuck!" shouted Howie. He stomped back to the table, waving his phone. "The airline says all the flights that came in today were empty because they're trying to get people back home. And because they were empty, no luggage got loaded on. And because our suitcases have been sitting around Chicago for so long, they sent them back home."

"So, they're never coming?" Chad asked.

"Once our stuff gets back home, they're going to put them all on the next flight back to Chicago. Then get it here sometime tomorrow. Maybe." He sighed and shook his head. "Shit."

Winnie came over from the table where he and Vic had been drinking wine with the troopers. "Can I help, dear?"

"The airline says we won't have luggage until tomorrow, at the soonest."

"Oh, I'm so sorry. And you wanted to go out tonight, didn't you? Let me see what I can find." He hustled off, tapping his chin thoughtfully.

An hour later the group was arrayed in Winnie's new finds. They looked mostly like country-club gigolos, out for the night to dance with cougars, but the cut and style of the garments did accentuate their best assets.

"Oh yes," Winnie pronounced, admiring his own sartorial handiwork. "I predict the next sound we hear will be panties hitting the ground en masse." He giggled joyfully. "Now, you all have fun tonight. Tomorrow Vic and I will be treating you to a gala farewell dinner in appreciation for all you have done to help us during the storm and its aftermath. Feel free to bring a guest, or guests, as the case may be, to join in the fun."

"That's very nice of you," Thor said.

"Least we could do, dear. You've been so helpful to us."

"Men," Paul barked. "Move out!"

The six walked out through the courtyard and down the beach steps, on their way to glory. Or getting Howie laid.

THE HOTEL Flamingo was located at the upper end of the main strip, farthest from the beach but with a commanding view of the ocean. Its higher position had spared it the flooding the beachfront establishments had endured, allowing it to shelter its guests more effectively.

The guys walked through the deserted town, glancing through windows at the darkened bars and clubs that lined the street. Most had been gutted, with piles of stools and tables blocking the sidewalk; waterlogged drywall and lumber lay about the streets. The gigolo posse walked in silence toward the Flamingo, the only building with more than a few lights on.

Once they neared the entrance, Paul drew them into a huddle.

"Men, the mission before us will test our very souls. It will take the last measure of our strength and our commitment. What we do today, men, will live in the hearts and minds of our generation. As God is my witness, this day we shall get Howie laid." They joined hands in the middle of the huddle, Howie reluctantly putting his on top, and gave a great yawp of manly vigor.

"All right, Bark, Ted, you lead us off. Acquit yourselves like the men I know you to be." He nodded solemnly to each of them. "God, you're so cute together," he said with a Winnie-esque inflection. Then he cleared his throat and his military bearing returned. "Good luck, and see you on the other side."

Bark turned to Ted. "One for luck?"

Ted smiled and nodded, and they kissed.

"Aww," Thor sighed.

They walked into the lobby of the Flamingo and then turned to enter the bar. It was about half-full, and they saw immediately that Paul's intelligence was spot-on. The bar was populated exclusively with college-age women, doing their best to fight off the boredom of an all-girl shambles of a spring break. The entrance of Bark and Ted sent a ripple through the room.

They walked to an empty booth and sat down.

"I think this is going to work," Bark whispered as he smiled at several of the young ladies who had watched him walk across the room.

"It's a plan that depends on your being irresistible," Ted whispered back. "How could it not work?" He felt a squeeze on his knee and smiled inwardly.

"Well, hello," Bark said to a trio of beautiful women who had sidled up to the booth. "Won't you join us?"

Ted hadn't anticipated how much fun it would be to watch Bark work. Previously, he hadn't paid much attention to Bark's moves because they had always landed him in bed with a woman. Ted tried to be happy for him on those occasions but was, for obvious reasons, not thrilled with Bark's success with women. Now, though, he knew they were leaving together, and he could sit back and enjoy watching his best friend—his boyfriend!—be charming and seductive and gorgeous.

But first, he reminded himself, he had a job to do.

"So, what's your major?" he asked the lovely woman sitting next to him, and soon they were engaged in genuine conversation. He had always found it easy to talk to women, and had actually done so a great deal, mainly because he had until recently hoped he might meet one who would distract him from the person he knew was the love of his life. Now that that person was sitting next to him, he found he could relax and enjoy the conversation.

Bark and Ted soon assembled a group numbering half a dozen; four were fascinated by watching Bark's biceps flex within the confines of his tight T-shirt, and two were engaged with Ted in a vigorous debate about the contributions made by last year's recipients of the various Nobel prizes.

Paul and Thor walked through the door right on schedule, and made a leisurely circuit of the room, attracting no small amount of attention. Ted noted that they indeed made a striking couple, if a couple they really were. They reached the bar, and again, according to Paul's plan, they were soon circled by a clique of interested ladies attracted by Paul's testosterone and Thor's puppy dog eyes.

Ted returned to his conversation, and kept an eye out for the next stage of the operation. He couldn't see Paul and Thor anymore, surrounded as they were, but when all five of their female spectators stepped back in unison, he knew the move had been made. Sure enough, Paul and Thor were nuzzled up together. Ted watched them for a moment and had to admit they were quite convincing. So much so, in fact, that he had to make a quick adjustment in his pants to remain comfortable sitting down.

As if on cue, Chad and Howie entered the bar. Chad's clothes, as his clothes always did, seemed to amplify the shape of his body in a way that was striking. Ted could finally appreciate what the model-wranglers saw in Chad—he made the clothes better simply by wearing them. Howie seemed, for once in his life, to have taken the advice to shut up; he smiled and listened as if Chad were the most fascinating person in the world, but he contributed little himself, and he refrained from reaching for his wallet for the first time Ted could remember.

Soon, many of the women who had been talking to Paul and Thor (who were still whispering sweet nothings and kissing each other every few minutes) settled on Chad and Howie, and the final phase began.

Ted couldn't tear his eyes from Paul—he simply had to see The Look. When it came, he felt an instantaneous heat in his boy parts, much like the one occasioned by Bark swimming laps naked. He could get used to this, he thought, not loading himself up with guilt when he found a man attractive.

Chad walked over to Paul and their little trio got very cozy. Several of the women around Howie rolled their eyes in frustration, but Howie was carrying on what seemed to be an engaged conversation with a strikingly beautiful woman; she had long, flowing brown hair and a brilliant white smile. Even as the others drifted away, she stayed, and to Ted's shock she seemed to hang on Howie's every word.

As Howie was locked and loaded, Chad worked up a classic movie-of-the-week sullen scowl and broke away from Paul and Thor, retreating to a table far away with his cocktail and his masculine dignity. And just as Paul had predicted, he was immediately set upon by no fewer than four empathetic women who seemed ready to offer their shoulders (at the very least) for him to cry on.

The only off-script moment came at the very end of the operation. Just as Bark and Ted were beginning to extricate themselves from their interlocutors, a new couple entered the bar. Ted recognized them as Abby and Ryan, whom Thor had helped out at the animal hospital and the free clinic. Thor, of course, welcomed them to join himself and Paul, and they were soon laughing and talking and carrying on like old friends.

"Well, buddy, I guess we should go take care of that thing," Bark said to Ted during a lull in the conversation.

Ted looked blankly at Bark but then felt Bark's hand groping about his crotch. "Oh, yeah, that thing isn't going to take care of itself," he agreed.

"Not anymore it's not," Bark murmured. "Now, if you'll excuse us, ladies, we really need to be going."

Disappointment showed on every face, but they charmed the lot of them with their sincere wishes for safe travels home. On their way out of the bar, Howie called them over to introduce them to Bella, who was delighted to meet some of Howard's friends. One more stop, to meet Thor's friends Abby and Ryan (Chad was more than capable of working alone) and they were out the door.

On the steps of the hotel, they high-fived. "We acquitted ourselves like men," Bark exclaimed.

"A fucking sexy man," Ted murmured, pulling Bark into an embrace that was part hug and part grope. "Watching you work was an inspiration."

"What about you?" Bark replied. "I could follow maybe half of what you guys were talking about. You could have had any one of those women, buddy."

"Thanks, but I've got what I want," Ted said, taking Bark's arm as they walked back toward the inn.

"And you've also got what *I* want," Bark growled, his hand once again straying into Ted's crotch.

"We'd better hurry, or that thing really is going to take care of itself," Ted said with a laugh.

They quickened their pace back to the Villa Hermes.

Chapter Thirteen
No Shame

Ted awoke happy for the first time in his life.

Sure, he'd been excited about Christmas morning as a kid, but that was mostly the excitement of running into the living room to see what was under the tree for him. In his post-adolescent life, waking up alone was just another reminder of how lonely he was.

This morning, though. This morning.

He was in the bed he and Bark had seriously deranged the night before—all night long, actually. The freedom and luxury of having all night and a room to themselves was intoxicating, and they had put the bed to good use. He and Bark went at each other as if they had been starved for contact for years, which in many ways they had. But now they had each other, and all the time in the world to explore the ways they fit together.

They fit together at the moment with Bark's head resting on Ted's chest, heavy and secure, and Ted ran his fingers through the spiky ginger hair. He had dreamed of this, but the reality of it was so much better than he had ever dared let himself imagine. Because it wasn't just the sensation of being here, doing this; it was the knowledge that he had a legitimate claim to this being and doing, and he could look forward to tonight when they could be and do until they exhausted themselves. It was pleasure with a future, and it was everything Ted wanted in the world.

"Mmmm," Bark murmured against Ted's chest. He moved his head in slow, gentle nuzzling motions and warmed Ted's nipple with his breath.

"Morning," Ted said. "Sleep well?"

"Sleep? When did we sleep? You were a monster last night, buddy. I may not walk normally again."

Ted laughed and riffled Bark's hair. "Toughen up, ya lightweight. I only did it three times."

Bark lifted his head and looked Ted in the eye. "Three times in addition to the time in the cave, remember? For my first day as a buttslut I think I proved myself beyond precocious. I think we gotta give my boy a rest."

Ted grinned. "There's still plenty of other stuff we could do…."

"And we will. But first let's get a few laps in, okay? I gotta work more of my body than just the dirty bits." He smiled at Ted. "And don't give me that look. You gave me a workout last night, so you gotta do my workout this morning."

"All right, you win. If that's the price I have to pay, then I'm willing to pay it. Lead on, coach."

DONNELLY STOOD on their balcony overlooking the ocean, basking in the morning sun.

"Do I hear someone in the pool?" Brandt asked Donnelly as he stepped out onto the balcony with two mugs of coffee.

Donnelly nodded as he sipped. "You gotta take a look," he said, motioning Brandt over to his side of the balcony, where a portion of the pool could be seen.

Down below, the sleek, nude bodies of Bark and Ted could be seen gliding from end to end of the pool, keeping perfect cadence with each other. Their smooth progress was only interrupted by periodic splash fights, which ended in laughing and kissing, and then they resumed their stroke.

"Mesmerizing, isn't it?" Donnelly asked.

"They do seem perfect for each other." Brandt smiled at his partner. "You kind of like the whole matchmaker thing, don't you?"

Donnelly held up a modest hand of protest. "I didn't do anything but give a little nudge. They were heading this way, but they were getting caught up on silly stupid societal stuff. It's sad to think of all of the best friends who really want what Bark and Ted have but don't know how to go about making it happen."

"Unless they happen to run into Archangel Gabriel," Brandt said with a laugh.

"I like to think that increasing the net happiness in the world is the only thing we can really call God's work, so I'll take it," Donnelly said with a graceful bow.

Brandt smiled and shook his head. "Get your halo over here and give me a kiss."

TED AND Bark stepped out of the pool and wrapped towels around their waists just as Winnie and Vic were beginning to bring breakfast out.

"Can we help with anything?" Ted asked.

"Oh no, dear," Winnie replied. "You're doing enough just being wet and naked." He smiled broadly and went about setting up the buffet.

Bark and Ted took their usual chairs and let the sun's rays warm them.

They sat up and turned to look when Chad came out of his room with one of the ladies from the bar the night before. But instead of the usual kiss-and-taxi routine, they strolled out onto the pool deck together. Chad was wearing a bathrobe, and his date had a large and expensive-looking camera slung around her neck.

"Oh, the light's perfect," she said. "You stand there." She placed him, then posed him so the golden sun shone on his back. She stepped behind him and took some readings with her camera. "All right, now look back at me." The shutter whirred. "Great. Now drop the robe off one shoulder. Awesome." More clicking. "Okay, slide it down farther, farther, farther... good, now off."

Chad dropped the robe to the pool deck. Chad was naked.

"Good. Now turn a bit... that's it, tease me with it. Good." She stood up and held the camera off to the side. "Now, you wanted to try a little side-peen, right?"

He took a breath and nodded. "Might as well go for it." He turned a little more toward the camera.

"Looks great," she said, as the shutter exploded with clicking again. Then she cocked her head to the side and closed one eye. "Here, let me...." She walked up to Chad and looked him in the eye while she frankly dandled his manhood. She looked down at it and smiled. "There's mama's little chubby." Her voice was gleeful. She stepped back and took more pictures. "Got it."

Chad put his robe back on and walked over to the table where Bark and Ted sat. "Morning, gentlemen," he said. "I'd like you to meet Libby. She's a photographer."

"So we gathered," Ted said, extending his hand.

"And to what do we owe the pleasure of this nudie photo shoot?" Winnie asked, hurrying over.

"Libby's helping me with a little project."

"It wasn't little from where I was sitting, dear."

Chad laughed. "No, I wasn't referring to that, but thank you. Do you have a browser handy? I can show you what we're working on."

Winnie dashed back into the office for his tablet, which he handed, panting, to Chad. He typed, and then handed it back to Winnie.

"Oh, it's a Tumblr," Winnie exclaimed. He peered at the title. "'The Real Chaz Mannington.' Well, that's lovely, dear."

"Scroll down," Chad said.

Winnie flicked down the page and gasped. "Oh my, you really are taking matters into your own hands," he exclaimed.

"I figure if there's already naked stuff out there, I might as well be sure at least some of it is quality. Libby took some shots last night, and I think they look pretty good."

"I cannot but agree," Winnie said. Then he tucked his tablet under his arm. "Of course, I'll want to take a closer look. Be back in a few minutes." He looked Chad up and down. "Maybe a bit longer than that."

Chad laughed and motioned for Libby to sit with him at the table.

"Do we have you to thank for bringing Chad out of his 'boo-hoo, everyone's looking at my wiener on Tumblr' funk?" Bark said to Libby.

"You know, it's funny," Libby replied. "I work as a photographer's assistant, and I meet a lot of models. It may surprise you to know that Chad's the most normal one I've ever met." She turned to him, clearly smitten. "And he's not bad to look at, either."

Chad smiled and kissed Libby. "She convinced me to get ahead of the Tumblr thing by getting my own images out there. I'm building my brand."

A thought occurred to Ted. "Hey, if you guys were in your room, where did Howie end up?"

Chad frowned. "I don't know. We came back before he did. Come to think of it, we left Paul and Thor at the bar too. You don't think…?"

"Paul and Thor and Howie all snug in a bed?" Bark uttered, horrified. "Holy shit, that would be the last sign of the apocalypse."

"Sorry to disappoint you, but it's not quite the end of the world," Howie's voice drifted over from the loungers on the other side of the pool. He sat up, hair disheveled, blinking in the light.

"Oh, dude, you ended up out in the cold again?" Chad asked. "That sucks, man, I'm sorry."

"We managed to keep warm," another voice came from under the pile of sheets on the lounger next to Howie. Bella sat up and shook out her mane of brunette hair. "Morning, everyone."

The three guys at the table exchanged a triumphant glance and then returned her greeting.

Bark raised his coffee cup. "To Paul, who knows the ways of the human heart."

They all raised their cups in salute.

"Speaking of," Ted said, looking around, "where do you think our Paul ended up?"

"Smart money says find Thor and you'll find Paul," Chad said. "You know, behind him. Working up a sweat."

"Shut up, you phobe!" Libby cried. "I thought they were such a cute couple."

"We're all just sort of getting used to them as a couple," Chad said. "Like Bark and Ted here. They've been an item for either twelve hours or four years, depending on how you count."

Libby laughed and congratulated Ted and Bark. They headed for the buffet to get some breakfast, as Howie walked toward his room.

"Ugh, need to take a shower," Howie said to Ted as he passed.

"Hey," Ted said. "Good for you. She's beautiful."

Howie glanced back at Bella. "I guess you do still have a straight bone in your body, somewhere. She's sweet, but one of my burdens is weeding out the ones who only want my money."

"And you do that by waving your credit card around?" Ted asked, laughing.

Howie put his hand on Ted's shoulder. "All women want money, Ted. But finding the woman who would love you even if you didn't have it… that's the hard part. She seems terrific, but as far as what really matters, well, the jury's out on this one." Howie smiled grimly at Ted and then continued on his way.

When he reached the end of the buffet table, Ted stepped over to check on Bella.

"Want some breakfast?" he asked her.

"Oh you're sweet. I'm good, though." She smoothed her hair and then pulled out her phone and began typing expertly. Then she tossed it off to the side. "Sit for a sec, Ted?" she asked him.

"Uh, sure," he said, lowering himself to the lounger Howie had occupied.

"Can I be straight with you?" she asked, then laughed. "Oops, that's kind of funny because of you and Bark. Howie told me all about you guys—he thinks the world of you, you know."

"Howie said that? We're talking about Howie, right?" Ted pointed to where they had just been talking.

Bella laughed, a bright melodious sound for someone who had slept outdoors on a pool lounger. "He can be kind of a pill, can't he? But his heart is in the right place, I can tell. I think he's got potential, but I need to know a couple of things to fill in the picture. So. He comes from money, right?"

Uh-oh, Ted thought. Howie was right. "Yes, he does."

"Let me guess. Enough that he never seems to worry about having enough but is always worried people don't know he has enough."

"Wow, you're good at this."

"Daddy issues? Love/hate, competing for the affection of the same women, that kind of thing?"

"Now you're scaring me."

She nodded. "Okay, bonus round. Always talks about hookups but never seems to have them; runs down anyone who's in a relationship but seems jealous of them at the same time."

"That's it. I'm dealing with a witch."

Bella smiled. "No, just someone with a lot of the same issues. Thank you, Ted. I can see why Howie loves you so much."

Ted was about to renew his opinion that they must surely be talking about different Howies, but Bella had picked up her phone and turned away.

"Carter, can you have the plane here tonight by ten-ish? ... Yes, there will be two of us. I'll be dropping him off at home ... Some little college town way up north somewhere. But I'd like to surprise him along the way, so can you get us into that little place I like? ... Perfect. Thanks, love. Ciao." She tossed her phone and lay back on the lounger, a contented smile on her face.

Ted walked back to the table, where he filled in Bark, Chad, and Libby on his conversations with Howie and Bella.

"Wow," Chad said. "Looks like Howie finally did it. He always said money loves company, and I guess his just made a whole lot of new friends."

"Good for him," Bark said. He tucked into his breakfast, and the group ate and chatted in the morning sun.

They were joined by a damp-haired Howie about halfway through their meal. He brought a plate piled high with Vic's good cooking.

"You're not going to eat with Bella?" Ted asked.

Howie shook his head. "Nah. She said she doesn't eat breakfast and just wanted to get a nap before they head out for home. Poor girl, having to ride a bus all that way. Do you think it would be too much for me to offer to buy her a plane ticket? She might think if I'm spending that much money on her, I want something in return. Which I kind of do, but wouldn't want her to think that."

"I wouldn't worry about it," Ted said. "She probably has her day all planned."

Howie shrugged and kept eating.

As they were finishing breakfast, the door to Paul and Thor's room opened, and Paul stepped out into the bright morning sun. He reached back his hand, and out walked Ryan, followed by Abby. Thor brought up the rear and shut the door behind him.

Paul and Ryan kissed, a dainty peck, and Thor kissed Abby.

"Oh," said Howie. "Nice."

Then the ritual was repeated, but with Thor kissing Ryan and Paul kissing Abby.

"Oh," repeated Howie, his voice darker this time. "Nice." He rolled his eyes sarcastically.

"You might want to ice that," Abby said to Paul.

He laughed and shook his head. "I'm keeping it as a reminder. For a girl you really follow through."

"And you are built like a brick shithouse," she replied admiringly. "That was all kinds of fun."

It was only then that Paul and Abby noticed Thor and Ryan's good-bye kiss had turned into a second-base makeout.

"Get a room, you two," Paul cracked, nudging them both in the ribs.

"Seriously," Abby agreed. "Men, right?"

"Can't live with 'em, can't get fucked without 'em," Paul replied.

"You might be surprised," she said, running a delicate finger down Paul's back all the way to his ass. "Hit me up sometime if you're interested."

Paul grinned. "I just might do that."

The couple took their leave, and Paul and Thor came to join the others at breakfast.

"And that, motherfuckers," Paul announced, "is the Guatemalan Flashback."

Once the laughter died down, Winnie came to the table. "Your new friends are welcome to stay for breakfast," he said. "Seemed like you didn't really want to say good-bye."

"I have a feeling we may be seeing them again," Thor said lightly as he filled his plate.

"So, Paul," Chad said, "try some new stuff last night?"

Paul nodded, but his mouth was full of egg and probably some bacon.

Thor answered for him. "Our Paul has proven himself fairly flexible, especially when spontaneous opportunities present themselves."

Paul looked askance at Thor. "It's not all that spontaneous when you ask everyone to sign a 'consent to penetrative sexual relations' form. That kind of ruins the flow, don't you think?"

"You had them sign a form?" Chad asked, looking astounded.

"Well, I tried, but first everyone laughed at me, and then no one had a pen, so we had to make other arrangements."

"What he means," Paul said, "is that he got out his phone and had everyone record a video message in which they said the sex they were about to engage in was consensual and what their safe word was. Which was still ridiculous, but at least it got us naked."

"You record any of the action with Abby?" Howie asked. "I'd watch that."

"No, of course not," Thor replied, a look of disgust on his face. "After I got everyone's statement, I put the phone in a drawer and there it stayed."

Paul sucked in his cheeks and looked away.

"Paul?" Thor said, his voice full of warning.

"I may have gotten it out again, just once," he said, grimacing guiltily.

"But no one gave consent to be videoed," Thor cried. "What did you record?"

Paul took a tactful breath. "Remember that time when he was all like 'arghgblarghgl'?" Paul made a growling noise and shook his head back and forth like a dog tearing into a juicy bone. "And then you're all like 'ungunh-unh-unh-unh'?" He lolled his head to the side, bounced up and down in his chair, and waved his arms about like a rag doll. "And then everyone was suddenly all wet?" He looked at Thor seriously. "Yeah, I recorded that."

"That's—" Thor's voice cracked. He cleared his throat and began again. "*That's* on my phone?"

Paul nodded.

Thor bolted to his feet. "Well, I'm stuffed," he announced, leaving his full plate on the table. "Paul, can I see you for a moment?" He walked toward their room.

"But I'm still eating," Paul cried.

"There's something I need you for." Thor looked at him with an intensity that startled the others. "Right the fuck now."

Paul grinned and stood. "Gentlemen, I must take my leave." He walked over to the door Thor was holding open. Then he turned back. "If you hear him call for help, just go about your business. I got this." Thor grabbed him around the neck and pulled him into the room, slamming it shut behind them.

A stunned silence fell over the group.

"Well, sounds like they had an interesting evening," Ted offered.

"So, are Paul and Thor...," Howie began. Then he shook his head. "Whatever. Long as they're happy." He got up to rejoin the snoozing Bella.

Ted smiled. He was starting to think Bella might be just what Howie needed.

THE GUYS spent their last day around the pool, finally taking some time to enjoy the sun and sea they had come so far to experience. As he and Bark swam and sunned, Ted reveled in the freedom of being naked under the bright sun and of being able to not only look at Bark, but to touch him whenever he wanted. He wanted quite often.

Chad had said a bittersweet farewell to Libby when her group texted her that the buses had finally arrived. He walked her back to the Flamingo, then returned to sit on a lounger by the pool. Bark and Ted swam up to him.

"Well, this is new," Bark said, looking at Chad's serious face.

"What's new?" Ted asked.

"Chad usually does a little happy dance when he sees off his latest conquest. Today, though, not so much. What's up, Chaddy?"

"I think something's wrong with me."

"What is it?" Ted asked, concerned. "Do you think you're getting sick?"

"No, it's not that. It's just that... well, Bark's right. When I said good-bye to Libby, I kinda didn't want her to go." He shook his head, his expression one of pure mystification. "That's never happened before."

Bark smiled. "I think Chaddy's in wuv," he singsonged.

"Don't tease him," Ted objected, sending a precision jet of water at Bark's head. "I think it's awesome. Good for you, Chad."

A half smile appeared on Chad's face. "You guys are so lucky."

"Why's that?" Ted asked.

"By the time you finally figured it all out, you already knew each other. Hell, you already loved each other. Now that you're together, it's like you've always been together. I've never even had a second date, and here you two are like an old married couple. You make it look easy."

"It is easy," Bark said. "You just have to relax about it and accept that you may have finally found someone you want to sleep with more than once."

Chad nodded. "We talked about getting together in a few weeks. I'm going to be in Chicago for the weekend doing a shoot, and she's going to be looking at grad schools. So I'll finally have that second date." He smiled sheepishly as if seeing the same woman twice were some kind of kooky scheme he was crazy to undertake.

Bark turned to Ted. "I think our little Chaddy is growing up."

"I think you're wrong," Chad said with a laugh. He stood, threw off his pool-boy shorts and shirt, and jumped naked into the water, soaking Ted and Bark with a masterfully aimed cannonball.

The three of them splashed and played like otters in the water for a long while, then crawled out onto loungers. Ted took one next to Paul and Thor, who were sunning quietly together.

Paul sat up and smiled at Ted. "Kiddie time over in the pool?"

Ted nodded happily and stretched out on the lounger.

"Hey, Thor, can you get my back?" Paul handed Thor the tube of sunblock.

"Sure," Thor replied. He hopped up and slid onto Paul's lounger, straddling it behind him.

"So, can I ask a personal question?" Ted asked.

Paul nodded, brow furrowed as if confused that anyone would ever consider personal questions to be off-limits.

"Is this… thing you two have going just because we're on spring break? Once we're back home, are you going to keep doing what you're… doing…?"

Paul grinned. "What do you think, Thor?"

Thor was busily smoothing the white cream into Paul's back, but he looked thoughtfully at Ted as he answered. "I think this week has been a spiritual experience. We have all grown so much. Look at you and Bark—your lives have changed completely. Chad found someone he may want to actually have a relationship with, and Howie has managed to keep the interest of a woman for longer than it takes to pay for her drink." He glanced across the pool, where Bella and Howie were entwined on two loungers. Thor smiled, then returned to his task. The sunblock was by now fully absorbed, but he kept stroking and kneading Paul's back, to his evident delight. "When I came here, I was still holding on to the violation I felt during that trip with Ilse and Pedro. I had no idea it was weighing so heavily on me. I thought it was because I had no essential interest in men that I had such a traumatic experience with Pedro. But Paul has helped me see that the bisexuality I had always assumed was there is real, and exploring it is spiritually rewarding and… physically? Well, it's fucking amazing." He wrapped his arms around Paul and pressed his head to the strong trapezius muscles. "What about you, Paul? How did you grow this week?"

"I fucked a girl," Paul said.

Ted burst out laughing at Paul's terse masculinity.

Thor rolled his eyes. "I know, I was there. But what about Ted's question? What are you taking back home from this experience?"

Paul turned his head to the side, and Thor shifted so that their cheeks pressed together. "I'm taking you back home with me. I know we want different things in life, but for right now, we just fit. And when we get home, I'm still going to want you in my bed. We don't have to be exclusive, and if we ask others to join us, I'm down with that. And someday I know we'll probably have to grow up and move on. But until then, anyone who tries to keep me from you is going to get seriously fucked up." He craned around a little further and kissed Thor softly on the lips. Then he smiled. "Is that what I think it is, creeping up my back?"

"Rock hard," Thor murmured. Then he moved his hand down into Paul's lap. "I see we agree. Shall we take this inside?"

Paul nodded and stood, then held out a hand for Thor. Their erections bobbed in front of them, leading the way to their room.

"Fuck," Ted exhaled.

"I only heard half of that, and I'm totally boned too," Bark said.

Ted turned his head and saw the throbbing evidence. "And you, Chad?"

Chad glanced down at his own hard-on, then shrugged. "Just happy for them, I guess." He closed his eyes and lay back on the lounger.

Two splashes in quick succession startled Ted, who was delighted to see the troopers gliding underwater from one end of the pool to the other. They reached the wall, turned, and stroked back to the other end in an easy freestyle.

"Oh, dude," Ted breathed.

Bark sat up. "How old are they supposed to be?"

"I have no idea. They're just so...."

"Yes, they are." Bark settled back onto his lounger. "That'll be you and me in a few years," he said happily.

"God, I hope so. They're gorgeous." He watched as the naked Brandt and Donnelly stepped from the pool and wrapped towels around themselves. "And, you know, awesome guys," Ted added, not taking his eyes from their impressive musculature.

Bark took Ted's hand and squeezed it. "Love you," he murmured.

Ted beamed, as all was right in his world for the first time in his life. "I love you," he whispered back.

That evening, as darkness fell, Vic and Winnie laid out a spread for dinner that was truly astounding. White linen cloths adorned the folding tables, and candles flickered from every surface. Vic presided over a grill loaded with the first fresh seafood the town had gotten in since the storm: lobsters and prawns and thick filets of salmon sizzled alongside filet mignon and skewers of vegetables. Winnie filled a table with salads and delicacies, and then endlessly fluttered around the pool deck topping up everyone's champagne flute.

The guys were back in their gigolo finery and were joined by not only Brandt and Donnelly, but also Abby and Ryan, back for a repeat engagement with Paul and Thor. Bella had had her luggage delivered and was striking in a long white dress and several pieces of brilliant diamond jewelry. Howie simply beamed at her constantly.

Winnie tapped his glass with a spoon and waited for quiet. "Now, before we partake of Vic's hot meat," he said with a roguish wink, "I wanted to say just a few things. First, I can say without fear of contradiction that we have never had a week like this one at the Villa Hermes. We started the week by welcoming to our gay little inn six straight boys, and we ended it with...." He looked around. "What's the current count? Are there any straight ones left?" He burst out laughing, as did they all. "We had the storm of the century and were beyond lucky to have two fine officers to bring law and order to our little backwater, defending us from utter destruction. Gabriel and Ethan, thank you."

Winnie applauded, and all joined in. Brandt and Donnelly waved to the group modestly.

"And after the storm, you all pitched in to help us get up and running again. Bark and Ted took care of the pool and cleaning up the deck, Paul got the shutters back on and did all of the other heavy lifting, Howie and Chad managed to get us back online, and Thor... well, thanks to Thor I have a new love in my life." Winnie held up the tiny Yorkshire terrier Thor had brought him from the animal shelter. "Isn't that right, Princess?" Winnie cooed. Princess, wearing a rhinestone-studded black leather collar, looked imperiously at the group from the height of Winnie's shoulder.

"You just happened to have a dog collar that would fit him?" Thor asked, scratching Princess's neck.

"Oh no, dear, that's not a dog collar. It's more of a...." Winnie shot a glance at Vic, who blushed. "Just something we happened to have around the house," he said with a smile. Then he was back to business. "I'd like to thank all of you for your help, your support, and most of all for all of your skinny dipping. It has been an uplifting experience for us, and I hope it has been for you as well." He applauded his guests, and they all smiled and laughed to be celebrated this way.

Howie raised his hand and stood to address the group. "I have to say something," he announced.

"Oh shit," murmured, well, just about everyone.

"When we got here, I thought our spring break was over before it started. Our luggage was lost, we were booked by my passive-aggressive travel agent into a gay resort, and no woman would come near me during our first night out. Now, at the end of the week, I can't imagine a better time could be had anywhere in the world. We have eaten like kings, had an underground adventure during which we learned a lot about each other, and have had the chance to pitch in and do some good instead of just get drunk and offend women. Two of us have discovered they love each other, and I wish them the best." He lifted his glass to Bark and Ted. "Two of us have discovered they enjoy each other's company horizontally as well as vertically, and I wish them the best." He tipped his glass to Paul and Thor. "Chad, you've discovered you are capable of a second date, and I wish you the best." He toasted Chad. "And finally, I have in the last twenty-four hours fallen head over heels for the beautiful Bella, who challenges both my mind and my body to accomplish more than I thought they could." He blew a kiss her way, which she accepted gracefully and sent back to him.

"So, at the end of this amazing week, I propose we return here in one year's time, from wherever we are, to renew the bonds of friendship we have built over the last four years and proven over the past week. Most of us will be going our own way in a couple of months; that's the way life is. But I want us to come back together next year to remember what great friends we have in each other. Will you join me?"

All cheered.

"Will you open your gay arms to our increasingly gay group?" he asked Winnie and Vic.

They nodded and laughed.

"And, officers, will you consider returning as our guardian angels? This week wouldn't have been the same without you, and we would love to see you again."

Brandt and Donnelly, blushing, shrugged at each other and then nodded their agreement.

"Now, I'm going to be heading out tonight with Bella, who seems for some reason to think I'm a pretty good catch. I've printed out your boarding passes, gentlemen, and I wish you safe travels. I'll certainly see you for class Monday morning."

The mention of Monday brought a groan from the group.

"Now I ask you to raise a glass and join me in toasting to the long life and success of the Villa Hermes and all who gather here!"

The group loudly acclaimed Howie's sentiment while Winnie and Vic held each other and dabbed at their eyes.

SATURDAY MORNING found the pool deck a rather more somber place, with the college crew (minus Howie) preparing to return home to the snowy north. As their luggage had never arrived, they didn't have much packing to do, so they ate breakfast poolside while they waited for the airport shuttle to arrive.

"Glad to be heading home?" Donnelly asked Ted and Bark, who as usual were sitting at their table.

Ted shrugged. "I kinda don't ever want to leave here because it's been so amazing. But then again, I'm taking the most amazing part home with me." He reached over and mussed Bark's hair, grinning widely.

"I'm so happy for you two," Donnelly said, beaming at them across the table.

"We were really lucky to have a guardian angel," Bark said, "who was willing to slip us lube and condoms at the right moment."

Brandt cracked up, because he knew that was exactly the kind of guardian angel his partner most wanted to be.

"You guys are getting married soon, right?" Ted asked.

The men nodded.

Ted turned to Bark, but with a faraway look in his eye.

"He's doing it again, isn't he?" asked Bark, not looking at Ted.

"What's that?" Brandt said.

"Looking at me like he's picturing me on the top of a wedding cake." He put a hand around his throat. "I can feel the bow tie around my neck when he does that." He turned to Ted. "Look, I've told you. I will marry you today if you want. My oats are sown, my heart is yours. I have committed myself to you, body and soul, for the rest of my life. I love you, Teddy."

Ted smiled. "I know. I just like hearing you say it. I love you." He kissed Bark, then kissed him two more times before returning to his pancakes.

"Dammit, something in my eye," Donnelly muttered, dabbing at the corner of his eye with his napkin.

"You are such a romantic," Brandt scolded, pulling Donnelly into a hug. "Best thing about you," he murmured, his lips pressed against the top of Donnelly's head.

"All right, listen up motherfuckers!" Paul's voice rang out over the pool deck. "The good news is that the airline has located our luggage, and is sending it to us on the airport shuttle." A mostly ironic cheer went up. "The bad news is that very same shuttle will be taking us back to the airport with our luggage." Mutters and expletives resounded. "The worse news is that the shuttle will be here in ten minutes." Groans from all corners.

"Well, I guess we better get our shit together," Ted said, rising. "Thank you both so much, once again." He extended a hand to the troopers in turn, as did Bark. "I hope we'll see you at the reunion."

Brandt and Donnelly laughed and shook hands with the boys.

"We wouldn't miss it," Brandt replied. "Another week in paradise. What's the worst that could happen?"

Donnelly elbowed him sharply in the ribs. "I keep telling him not to provoke the universe that way." He scowled playfully at Brandt. "Now, you two should check that you have everything."

The college guys scattered, gathering their few possessions. Winnie begged them all to keep the pool boy/gigolo clothes they'd been wearing, and they seemed glad to have some souvenirs of their time at Villa Hermes. All too soon, a horn announced the arrival of the airport shuttle in the circular driveway out front.

"Let's move it, bitches," yelled Paul. Then he turned to Brandt and Donnelly. "It was an honor to meet you," he said, his voice deep and serious.

"It was great for us too," Donnelly said.

"Thank you for showing them it's possible to be gay and... guys like us," Paul said as he shook Brandt's hand.

"You give me hope for the next generation, Paul. When labels no longer apply, we need strong leaders to show people the way."

Paul seemed deeply touched and nodded his acknowledgment of Brandt's praise. Thor joined the group, carrying his well-worn pack.

"Gentlemen, it was a pleasure to meet you both," he said, shaking the troopers' hands. "I haven't always had the highest esteem for law enforcement, but you two changed my mind."

"Lots of mind changing going around this week," Brandt said, looking from Thor to Paul and back again.

Thor burst out laughing. "Yes, we are returning different people. But that's what travel is supposed to do for you, isn't it?" He nudged Paul. "We should get going, hon."

Donnelly's eyebrows shot up at this.

"He just does that to push my buttons. I ignore it and hope he'll grow out of it."

"Not gonna happen," Thor said under his breath, smiling at the officers as he and Paul took their leave.

Chad approached the officers, as if he'd been waiting his turn. "I wanted to thank you," he said, shaking their hands. "That first day, when I was freaking out about finding those pictures on Tumblr… well, you helped me a lot. Thank you for that."

"Happy to help," Brandt said.

As Chad walked out through the courtyard, Brandt reflected on how it was usually Donnelly who helped people, while he watched from a distance. This time he had done some good himself, and it felt wonderful.

Ted and Bark were the last to head for the shuttle, but not before stopping to say good-bye.

Ted dropped his backpack and practically flew into Donnelly's arms. He gripped the officer tightly and made no sign of wanting to let go. "You saved me," he whispered, just loud enough for Brandt to hear. "I wouldn't have been able to…."

Donnelly ran his hands up and down Ted's back, waiting for him to catch his breath. "You are an exceptional young man. It was an honor to see you take control of your life."

"I hope my family is half as supportive as you are," Ted replied, releasing Donnelly from his grip.

Donnelly held Ted by the shoulders. "Even if they aren't, you hold strong, okay? They may need some time, but no matter what, you are a good person, and a strong one, and you will be okay."

"Thank you," Ted whispered.

"Now, you take care of each other," Donnelly said as he hugged Bark in turn. "And if you do get married, you have to send us an invitation."

"Would you come?" Ted asked, eyes wide.

"From the very antipodes I would come," Donnelly said, smiling broadly.

Brandt put his arm around his partner, touched by his Shakespearean devotion, then shook hands with both boys, each of whom pulled him into a hug. He was not naturally a hugger, but years with Donnelly had made him appreciate it more than he ever thought he would. He held Ted and Bark, feeling their warmth and strength and hoping they would be happy.

Donnelly smiled, a tear still in his eye. "Now, you guys have a safe trip, and I hope we'll see you in a year." Then he added with a wink, "If not before."

Ted and Bark nodded and made their way out through the courtyard. As Brandt heard the shuttle pull away, Winnie came to their table to pour more coffee.

"It's going to be awfully quiet around here," the innkeeper said. He sat down to join his last guests.

"No one checking in today?" Brandt asked.

"No, I'm afraid not," Winnie replied. "Most of the bookings evaporated with the storm. The town in general won't be ready for tourists for another month or so. We'll stay open, but few people are going to want to tour a war zone on vacation."

"So, would you happen to have our suite available, say, during the month of June?" Donnelly asked, casting a glance at Brandt. "Perhaps starting the week of June eight?"

"Oh, as of this morning the entire month of June is available. And June is so lovely here! Early in the summer before school lets out the town is just so peaceful, and the weather couldn't be more beautiful." Winnie took a breath and looked at the men. "Are you planning another trip so soon?"

"We get married June seventh," Brandt answered. "We've been trying to think of a place for a honeymoon. In fact, that's one of the reasons we came here."

"That would be lovely!" Winnie exclaimed, bouncing up and down. "We would be delighted to have you back. You simply must come. It will be on us, in appreciation for all you have done for us. You simply must stay two weeks next time. And I promise: no acts of God to get in the way of your enjoyment. Oh, please say you'll come!"

Brandt and Donnelly had been trying to stifle their laughter at Winnie's overwhelming excitement but failed in the end.

"We are touched by your generosity," Brandt said and meant every word of it. He turned to Donnelly, eyebrows raised in question, and got a vigorous nod in response. "We'd be thrilled to spend our honeymoon here."

Winnie sat back, hand on his heart. "You have made this old man so happy," he said, a catch in his voice. "So very happy."

"You are so generous, Winnie. We're very grateful."

Winnie cast his eyes to the heavens. "Gorgeous, brave, and chivalrous," he cried. "Oh, to have met you when I was in the bloom of youth myself."

"I'm sure you have many years of pool boys in your future, Winnie," Brandt said, laughing.

THEIR PLANE tickets were for the afternoon flight home, leaving them a leisurely Sunday morning. They spent the early part of it swimming then relaxing in the hot tub.

"Penny for your thoughts," Brandt said through the steam rising from the tub, tinted gold by the sunrise.

"Where are you keeping your change? You're naked."

"Figure of speech, dumbass. Tell me why you have that goofy look on your face."

Donnelly chuckled. "I'm just thinking about all of the changes this place has seen this week. Everyone's gone home different than they were when they arrived."

"How about you? What changed for you this week?"

Donnelly tipped his head thoughtfully. "I found out I could fuck a straight guy until he shoots all over himself."

Brandt splashed steamy water at him. "Nice," he muttered.

"Sorry. It's just that that was one of the hottest things we've ever done." He gave a little shiver at the memory. "Awesome." He seemed to collect himself. "How about you?"

"Well, first I learned that you like to fuck straight guys."

"Just one, actually."

"Let's hope so," Brandt said with a raised eyebrow. "Anyway, it was really amazing to watch the guys dealing with a lot of the same issues we faced when we got together, but doing it in a way that seemed much more... normal? There are times when the fight for equal rights seems like it's never going to be won, and then I look at the next generation and it gives me hope that what we're fighting for may already be won. I mean, Thor, right?"

"Yeah, that whole situation with Paul was fascinating. And that everyone else seemed to take it in stride." Donnelly looked out over the ocean. "It kind of restores your faith in humanity, doesn't it?"

"That it does," Brandt agreed. "That it does."

After a long moment of soaking and reflection, Donnelly broke the silence. "So, next time we sit in this hot tub...."

"We'll be an old married couple," Brandt finished for him. "I can only imagine being completely exhausted."

"Why?"

"Are you kidding me? After what we went through finding a wedding planner, and then the week we've spent here? And don't forget my brother is coming down to throw us a bachelor party next month. If our luck holds, a simple party will turn into some kind of madcap adventure only a truly demented novelist could come up with."

Donnelly burst out laughing, but he nodded along.

"By the time we manage to beat back whatever alien invasion accompanies our wedding, I can only imagine we will arrive here, bruised, battered, and still stomping out the flames."

"But we'll be married, and so it'll all have been worth it."

Brandt floated his way across the pool to come to rest on Donnelly's lap. "Still glad you proposed to me?"

"Definitively," Donnelly replied. "I would do it again in a heartbeat. In fact, I was just about to propose something to you."

"Might this proposal of yours have to do with the thing that is poking me in the buttock at this very moment?"

"It might indeed. Would you like to come up to my suite to achieve confirmation?"

Brandt grinned and then leaned in to kiss his partner. "Do it right and I may achieve confirmation all over myself."

Donnelly's grin was twice as wide as Brandt's. "Must be going now—I have a date with a straight guy."

"The straight guy thought you'd never ask."

They stepped out of the hot tub, naked, and walked in the golden morning light into their future together.

XAVIER MAYNE is the pen name of a professor of English who works at a university in the Midwest United States. Versed in academic theories of sexual identity, he is passionate about writing stories in which men experience a love that pushes them beyond the boundaries they thought defined their sexuality. He believes that romance can be hot, funny, and sweet in equal measure.

The name Xavier Mayne is a tribute to the pioneering gay author Edward Prime-Stevenson, who also used it as a pen name. He wrote the first openly gay novel by an American, 1906's Imre: A Memorandum, which depicts two masculine men falling in love despite social pressures that attempt to keep them apart.

Website: http://www.xaviermayne.com

Don't miss how the
story started!

Frat House Troopers

A Brandt and Donnelly
Caper

By Xavier Mayne

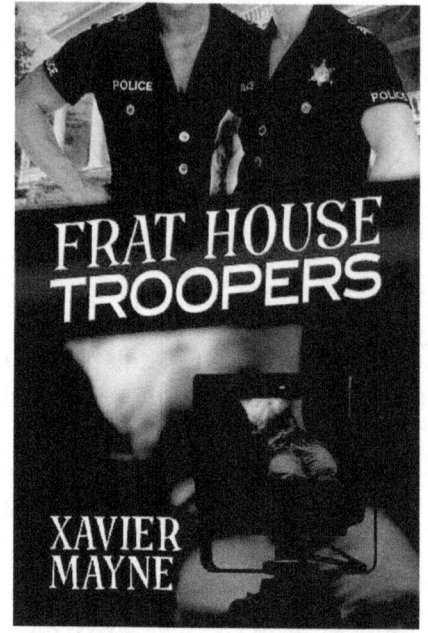

State trooper Brandt's new
assignment to infiltrate a sex-cam
operation puts him in a very
uncomfortable position, especially since he'll have to perform naked on
camera for his audition. Fortunately his partner and best friend,
Donnelly, has his back—whether that means helping Brandt shop gay
boutiques for sexy underwear or offering Jäger and encouragement while
he researches porn.

Despite his mortification, Brandt gives the audition his best "shot"—
and becomes an overnight sensation. But to meet the man behind the
operation, he'll have to give a repeat performance, this time live on
webcam opposite the highest bidder. Donnelly makes sure to win that
auction for his partner's sake, but their plan has a flaw: faking it is not
an option.

In the aftermath, Brandt is a humiliated mess trying desperately to
come to terms with what he's had to do for the job and his own mixed
feelings. But Donnelly has been on a journey of discovery of his own.
Suddenly everything the two men thought they knew about themselves
and each other gets turned inside out. Meanwhile, they still have a case
to solve… but it may not be the case they thought it was.

http://www.dreamspinnerpress.com

Don't miss how the story started!

Wrestling Demons

A Brandt and Donnelly Caper

By Xavier Mayne

Jonah Fischer's high school wrestling career has been stellar, but now he's the unwilling star of a series of videos that have hit the web. The whole world may have seen the evidence that his best friend turns him on. Jonah's conservative family wants him cured, and his conventional town and school want him normal. The only person who still wants him just the way he is is Casey Melville, the same best friend who turned him on for all the world to see. Meanwhile, Casey begins to wonder if there's more to his feelings for Jonah than he thought.

Officers Brandt and Donnelly—lovers as well as partners on the job— have been assigned to find the culprit who posted the video. While investigating the case, they also help Jonah and Casey find their way through their feelings, and steer them toward refuge when Jonah's family turns against him. But the mystery remains: who wants to hurt Jonah badly enough to post those videos, and why? Thank goodness Jonah and Casey have found friends—they're going to need all the help and support they can get.

Husband Material

By Xavier Mayne

Husband Material is a long-running reality show, where eighteen lucky guys compete for the hand of one lucky lady. Meet contestant number one, Riley. Since being left at the altar, he's hit the gym to get into the best shape of his life. Now he's in it to win it. Contestant number two, Asher, doesn't really want the bachelorette; he needs the prize money for his sister's cancer treatment. Asher's upbeat personality brings Riley out of the funk he's been in since his breakup. They make a formidable team, with one complication: Asher's falling for Riley.

Producer Kaitlyn has her hands full when two bachelors are found in the shower soaping up inappropriately, then another live-tweets the entire debacle. If another scandal erupts, the network will cancel the show.

The two bachelors are on a collision course under the watchful eye of a producer torn between wanting them to find true love and trying to keep her show going. In the end, Riley must choose the bachelorette or the bachelor.

http://www.dreamspinnerpress.com

NOT JUST FRIENDS

JAY NORTHCOTE

http://www.dreamspinnerpress.com

SHADOWING *Mace*

CHEYENNE MEADOWS

http://www.dreamspinnerpress.com

ILLUSIONS

S. A. Ozment

http://www.dreamspinnerpress.com

BA TORTUGA

Say SOMETHING

http://www.dreamspinnerpress.com

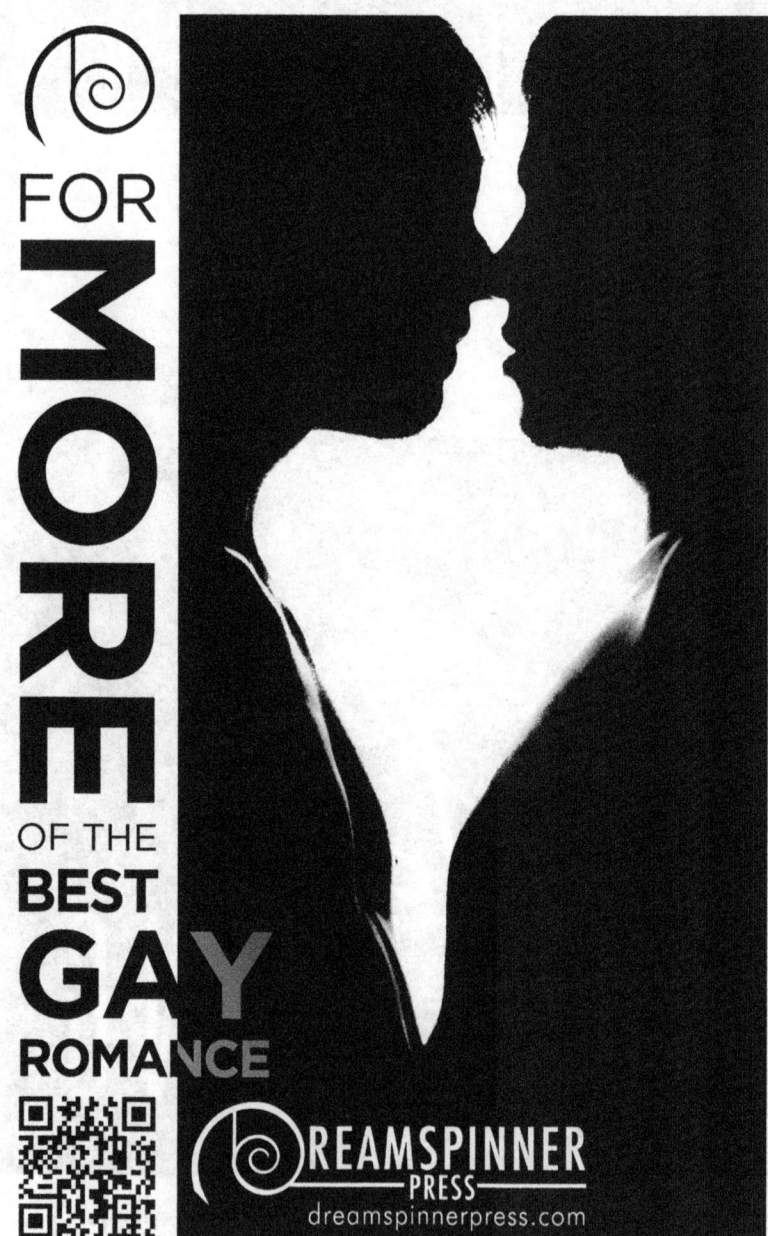

Made in United States
Orlando, FL
22 March 2026

79559072R00138